THE SPY HOUSE

To Left Bank
Pictures –

M. F. Kelleher

THE SPY HOUSE

M.F. KELLEHER

ISBN 9798721718212

First Edition 2021

Cover artwork by Claire Meczes

PROLOGUE

The first glow of dawn hangs in the air. The lightness of the sky creates breaking flecks across the walls of the bedroom. The city is peaceful now, unusually quiet. Soon the traffic and the chatter will well up into a crescendo of ideas and travel, emotion and organisation, bringing the place to life. Gabrielle wakes suddenly and surveys the room around her. A man is next to her, naked, under the quilt. She silently rolls out of bed, pulls on her clothes and stuffs her handgun into the back of her jeans.

She watches the sleeping man. He isn't all bad, she thinks, just got in with the wrong crowd. She has learnt enough about his life in the past three weeks as his new girlfriend to know that he wouldn't be missed by his colleagues or his family. His youthful hopes of success have nearly faded in his head, his aspirations to be something have faltered, but he is still hopeful enough to be dangerous. Men like him have the potential to be uncontrollable, they still believe in something, but don't have the skills to pull off the kind of crimes that would make them feel happy.

London Centre had been quite clear with her, penetrate the cell, befriend Franz Keneely and report back to them. London are never ready to give control to the field agents to allow them to make decisions. She screws the silencer on to her Smith and Wesson, presses the barrel against his cranium and gently pulls the trigger.

CHAPTER ONE

A normal flat of an ordinary family; lounge, TV, kitchen and two bedrooms. Gabby is late and crashes through the front door, picks up the TV remote and pushes channel 476. A hidden door in the sidewall opens, she goes through and descends the stairs two at a time then pushes a large steel door at the bottom of the shaft. She enters a grey equipment room with a single, red emergency light providing the only illumination. She flips a power button and four screens light up in front of her. She types in a password and a video link stutters onto the main display. The screen shows an empty meeting room in London.

After thirty seconds, the door opens on the screen at the far end of the remote room and Sir Stephen Laughton, Head of MI6 Field Operations in Europe enters, and slowly makes his way towards the screen, then takes a seat in the centre of the table. His three-piece suit an echo of past times in the security service, his mop of salt and pepper hair sits atop a tall frame.

"Good morning, Blackhawk."

"Sir."

Laughton opens a file of papers with deliberation, and takes time to prepare himself.

"Apologies, I only have five minutes, but I'm keen to hear about your report on Hillbank."

"Of course, sir," she says. "Target Raleigh has been terminated, as per plan."

"Which plan was that?" says Laughton.

"I managed to get intelligence from Raleigh last night on the cell and the funding routes they use."

"I don't remember a kill order being issued."

"It was a code 12.8, sir, field operative in imminent danger."

"What's your intel?"

"The cell is led by Martin Teileter, he's a long-term criminal in Germany and the Baltic, local prostitution and drugs mostly; this is a bigger game for him. Elias Müller is the financier of the cell and connected through to organised crime in the Eastern bloc. Their armourer is Tobias Teergarten, well known to us. The cell is five strong, their intent is high-level crime driven by financial interests; this isn't a gang driven by ideology, just money. The commands come from a controller in the south of France."

"Who is the controller?" asks Laughton.

"We don't know yet. They must have a range of interests and criminal operations or they wouldn't be able to maintain authority from outside Berlin," she continues. "That implies a significant player, and they must be known to us or the French security services."

"Are the French in on this?"

"Yes, I have talked to Bernard Atelier in the DGSE crime division," says Gabby, referring to the Direction Générale de la Sécurité Extérieure, France's MI6.

"What are this gang's weaknesses?"

"They're new, only formed in the last three weeks, so they're not familiar with working together yet. So, they won't trust each other at all; we can use that as a lever."

"What about personalities?" says Laughton.

"Teileter is a nasty piece of work, won't think twice about murder. That will give them all an uneasy feeling that he could turn on them at any time. The others are not big players. Keneely, who was Raleigh, was the one who would have seen through infiltration so his death is a benefit.

"Any potential sources?"

"I have built up a strong link with Raleigh's younger brother, Alexander. He is ready to talk, or at least drop information to us. They think I am Raleigh's girlfriend. They'll discover he's dead in the next 12 hours, so I will need to be somewhere they can find me, tearful of course, in the next few days. But I am not trusted with information like Alexander is, I'm not one of the gang, just on the periphery. If we turn him, we have a solid source on the inside."

"Sir Bernard has asked me for a report on their plans," says Laughton.

"I have worked on Alexander, but he needs to know there's someone he can trust before he gives us anything," she continues. "He'll be upset about Raleigh so that will be the lever, we can get closer over our mutual sorrow for his brother and my ex-boyfriend. I have played on his insecurities and his fear of being caught. I told him that a friend of mine was given a deal on prison sentencing by leaking information, so we'll work on that angle."

"The gang isn't operational yet are they?" says Laughton.

"No, but any day soon would be my view. They won't hang around."

"Alright. Thank you. I need to go," he says, and the screen in front of her goes blank before she can say any more.

Gabby sinks back into the chair and exhales. She takes a shower to remove the sweat from the previous night and wraps her dark hair in a light towel. She makes coffee in an over-sized cup and sits on the balcony of her apartment.

Deep undercover takes its toll over time, you don't know who you are; even start forgetting your real birthday. A requirement of the job is total immersion in another life. You have to believe in your cover story or they see through it. She sips her coffee and looks across the city. Berlin excites her still because it sits strategically between East and West and is the crossing point of so many spy networks. But this is the start of her third year here and she needs to move on soon or London will leave her hanging in one place for too long and forget about her.

She wonders how long she can go on doing field operations. Maybe she has been doing this job too long already. One day she knows she will reach the end of what is bearable; one human can only take so many deaths, so much violence and so much pain. Too many field agents she knows say the same and have been saying it for years. Maybe that is the only escape you have in the field, inside your head you can get away, but never in real life.

Gabrielle trained to kill ten years ago in an SAS training camp in Ireland. The sergeant had tried to break her; too pretty, he had said. What's a girl like you want to be here for? Give it up and go back to shopping. On the last day she had gone in to his office and delivered a sharp blow to his testicles. She wasn't going to be forgotten quickly.

She thinks about the people she has killed. All have been justified in her mind. They were all violent men and women; the world is better off without them. She regrets only one death, a 17-year-old bomber. She had been turned by a gang who were much older than her and she genuinely believed in what she was doing. But Gabrielle had a job to do and shot her where she knew the girl would die immediately in the least amount of pain. As her instructor had said on the last day of basic training, "For every operation you are sent on, just deliver it and move on. It's the only mantra that is allowed when you're in the spy house."

She has no more time to sit and think as she has work to do. The old school luxury of an agent being allocated to only one case at a time is long gone. As well as the Hillbank op she has day to day work on top of that.

She checks her encrypted messages, and a kill order has come in while she was in the shower. She researches the details then in the early afternoon drives out east to the very edge of the city. The target is a man of routine and that makes it much easier to find the best location for his death. She scouts his home but it has too much security and too many backstreets around which you could get lost in an escape route if you aren't familiar with the area.

She heads back in to the centre of Berlin, parks on a side street near where the target has his office and walks the pavements for three blocks around the site. It is her call on the method of assassination. Gabrielle has been trained in hand-to-hand combat and is comfortable with knives, guns and hands as her weapons. She favours operations where she is the killer, it is neater. Involving other people in an op always makes it difficult but she accepts that it happens. Working solo in operations over the last ten years has given her a lone wolf mentality; 'trust no one' is one of the truths of MI6. You never know who is reliable, or has been turned as a double agent, or has just lost it.

She puts her phone to her ear and acts out calling someone while she walks passed the main entrance of the target's office block. Mobile phones are a spook's godsend, it allows her to stand and survey all of the details of the office reception layout without attracting suspicion. A security guard sits reading a paper and doesn't even look up at her. She considers close-range knife as the solution rather than a handgun as that would be audible even with a silencer. The street has tall buildings along both sides which is always good for sniping but she isn't a trained sniper so it would involve a CT72 order for resources, and paperwork is always something that she avoids at all costs.

She goes to a local bar to consider the options and after going through all the possibilities she concludes that close-range is not viable. The target will have bodyguards and a near-in kill is out of the question. It will have to be a sniper. She just hopes it will be a good one.

It is getting dark when she returns to her flat. She goes online and puts in the CT72 order – a sniper for the next day. Gabrielle can't remember if she slept the previous night and crashes out fully clothed, then wakes at 11pm, takes off her clothes and retreats beneath the duvet.

Her phone buzzes at 10 the next morning.

"Gaby, you old tart, how are?"

"Mac! Thank God it's you. I never know if I'm going to get a proper killer or some 25-year-old with a gun they've never used."

"Always happy to be wanted, old thing. Got this order on my phone at 5am and knew I couldn't let you."

Mac's propensity not to finish sentences is annoying at first then becomes endearing.

"I had to sort this all out myself, Mac. Bloody London were as useless as ever."

"I need to go and give them some."

"You are just the man to do that, Mac!" She laughs for the first time in months.

"Berlin looks sunny but slightly cold, not unlike your good self."

"Where are you, you old bugger?"

"Military airport in the north, can't remember the."

"I know it. I'll come and pick you up."

"You are a wonderful."

Mac is a veteran of Afghanistan, one of the three best snipers in British Military Intelligence. Apparently 300 kills in war zones, which she had tried to verify one long night in a bar in Vienna with him, but they only got to 83 before the vodkas prevented any further intelligent conversation.

He is sitting on a bank on the right-hand-side of the main airport entrance as she pulls up, his black hair is short and his large limbs are sprawled over the grass.

"Looking for a good time, soldier?" she shouts from the car window.

"Always." He saunters across to her and throws his bag into the back seat.

"I thought lunch might be in order."

"You know, food has always been one of my."

They drive to a pub in the countryside and she orders beers and huge German sandwiches. She thought American food was big until she came to Berlin. They sit in the September sun and talk about their lives and the people they have killed.

"Remember that woman in Hungary?" he says almost absent-mindedly.

"Hanna Matto."

"That's the one op I almost abandoned. Couldn't bring myself to."

"You were young and she was beautiful, that's all," says Gabby. "She was a nasty piece of work, we had to stop her."

"I guess."

They sit in silence for half a minute. His hand moves across his two-day-old beard.

"You know I chose sniping because I couldn't face hand-to-hand combat?"

"What didn't you like?" she asks.

"The look in their eyes, just before they die. I was put on a couple of ops straight out of that training we had in Cleveland. I wasn't ready psychologically. Not ready at."

A headstrong breeze buffets across the river and up the grass bank to the table where they sit in the dappled light. Her blue-green eyes watch the memories run across his face. For a second, she sees the man beneath the sniper; then it has gone, faster than a bullet tumbling through guilty flesh. She is aware it is a moment that Mac wouldn't share with anyone else. They have a bond between them. Two isolated people, two killers, drawn together by death.

"Time to go, Mac."

She drives them to the kill location and they pose as a couple in a local café. He over-acts and takes the role of boyfriend in the scene very seriously, insisting on holding hands.

"Brief me, darling."

"Herbert Klingerfeld started as a gang master of foreign labour and worked his way up to extortion and eventually arms trading," says Gabby. "Sold surface to air missiles to the Israelis four years ago and now habitually sells anything to anyone."

"Gun whore."

"He is now planning a deal with the North Koreans, selling automatic weapons, and more importantly parts for surface to air missiles."

"When is he expected here?"

"4pm; you've got about 45 minutes to set up. He'll arrive in a car and it will pull up in that block opposite." Mac doesn't look immediately but glances over in the flow of their conversation a few minutes later.

"Shouldn't be too difficult to get a good line. These offices empty on this side?" he asks.

"Exactly; here's a key to the back door of this block next to us, number 51." She places a key on the table between them.

"All good, honey. Just let me get to it."

They get up and stand near each other, face-to-face, outside the café. She kisses him on both cheeks then turns and walks back to her car without looking back.

Later that day, in the early evening, Gabby gets the news on her phone that Mac has been shot dead.

*

CHAPTER TWO

Gabrielle feels her stomach pull. She is used to killing but they're all strangers to her; this is different, someone she knows, a real life that has been taken.

She immediately suspects the message about Mac is rogue, either intercepted from London Centre's comms network or Mac has been captured and the captors want MI6 to think he is dead. She sits in her kitchen. She has seen and heard enough death to know that what you read about it, and are told, is seldom true.

She descends to the comms room. Her reflection in the glass of the monitors looks strained and she turns away to the keyboard in front of her. Gabrielle types furiously, 'Stranraer, status?' The main screen shows her words and the encrypted version next to them. Stranraer is Mac's codename.

Gabby taps her fingernails on the desk and paces the room before the screen changes.

'Terminated,' comes the reply.

She spins round on the chair to sit in front of a side desk with a mass of buttons and switches. She flicks switches and turns dials until a ringing tone pushes out from the speakers at both ends of the room.

"Hello?" A voice comes from speakers.

"Blackhawk, encrypt request."

"Registered voice profile," says the voice. "Passcode?" She says the word. Five seconds later the screen flickers and the words "Encryption Enacted" appear, then it fades to a picture of an Ops Controller in London Centre.

"Hello, Anglesey."

"What can I do for you?" he says.

"Stranraer, I had a message."

"What message?"

"Terminated?"

"That's right. GISS called it in about an hour ago."

"The Belgian security service? Why them?"

"They were on the scene apparently."

"In Berlin?" she is sounding incredulous and suddenly realises it.

"What happened?"

"Stranraer was ambushed in the kill position is all we have."

"I personally vetted the site. It was secure."

"Evidently not."

"And has anyone asked why the Belgian security service was on-site?"

"No intel on that, sorry."

"Is anyone actually doing anything to find out why?" She is angry now.

"We know you and he were close, Blackhawk."

"Which means what exactly?" she says.

"Take a break, Gabby," says Anglesey. "We're moving as quickly as we can. You know these things have protocols."

"Asset down in the field should be a bloody top priority." She is emotive but in control. "There's only one explanation with this sort of event."

"And that is?"

"We've got a leak."

"Network status is secure for normal operations, Blackhawk," he says.

"Someone must have leaked, I only confirmed the kill location at 10pm last night. It was accessible to anyone with Top Secret clearance on the network."

"There's a briefing at 8 tonight with Scarlett. You should be on it. Got to go. Speak later." The screen goes blank.

Gabrielle lived through the mole purges of 2004 in MI6 and it was not a pleasant experience. She knows what it means for her as field ops. She is utterly alone from now on, until the mole is found.

The briefing at 8pm reveals nothing and Gabrielle drives to the river district of Berlin where bars and cafés light up the evening sky. Her mind buzzes with options about what could have happened. Half of her does not believe Mac is dead at all; maybe he fabricated the story, he has wanted out for as long as she can remember. An old dog, too tired for new tricks.

That's what she will do when the day comes, go to Rome, get plastic surgery and only speak Italian. She has started to create her back story already, planting evidence she will need to form a complete record for a fictional individual: birth certificate, parents, pictures and school records; waiting somewhere online for any prying eyes in the future. But there always seems to be one more important op to complete, one more criminal network to destroy, one more guilty life to end. But she will get out, one day, she will do it.

Schiffbauerdammstrasse runs beside the River Spree in the centre of the city. She parks and spends few seconds observing what is going on, checking for normality; nothing appears to be out of place. She pulls the door handle and steps out. The Mett Bar has been an MI6 haunt for years, since before the fall of the Berlin Wall. Deep undercover agents penetrated East German intelligence in the 1960s and double agents held the three top jobs before the collapse. Gabrielle pushes the door and goes in.

The long, low room is populated with tables and chairs that have seen better days. The décor is decidedly retro but still there from the first time it was fashionable. No more than half a dozen groups of ones and twos sit huddled over mostly beer. She surveys the faces as she passes but there's no one she knows or wants to avoid.

"Long time no see," she says too casually to the barman. "What's been happening, Hans?"

Hans is in fact Gordon Rathbone, The Honourable Gordon Rathbone, a graduate of Oxford, then the Guards and the Home Office and now the Foreign Office. He is a fixed deep cover operative, has no official information given to him and it is against the rules to give him any. He is formally a one-way source of information from the street into the security services. Informally however, he is a mine of information and one of the few people she trusts absolutely.

Hans puts down a bottle in front of her and leans into her personal space. Their eyes stare straight at each other, decoding, as per training. After five seconds, he kisses her on the lips. That is a signal that they can talk openly.

"I heard," he begins. She raises an eyebrow. "Risk level has been raised."

"I haven't received anything."

"There have been incidents."

"Worse than normal?" she says.

"Getting that way."

"Did you hear about Stranraer?"

"That's the latest gaff. There've been three or four in the last month."

"Terminations?" she almost mouths the word without sound.

He faintly nods.

"It's a leak, got to be," she says. "One mistake is understandable, but three or four means we're busted."

"Don't rock the boat, old girl."

"It's what I do, Hans."

"A lot of activity in London and high up, I heard," he says.

"I don't know what I'll do yet," she says and locks her eyes on his, wishing she could ask Hans all of the things that are in her mind in that instant.

"Got any options?"

"All I know is, I'm not going to sit back and wait for a knock on the door."

"Why would that happen?"

"I called London, they told me ops level is normal, I'm already being kept in the dark."

"Because of Stranraer?"

"Maybe," she says. "I'm going to have to find out myself."

"Trust no one," he whispers.

"I know." She smiles. "I may need you, Hans. Check our drop point 23G every day at 4pm for me."

Gabby finishes the beer and beckons him with her forefinger. He leans in close. She kisses him on the cheek and presses a USB into his hand, then gets up.

"Look after baby for me," she says and turns away toward the door.

"Liebe dich," he shouts across the bar as she walks away.

Gabby pushes the door to the street and lets in a rush of northern air that makes her eyes water, but only for a moment. Then she is gone. Hans leans down beneath the counter and lodges the USB in a crevice against the underside of the bar.

*

A flock of pigeons bursts up in front of Stuart Palmer and flies off across the small square where he sits at a café table. The German capital city bustles the other side of the buildings in each direction of the compass. It is rare for him to take any time off, but his boss had insisted on him taking leave before the end of the year. He pushes back his blond hair from his forehead and tries to relax, his face is kind, innocent even; his brown eyes looking out from a boyish face.

Stuart looks across at a woman twenty feet in front of him, she is scouring her mobile phone for enlightenment; she looks up briefly at him then back to her oracle. Another woman on another table is drinking some sort of yellow liquid from a tall glass; she is about forty, well dressed, and looks nervous as though she is waiting for someone or something. Stuart thinks he recognises her. He wracks his brain, but it's no good, he can't remember. She picks up the glass and empties it then collects her belongings and walks away to the far side of the square before disappearing up a side street.

A small car arrives from a road behind him and moves at walking pace through three sides of the square. It stops near another café on the far side of the place but no one gets out. After a gap of time long enough for Stuart to start thinking about something else, a man dressed in black gets out from the rear passenger door of the car and calmly walks to a table where a man is sitting reading a newspaper. The man in black takes out a handgun and shoots the sitter in the head once, then again, and runs back to the car. Screams and shouts rise up all around the walls of the houses; the car screams away around the corner and is gone. Blood pumps out on the table in front of the victim and drips down onto the cobblestones beneath.

Stuart's body is solid, he cannot move anything, even his eyes are locked onto the scene before him of the old man slumped at the table. His brain is screaming at him to move, do anything. He strains all his sinews to move one leg, it won't budge. He can feel his blood pressure rising. At last his leg moves, then the other; he is up and he is running. Stuart feels the cobbles beneath his feet and the air around his face. All he knows is he needs to get away.

He is sweating now, around each corner, away from the gore. He steams out into a narrow street that slopes away to the main road fifty yards beyond. A man is coming the other way, Stuart steps to one side to avoid him and the man steps the same way,

Stuart steps the other way, so does the man. Stuart and the man are two feet away from each other now. The man brings his arm up and the knife rips silently through Stuart's coat into his beating skin beneath.

*

Gabrielle knows that from now on, everything she does must be unpredictable. She adopts Operational Protocol 15, where a field agent needs to be untraceable for a period of time. The protocol includes randomising your travel patterns, so she leaves her car at home, catches a cab and a tram, then checks into a hotel on Mohrenstrasse.

She dumps her bag and emerges into the autumn sunlight. Gabby needs to get some clarity in her head to think through her plan. She walks through the Berlin backstreets, turning whichever way she feels at each junction to create a challenge in her mind and raise her level of brain activity. Within five minutes, she registers that she is being tailed by a guy in a black jacket. She doesn't recognise him and needs to know if he is BND – the German domestic security service – or something more deadly. She deploys a set of simple techniques to test if someone is following her, or whether it is just her own paranoia. He passes the tests; he is indeed a tail.

She returns to the hotel but instead of going to her room she takes a right hand turn to the rear staircase. There is a fire escape on the outside wall and she climbs out and up to the roof to get a view of the street below. Looking down from the top, she can see her tail waiting in a café across the street. She takes her phone and photographs him, then runs the image against the MI6 Oberon database of all known people of interest but it doesn't match with anyone.

She walks across the roof to the next building and breaks in to the access door for the lifts before climbing down through the lift machinery to reach the top floor. It is an advertising agency and she makes her way down through the building, passed desks with cool people talking about creative ideas and through colourful brainstorming areas. It reminds her of why she baulked at the idea of an office job when she was a young woman.

She walks out through the reception area to the street and turns west, after a minute she checks for her tail in a shop window. She has lost him. She walks on, finds a café and orders a coffee.

It takes her tail fifteen minutes to find her. That means, she knows, that they have GPS on her. They cannot have known where she is unless they have tracking deployed. It tells her that she is important to someone, the only question in her mind is who. If it's MI6 and associates then she is concerned but it's manageable. But if she is being tailed by private interests that is much more difficult to control.

She plays it cool and takes half an hour to finish her drink. She leaves 10 Euros on the table and slowly gets up. She saunters across the street and into an alleyway that she scouted while sitting in the café from behind her sunglasses. She drops into a doorway recess on the left-hand side and waits. The tail turns into the alleyway, stops when he cannot see her, and then walks more slowly towards the dead end.

As he passes her doorway, Gabrielle delivers a high kick to his stomach, winding him instantly. He bends over and then rights himself; he is a professional and can cope with some onslaught. She steps back and kicks again, this time to his kidney. She has the upper hand; he groans and she grabs an arm, twists it behind him and pushes him down.

"Time to talk," she whispers in his ear, pressing him into the road.

With a single movement, he spins and grabs her neck and thrusts his thumb against her throat. She is caught off guard and gasps. He presses harder. The air stops flowing. She falls back, feeling light headed; the man keeps his hand in place. She is fainting now; her brain is running at double speed. She has to get his thumb off her windpipe. It takes all of her energy to bring her knee up to his groin. He is stunned for just one second, but that is enough. She pushes him hard, he falls back and hits his head on the ground. She gets up and kicks him; he rolls away, gets to his feet and runs off back up the alleyway and around the corner.

She is annoyed with herself, as she should have held him and found out who he worked for. Just winning the fight is not enough, you have to win and get the information. She swears silently at her lack of concentration.

Gabby arrives back at her hotel at 5pm. She knows someone has been in the room the moment she enters. She checks her things, nothing missing, but what had they been looking for? She pulls out her phone and autodials BND.

"Robert Bolt please; Gabrielle Lane." she says in to the phone, then waits while the call is put through.

"Robert, old thing, how are you?" She listens to the answer.

"Look, you had a tail on me today. I wanted to know if you have also trashed my hotel room."

She listens.

"I thought we had a joint working agreement, Robert," she says, getting angry. "You know what? I don't believe anything you've just told me."

Gabby ends the call, steaming inside. She can tell when German people lie, something she picked up quite quickly in Berlin. The fact remains that she has become a person of interest to at least one security organisation and she can't think why.

She eats in her room and researches anything she can find about the hours before Mac was killed, anything at all. She goes through the known sites used by the German criminal underworld to leave their messages for each other – Munich Flower Market.com and Belinda's Weekend Travel Company, but there is nothing. Now is the time that she needs to maintain her cool. In these first few hours after an unplanned incident where there is no framework and no structure to rely on, she can feel vulnerable, she knows from numerous psych tests she has completed. She must find out more, and quickly, to stop the feeling of insecurity; until a pattern forms, her brain will keep telling her she is unprotected whether she tries to consciously believe it or not.

*

The nurse gently lifts Stuart Palmer's left wrist and feels his pulse. Steady now after 48 hours of touch and go. She lowers the limb back down on to the bed covers, turns to the intravenous drip and taps the outside of the casing. She takes a syringe from her pocket, removes it from its packaging, fills it, and injects liquid into the tube. She writes something in the notes at the end of the bed and glides out of the room. Palmer's breathing is steady, the lights on the monitors indicate his heartbeat and vital rhythms. It is mid-afternoon and the sunshine floods in through the window next to his bed. An hour passes. Nurses walk along the corridor outside. The lights on the monitor slow and suddenly an alarm crashes the peace. Two nurses come running in and check the dials on the monitor. One starts resuscitation; the other messages the on-call doctor. Within a minute, a tall, dark woman in her fifties arrives and inspects Stuart. One nurse leaves the room and the other continues resuscitation. His breathing is shallow; his body starts to convulse, he vomits and it stays in his mouth. They turn him, the doctor calls for drugs and a syringe. She thrusts it in to his right arm. The convulsions stop. He cries out in pain; then settles.

"What was it?" asks the nurse.

"Do you have the last test results?" says the doctor. The nurse dips her hand into the patient records folder on the bed, draws out a single sheet of paper and hands it over and the doctor reads.

"It doesn't make sense to me. These results show all clear, but these symptoms now show some sort of poison. Has anyone been in here? Anyone who is not staff?"

"No one has been here. We've been at the nurses' station, right outside, since nine this morning."

"We'll need this investigated," says the doctor as she goes to a telephone at the nurses' station outside and dials a number.

"Herr Professor? Dr Blumhof. There is something you need to see on the wards." She listens to his reply.

"Now, if you can." She replaces the receiver and goes back to Stuart's bedside. She looks at his pupils, watches the monitors and looks through his notes again.

"What are you all about, Herr Palmer?" she says under her breath.

*

CHAPTER THREE

The grey waters of the Thames sweep passed the windows of the MI6 Headquarters at Vauxhall Cross in London. A telephone buzzes in front of Sir Stephen Laughton from a row of three positioned just off centre on his vast, polished desk.

"Yes?" he says.

"Sir Bernard for you, sir."

"Thank you, Martine." The line clicks.

"Stephen."

"Sir."

"Stephen, you have a field agent - Blackhawk?"

"Yes."

"Is she under our control?"

"She is, sir. She is running OP15, if you have intel about untrackable actions that would explain it."

"OP15?"

"She suspects a comms network breach, sir."

"Is she right?"

"Not at all, sir. Network status green," says Laughton.

"She's the one on Hillbank isn't she?"

"Sir."

"Am I getting my special report, Stephen?"

"In the works, Sir Bernard." Laughton knows that the extra work for his staff to run Sir Bernard's requested special comms report will not be popular with the section comms team who are already overloaded due to breach investigators on site. This is just further hassle.

"Tomorrow please, Stephen."

"Sir."

The line goes dead.

Laughton gets up and goes to his drinks cabinet between the two bay windows on the right-hand side of his office. He pours a single malt and looks out across the running tide; his fingers touch the arsenic capsule in his pocket. You never know when you might be caught. Every day is a high wire act, all the people you meet that you have to lie to. A man can only keep going for so long and Moscow has become increasingly demanding in the last few months. Something is happening, Laughton can tell. It feels like an eyes-only operation is bubbling through MI6, but not for his eyes. He has heard nothing, and that makes him wary. Laughton has been very careful to leave no trace of his leaks over the years, but that doesn't mean his luck might run out one day. He drinks the malt straight down and pours another.

*

With her overnight bag on one shoulder, Gabrielle makes her way onto the train in Berlin Hauptbahnhof. Her sleepless night has made her feel tired but not enough to alter her perception levels. She will be weaponless until she picks up a gun in London due to the Eurostar leg of the journey having customs checks. As the train speeds through the countryside, she stares out of the window and remembers her first train ride as a girl. She had been very excited; her parents picked up her and her sister from school with large suitcases in tow. They went to Paddington Station and took the train to Exeter. Their father had hired a car, another first; then they drove to Dartmouth. They stayed in a tiny cottage overlooking the sea and spent what seemed like forever walking the coast paths and playing on the sand. She remembers the way her mother looked on that holiday; she must have been in her mid-thirties. Gabrielle could not remember seeing anyone as happy ever again. After her father was killed at sea on an August morning two years later, Gabrielle's mother was never quite the same woman again, as though she lived in shadow. She had remarried when the girls were teenagers but their step father was never going to be good enough as a stand-in.

The train draws in to London St Pancras and Gabrielle decides to walk. Within half an hour she has reached an off-grid safe house that she knows can be a base for a few days. The place is three high-ceilinged rooms within a Victorian mansion near Green Park. It has been an MI5 property for forty years and, she being MI6, means that her official network doesn't register the MI5 location. A beautifully British weakness, she thinks. She taps in the front door code and disappears inside.

*

A group of doctors enter the room like sheep and the tallest man starts speaking with authority.

"This is Herr Palmer. Knife wound to the stomach initially but then he was poisoned whilst on hospital premises. We have launched an investigation."

"What do we know about the poison, Herr Professor?" says one of the group, a small man; his curly hair amassed on the top of his head to make him appear taller. He has thick-rimmed glasses and carries a hard-backed file with papers in it.

"It was plant-based and injected into the IV. We don't know how it was transported or administered without detection, but we will know that soon."

"We have a poisons specialist in my team now, Herr Professor," says the other. "I am happy for him to be used immediately to help."

"Thank you, Dr Langer. Your help is very welcome," he says barely hiding his contempt.

"What do we know about the patient, Herr Professor?" says Langer, picking up the patient record folder. "How did he get stabbed in the first place?"

"Attacked in the street."

"No history?"

"He is a British civil servant. We approached the Embassy for patient records of his background but they say they didn't have any records. He hadn't been to a doctor in the UK for years and all records had been destroyed."

The group smile to each other, jointly not believing.

"Did we give him a full body review and a full test set?" asks Langer.

"All as per procedure, Doctor," says the Professor getting mildly frustrated at Langer's implication that somehow the Professor's team had failed in some way.

Langer pauses his onslaught for a second. "I have utmost respect for your team, Professor. My point is only that we need to be sure for the sake of the hospital."

"Of course, Langer, this hospital and its facilities are excellent and our procedures are always followed, rest assured." He smiles but not honestly.

"Let us move on ladies and gentlemen," he says to the group and they all move out of the room in a pack except Langer who holds back for a few seconds. As the last student goes out through the door, he opens his own file of papers, draws out a sheet of paper and exchanges it for the top sheet in the folder, then hurries after the group down the corridor.

*

Thames House is the building widely known to be the headquarters of MI5 but is actually a decoy building. The real headquarters is far more secure and far less obvious. Thames House does though contain some of the middle to senior level operations staff, and the Hot Ops Control Centre. The first name on Gabrielle's list of people to talk to is a woman who she knows will give her real and truthful information. Marjorie Allardice was the Operations Controller for Alpha Branch in the past, the part of MI6 that is focused on Europe. Marjorie had befriended Gabrielle on her first day. "There are not enough girls here," as Marjorie had put it. "We need to stick together."

Marjorie is one of a core of well-connected women who have come into the British security services since the turn of the millennium. Educated at Roedean and Cambridge, she had slept with her first year Professor then they had an almighty argument at the start of the second year and Marjorie got her sacked. She went on to gain a First in Economics. She was officially picked up for MI6 at twenty-five, some say she was recruited while still at Cambridge, but that is a rumour driven by the Service's reminiscences of Philby and friends. Security operations in the 21st Century require finding people who will fit in to a wide range of different groups in the field and so the service is diversifying but is still overly reliant on Oxbridge as the source for senior staff. Marjorie made the move to MI5 in her thirties when her father had died and she needed to cut down on travel to look after her mother in St John's Wood.

From her vantage point in the coffee shop opposite Thames House, Gabrielle can see the main doors and the two side doors used for access. At exactly 3:32pm, Marjorie emerges in to the daylight from a ten-hour shift leading an op in the North of England. Gabrielle waits, then gets up, leaving a fiver on the table, and follows Marjorie to the tube station.

Westminster Tube station is a spy's paradise; it is designed to not have any hiding places for people who might want to attack MPs coming back late at night from a party and the worse for wear. Gabrielle can see Marjorie all the way down the escalator to the lower level. They stand, thirty feet part on the Jubilee Line northbound platform. Gabrielle steps back behind a group of Italian tourists for camouflage. The train arrives, Gabrielle waits for Marjorie to move, which she does. Gabrielle takes the car that is one along from her target.

They reach daylight as they step on to the street at St John's Wood; a busy road junction. Marjorie navigates the traffic and walks quickly toward the mansion flats where her mother now lives. Gabrielle speeds up. As Marjorie turns into Victoria Mansions, Gabrielle draws level with her friend.

"Marjorie?"

The woman doesn't turn to look but slows to a saunter.

"I saw you Gabby, back at Westminster."

"I thought you might have done. I need to talk."

"I heard."

"What did you hear?"

"That you are off-grid."

"I am."

Marjorie takes a side long glance at Gabrielle, the first time she has looked at her.

"You'd better come in," says Marjorie.

They go through an enormous Victorian portico to the flats and up the stairs. Marjorie puts her forefinger to her lips as she and Gabrielle enter the flat. "Don't want to frighten the horses," she says, her eyes widening. "Mother?" Marjorie calls gently from the front door.

"Conservatory, Marjie," bellows a distant voice. They make their way down a long corridor and into the conservatory of 17A Carlisle Place.

"You remember Gabrielle?"

Lady Allardice turns an aged head and peers at Gabrielle.

"Oh yes, the thin girl. How are you, my dear?"

"Very well, thank you, Your Ladyship."

"Don't bother with all that, call me Fi."

"What's been going on, mother?"

"I was just tracking these Chinese websites that issue statements apparently independent of the Government, but it's all bloody transparently the bloody Chinese security service. Think we were born yesterday."

"Mother was in 6 for thirty years from the 1960s and still dabbles," says Marjorie.

"What are they saying, Fi?" asks Gabrielle.

"Just reeling off names of individuals who are of interest to the authorities, making out they are trying to protect them. I invented this technique in '68, we used it against the Soviets very effectively if I recall. Brought in a large number of their double agents that they were running in London by appearing to be a pro-Soviet newspaper. Fell right into it." She lets out a sharp laugh as Marjorie disappears to make some tea.

"How do you find the sites, Fi?"

"Easy for me, my dear. This technical chap I know set my computer up with something..." She stops, completely still for one heartbeat, then reanimates. "No, gone. Anyway, it allows me to track covert ops very easily so I can get in to places I'm not supposed to." The old lady's eyes glisten.

"Could I take a look at your computer? I'm always interested in gadgets," says Gabby.

"Be my guest, my dear. In the study, second door on the left, back towards the front door."

Gabrielle finds the study and sits in front of the desktop computer. She pulls out a micro drive from her back pocket and plugs it into the machine to run a strike analysis which will find any tracking devices that need to be disabled before she can do what she wants to do. She creates a false user and a mask environment, and brings up the log in screen for the MI6 main database. To make a covert enquiry into the mainframe, she must leave no activity threads within the tracer paths across the network. Tech Branch will spot the activity within 60 seconds so she has to get in and out before the alarms trigger. She logs in and starts a timer on her watch.

Gabrielle is looking for the patterns of comms activity just after Mac received his reporting instructions, to find anyone who was unduly active around that time. A list of messages is displayed for the seven-hour period between her ordering the sniper and Mac being notified of his reporting information. She runs a duplicate search against kill location and matches the two. A list of match names comes up of active people in that period of time:

Smethwick, Laughton, Barlow, Martin, Bhaskar, Allardice, Raleigh, Laughton, Morris and Shah.

Some are field ops requests, some are within her ops section and others are London Centre messaging. She copies the whole bulk data file onto a USB and pulls it out. She closes and destroys the false user she had created and runs a shadow program to remove all traces of activity on Fi's computer. As the last screen disappears, the alarm bleeps quietly on her wrist. She breathes out. Something will be in the data and now she needs a specialist to do the analysis. She knows who will be perfect; Jim Cartright is her next port of call.

In the conservatory, Marjorie and her mother are drinking tea and eating tea-cakes.

"Thank you for use of your computer, Fi," says Gabby.

"You're very welcome, my dear. I hope it helps you."

They all chat for an hour and get on to the old days in 6. Fi entertains them with stories that Marjorie has heard many times.

Fi needs to check the horse racing results and leaves them to chat. Marjorie and Gabrielle's conversation eventually returns to the present day. She tells Marjorie about Mac's death and her theory about the mole.

"What's your next step, Gab?" asks Marjorie quietly.

"I need to talk to a few people who have the information I need. There's evidence out there, I just have to find it and piece it together."

The time ticks on and the two friends enjoy each other's company. Eventually, Gabby looks at her watch. "I need to go," she says, then pauses. "I was never here, Marj, it's better like that, I don't want you and Fi caught up in my mess."

"You can trust us, Gab," says Marjorie. They walk to the door.

"I'll see you," says Gabby kissing Marjorie on the cheek. She walks down the stairs and pushes out into the dark. Inside the flat, Marjorie goes to the study and starts to file her contact report with London Centre with an update on Gabrielle's latest information and state of mind.

CHAPTER FOUR

Catherine pulls out her mobile phone and taps in the decrypt key. Only three other people are sitting in the restaurant on Nüschelerstrasse in the centre of Zurich city centre.

Her boyfriend has sent pictures of his new flat, Park Street in Mayfair. She doesn't trust him, too confident by half; she is sure he is cheating on her and fully intends to return to England as a surprise to catch him out.

A message pings in. "Damn it," she murmurs, pulling one hand back through her blonde hair. She has been hoping for no more work this week. The screen shows a subject line "653/6.1."

She opens the message and it contains the usual instructions, a grid reference and time, 6:30pm tonight. The location is a villa on the outskirts of Zurich. Catherine would have given anything not to go, but once you sign up, it is impossible to get out of work when it comes through. The target is Marco Estaves, a small-time gangster who runs prostitutes on the western side of the city. He has aspirations for more involved crimes including supplying mercenary soldiers to the Middle East and it is time for him to stop, or so London and the Swiss security services have decided.

She reads the brief attached to the message. Estaves has personal security and the kill will have to be close range. She will use her favourite handgun, the Beretta M9, she thinks, and walks out; her long legs striding purposefully up the hill to her apartment, ten minutes away.

MI6 have allocated her to Northern Italy and Switzerland. The dedicated patch strategy is a change from the old days of assassins, where they were deployed anywhere across the world and had to fly long haul to complete a kill order. Long haul isn't the best experience just before you have to work, and you have to be fit in this job, almost like an athlete. She takes care of her diet and only eats things that will keep her weight within four pounds of her optimum. She goes to the gym every other day and can outrun all the men on the treadmill.

She takes her Jaguar F-Type up through the hills, parks, and makes a wide sweep on foot of the valley where the house lies. She has maps on her phone from London Centre and a floor layout. She is wearing camouflage leggings and a running jacket, her hair swirled up and hidden beneath a woollen beany. Catherine gets back to her Jaguar and drives to a clearing in the wood that sits just beyond the house. She walks through the trees until she reaches the top of a wooded slope that leads down to the rear of the property. There are two guards that she can see, one on each side of the terrace, but she can tell that they're amateurs from the way they stand; no military training is apparent. They mostly stay in the same spot, but occasionally one of them goes off for a cigarette down one side of the villa.

She re-positions herself along the slope so she can see his smoking place, and as he walks there for a second time, she silently drops from the top of the rise, fast, almost flying. She appears from the wood, ten feet from him, runs up behind him and pushes the knife in between two ribs. The lights in his eyes dim instantly and he slumps to the ground. There is a side door; she tries the handle; it's locked. She withdraws a wire from her watch, inserts it in to the lock and waits for the tiny click. Catherine silently opens the door and steps inside; she can hear Marco on the telephone in the sitting room. She pulls out the Beretta from the holster strapped to her back, screws on the silencer, and treads silently across the room until she is against a doorframe within twenty feet of him. The shot will have to be point blank to be effective. She has one shot to make this work as the other guard may hear the shot and block her exit route.

Estaves is pacing the room, talking about some arrangements for importing something or other. He is facing the doorway where she is hiding.

"Come on, Marco," she whispers under her breath, "Just move round a tiny bit."

He moves. She takes three paces, pushes the Beretta into his torso, and pulls the trigger. A dull thud echoes around the room; he tries to call out. She takes the weight of his body and lays him down. He holds her gaze for a second, then his eyes close. That is half the job, as her instructors have always told her, the other half is getting out.

Catherine turns back to the doorway and runs silently across the room, out through the side door and across the garden to the wood. She stops for a second to check she isn't being followed then runs up the slope and swings back around the hill to the place where her car is parked. Her body slips down into the driver's seat, she stows the Beretta in its housing alongside the seat and the engine roars. She drives back to the main road and turns to the city; as she does so, a black Porsche pulls out behind her, and she puts her foot down.

The Jaguar pulls away easily and she is comfortably a hundred yards in front, she steadies her speed and enjoys the evening air. The Porsche is still there; when they approach a long straight stretch, it suddenly accelerates and comes up close behind her, she pushes her Jag faster but the Porsche stays with her. It has blackened windows so she can't see the driver. It pulls out and draws level with her as they both hit 70mph. The straight stretch will end in ten seconds. The passenger window of the Porsche slides down and the passenger raises a hand gun to her; two shots rang out, the first hits the door beside her and the second smashes the side window. Catherine brakes right at the start of the curve in the road, the Porsche doesn't slow and barely makes the corner before re-gaining control and speeding off. She pulls over and sits motionless, taking in the events of the past minute. A trickle of blood drops down her cheek from glass fragments that have grazed her cheek. She looks in the rear-view mirror, she has three or four cuts across her face.

She stabs a button on the car's console.

"Message for London Centre," she says out loud.

"Message for London Centre," repeats the electronic voice. "Go ahead."

"Message to London Centre from Coniston. I have completed job 653/6.1 successfully. The job itself was fine but I was chased afterwards and sustained fire, 2 rounds; no injuries. Attack was not at the job location but the assailants appear to have been waiting for me, and the location seems to have been leaked, suggest you explore. Message ends."

She wipes the blood from her face, drops the clutch and heads for the airport.

*

Gabby pushes back the wardrobe door in the safe house and enters a small room hidden behind it that contains the comms equipment. She goes to a bank of computers on the left-hand side, pulls out her mobile and plugs it directly in to one of the servers. She opens an app and a range of proxy locations appear on the screen; she selects Barcelona and runs the program. A message is displayed on the phone, 'Network proxied to Barcelona node 238DT'. She pulls out the connecting cable, puts in a wireless earpiece and stabs the final connecting switch to bring her on grid.

A voice comes through the speakers.

"Blackhawk, nice to hear from you at last."

"Morning, Cabinetmaker. How goes it?"

"Mustn't grumble, you know. How is Barcelona?"

She pulls up the Barcelona weather forecast on a second screen.

"It has been lovely these past couple of days but looking a bit shit now to be honest. Spoiling my suntan."

Gabrielle is running a voice stress detector on the screen to her right to tell if Cabinetmaker is relaxed or under pressure. The stress chart is climbing; he is being puppeted, taking direct orders from a senior officer into his earpiece.

"We were worried about you."

"I'm fine, just being careful after the news from the other day."

"We were wondering if you could come in to the Consulate in Barcelona and debrief your Hillbank op."

"More than happy to do that in a day or two, Cab."

"We were hoping for sooner." She gets up from the seat and paces the room.

"Not possible I'm afraid, my other boyfriend needs to see me."

The stress chart jumps on the screen. Cabinetmaker is a junior ops room clerk, she met him once and he was timid. She cannot be sure if the jump was just his natural nervousness or a translation of her words as having any double meaning.

"Just some stuff I need to do," she adds. "What intel on Stranraer?"

"The location was leaked, Blackhawk."

"Anything on how that happened yet?

"We're checking, all the protocols seem to have been were followed."

She is getting frustrated. "Don't tell me you lot have been sitting on your arse for two days after we lost someone in the field?"

"We have nothing more. The Crows are all over it but have come up with nothing," he says, referring to the MI6 Investigations Branch. The nick name is a wartime one from when they all wore black bowler hats that made them feel separate and slightly superior to the other staff.

The stress chart is right at the top of the screen now; Cabinetmaker isn't used to puppeting or is just out of practice.

"I need to go, Cab."

She switches off the comms, pulls out the earpiece and throws it down on to the desk. They are running her as a rogue agent now as the Americans call it, she knows the protocols for a field agent who you don't trust as well as they do. She is even more aware now that she needs to plan her approach very carefully over the next few days and stick to people she can trust, or at the very least, the people she thinks she can trust.

*

Stephen Laughton was recruited as a Russian agent at Oxford in the 1990s; he studied Social Urbanisation Patterns of the 19th Century as his final thesis. He became convinced that communism is the better option after many late-night meetings in the pubs of Oxford. Covert visits to Moscow followed, all arranged through his sole Russian handler, Ivan. A name that Laughton has always been amused by; he can't believe that the Russian security services chose such an archetypal cover name. By his mid-twenties, Laughton had a good job in the Home Office and made the application to the Foreign & Commonwealth Office at the behest of Ivan. Once inside the FCO, with his Oxbridge background and cut-glass accent, it had not been difficult for Laughton to speed through the levels of seniority. He had joined MI5 as a Higher Executive Officer and was a key part in the Northern Ireland operations for which he was promoted. He moved to MI6 the following year.

Moscow likes to think they have not demanded a great deal from him. They encouraged him to 'live like a normal man' and he met Caroline in his early thirties. Neither wanted children and Linny, as he calls her, is a successful Barrister in the Inns of Court. They travelled to New York and Bali to celebrate her becoming Queen's Council. They live happily in Highgate, overlooking Hampstead Heath. His biggest regret is that Linny knows nothing of his Moscow connections; he has spent a lifetime lying to the woman he loves so much that he would lay down his own life to save hers.

Laying down his life is not so far-fetched an outcome, he thinks, it would put an end to the strain of pretence and the deaths that he has been responsible for – the men and women from MI6 who he had leaked information about and so put them in danger. Moscow had completed the task and killed many of them. A vision of another Stephen flashes momentarily across his mind, the one who declined the offer of dinner with Ivan all those years before, the one who followed a career in journalism and then as a writer, the one who has not been lying to Linny for decades.

Laughton walks up Dean Street from where the taxi drops him and turns right into Quo Vadis, a restaurant where he has met Ivan many times over the years. Ivan is sitting in the corner, just as he always is.

"Ivan."

"Petrov," says the Russian, using Laughton's SVR code name. "I ordered the sea bass for us, I know you like it."

Laughton sits. "How are things?"

"Interesting activities going on that you don't need to know about, but good for Russia."

"How long have we known each other, Ivan?"

"Many years, comrade."

"Don't call me that," snaps Laughton.

"After your years of service? You deserve it."

"For over twenty years, I have done everything you have asked of me, haven't I?"

"You have, Petrov."

A moment's silence languishes between the two men.

"I want to stop, Ivan," says Laughton without emotion. "I have had enough."

The Russian is silent for a few moments. "I'm not sure what to say; you see, there isn't a way to stop." He pauses, selecting the right words. "This is a job for life."

"Nevertheless, I want to stop; I want you to arrange it."

"Go on a holiday with that beautiful wife of yours,"

"Keep Caroline out of this."

"You need to rest."

"I need to stop, Ivan." Laughton is dead serious now. "Did you hear me?"

"I heard. But they won't like it."

"Tell Moscow, they have had many years of loyalty," Laughton drops his voice. "And now that is coming to an end. I'll do one more op, that's it. Then it must stop."

"Alright," says the Russian. "I will tell them, one more operation."

"I need to go," says Laughton.

"The sea bass, you have to stay for that."

"Give it to your contacts in Moscow, Ivan." Laughton gets up and strides out of the restaurant.

*

The light from the upper window moves across his face. Stuart opens his eyes for the first time in what seems like months but isn't. He looks around the hospital ward as it comes into focus. Lying still, his brain automatically starts to go through what he can remember of the events that led to him being in this bed; the café, the car, the running, the man with the knife.

"Herr Palmer." A voice comes from the doorway. "Good to see you awake."

A nurse walks in. "The doctors weren't sure how long you would take," she says. "How do you feel?"

"Tired."

"That's to be expected. Have some water."

She pours liquid into a glass beside his bed and puts her hand behind his head so that he can drink.

Over the next two days, Stuart sleeps, drinks, eats and gradually feels better. Doctors come in and out, inspect his charts, speak efficiently and briefly to him, and write more notes.

By the third day, he is feeling relatively normal. Another nurse comes in.

"Good news, Herr Palmer," she says breezily. "You will be allowed to go home today."

"Thank you, nurse. That's very good news."

She smiles politely. "I will get your clothes and you can get dressed."

Doctor Langer enters the room from the corridor. "Nurse?"

"Yes, Doctor?"

"I couldn't help over-hearing. I'm afraid there's been a change of plan." He turns to Palmer. "I'm sorry to disappoint you, Herr Palmer, but I have taken on your case now and we have had some more test results back. I'm afraid you have an infection that we must treat before you can be discharged."

Stuart in fact is glad as he doesn't feel ready to go back just yet.

"Can I make a telephone call?" he asks. He calls the office. Geraldine is pleased to hear from him and tells him that everything had been sorted out while he's been away. Malcolm took on the policy paper about trade and Sally from accounts found someone else to do the analysis of health care services for British expats in Germany. She speaks as though he has been away on a business trip rather than the victim of a stabbing.

"How do you feel, Stuart?" she asks eventually.

"OK." There is a British pause as they struggle to find any words that show some caring without being too forward.

"We've all missed you, Stuart."

"Thank you, Geraldine, it will be good to get back and see you."

"When are you coming out?" she says.

"A while yet, there's an infection apparently."

"Do they allow visiting?" asks Geraldine.

"Yes."

"I might come to see you then."

"That would be nice," he says. They hang on the telephone line, each wanting to hear themselves say something more deeply felt.

"I'll come in tomorrow," she says.

"Right."

They ring off and, in the office, Geraldine pushes her hair back from her eyes and is lost in her thoughts.

*

Jim is late. He arrives in a fluster, having been held up by some last-minute analyses needed before the opening of the Asian markets.

Gabby hasn't seen Jim Cartright for six years. They worked together in the Metropolitan Police Specialist Decryption team during her training. Jim borders on genius when it comes to numbers and finding patterns in data. He left the police and moved in to banking in London's Docklands area. She booked a table at Elephant Royale Restaurant as she knows he likes Thai food. She asks for a table overlooking the river so she can see the horizon.

They chat for an hour about people they know and their lives. Gabrielle, like all field agents, has a number of fabricated cover lives that Comms Branch create for everyone who needs to form a false impression of how they spend their days. Her cover story for Jim has always been that she works in a law firm as an investigator. She has a fictional boyfriend, Ralph, and they have a flat together in Fulham. When she first started in field ops, it seemed very odd having to learn about her cover lives, but over the months and years, she has become used to it and is quite fond of some of the people in her stories. When in Berlin, she has a particularly lovely fictional uncle who lives in Munich who she visits regularly. He sounds so kind and the sort of person she wishes she knows in real life.

After a while, Gabrielle thinks the time is right.

"I wanted to ask you something, Jim."

"Fire away."

"We have a legal case currently running and I have to find out if there are any patterns in the emails being sent between various people in this company."

"What's the data type?" he asks.

She pulls a second USB stick from her pocket. "Data strings with time stamps and routing codes," she says. Gabrielle has anonymised the original data so that no trace of real names exists within the version on this USB.

"What do you reckon?"

"Let me have a go, Gab," he says. "How much data?"

"4 terabytes." He widens his eyes.

"How long would it take?"

"A week?"

"Three or four days would be good if you can, we've got a court date coming up." She flicks her eyes up to his and smiles.

"I'll do my best, Gab. But I need to go back, sorry. Chinese markets are having a big announcement and I'm needed." He pauses. "Really nice to see you again."

"You too, Jim. Look after yourself."

"I'll message you when this is done," he says, then walks away.

Gabrielle raises her hand to order another glass of wine as she wants time to just think. She has started to feel lonely for the first time in a long while and gets out her phone. She flicks through her contacts, chooses one and autodials. A man answers.

"Rich, it's Gabby. What are you doing tonight? Fancy a drink?" A pause while she listens. "Great, new flat? Ping me the address. I'll be over."

She sits staring for a few moments thinking about her life. The waitress comes up; she cancels the wine, pays the bill and goes out to the street.

Gabrielle clambers into a waiting cab. "Park Street, Mayfair please."

*

CHAPTER FIVE

Streaks of a London dawn linger across the sky as Gabrielle gets back to the safe house just before 9am the next day. She packs her bag and takes the tube to Heathrow Terminal 5, pays cash for a ticket and boards a flight immediately.

Brussels airport is bathed in sunshine as the plane swings round to make the final descent. She takes a cab to Rue Souveraine in the centre of the city and checks her phone for the address she needs. Rue Souveraine is like a hundred roads in Brussels, tall houses from la belle époque creating a beautifully decorated ravine up to the sky.

She finds the building she needs and pushes at a large door which leads to a roofless square with steps to the flats above. She finds the staircase to number 12, silently makes her way up to the second floor and lets herself in through the front door. The sitting room has a panoramic view of Brussels, rooftops stretching out north-west to the Parc du Cinquantenaire. Gabrielle goes through the rooms to check nobody is sleeping late. There is no one there; she is alone in the place.

Gabby goes through some files in a cabinet next to a large rosewood desk that sits squarely across the end window. She finds nothing; he is being careful. She knows he will not be home for several hours and so it's a waiting game. She realises she is hungry and opens the fridge, takes meat and cheese and sits in an armchair that faces one of the windows. After last night she is tired and closes her eyes. Gabby is woken by the sound of a key in the front door. The chair she is in is high-backed and she is invisible to whoever is coming in. She waits; the person arrives with shopping bags and makes their way to the kitchen. They start to put the food away; Gabrielle gets up from her hiding position but forgets the plate she took for the food and it clatters on the floor. The man in the kitchen turns and draws a handgun but Gabrielle is quicker than him and by the time he turns, she has raised her Smith & Wesson to his temple.

"Ca fait, longtemps, Jonas," she says.

"Blackhawk, it has been a very long time," he says. "What brings you to the world's greatest city?"

"We're not in London, Jonas but I'll let it pass. Put the gun on the floor." He does so. "Sit down in the chair by the desk."

Jonas Geelan steps across the room with his hands showing, and sits down.

"What can I do for you, Gabrielle?" he says calmly. She keeps the gun trained on him.

"Information, Agent Geelan," her voice is monotone. "Information about an op that your GISS Security Team carried out a few days ago."

"Any particular operation?" he asks.

"I need you to take me to your HQ and we're going to find out together."

"You want to come with me to Rue Royale?"

"Oui," she replies.

"Why would I do this, Gabrielle?"

"Because I know you're running a double agent between London and Brussels, and I know her name, and because you don't want that to get out because London would get annoyed."

"I don't know anything about a double agent." He holds her stare.

"Oh, how dull, I thought you would be more of a man about this. Do I have to show you the evidence?"

"I don't know anything about a double agent, Blackhawk." He repeats and blinks slowly.

She reaches into her jacket, pulls out a sheet of paper and unfolds it. "Names, dates, locations," she says, holding the paper in the air.

He is silent for five seconds. "I'll help you," he murmurs.

"That's my boy. The master copy of the information on that paper is in a letter that has already been posted to the Director General of your security service and is on the back of a motorbike coming from Berlin. It will take that bike about two hours to arrive. That's how long we have to get the information. The motor cyclist will call my mobile when he arrives at the address to check if he should not deliver the letter. No answer from me will mean he will deliver the letter. If I answer, I can tell him to go ahead or stop. That is the only way he will abort the delivery. Also, just in case you're thinking of any funny business, the motor cyclist is also a field agent from MI6, armed and has orders to kill on sight if he is attacked or stopped en route."

Geelan is silent. She lowers the gun. "Let's go," she says.

They take a cab to the GISS building and emerge from the lifts on the fourth floor. Jonas lets Gabrielle into his office and they sit in front of the computer.

"Give me the keyboard," she says. He moves it over.

"Stand over there," she orders, typing a string of characters in. She hits enter and a list of flies comes up on the screen.

"If you tell me what you're looking for...," he starts to say.

"No need for you to know anything more, monsieur," she says. "What does the suffix Ge-26H mean?

"It's a hard disc location downstairs, Gerlain archive room, Row 26, Location H."

"Right, and so La-83D is another archive room?"

"Laborde," he replies. She writes down the two references.

"Show me the archive," she says. They take the lift to the basement and enter a labyrinth of connected rooms crammed full of paper files for the old cases and hard disc storage devices for the more recent work. They pass three rooms before they arrive at Laborde.

"Here," he says. They go down one of the long rows of shelving, lined with eight-foot-high cabinets. Section 83 is on the corner.

"Location D," she says under her breath. She reaches up to pull out the drive. At that moment, he grabs her arm and twists it behind her back, pinning her face against the cabinet. Gabby's body is more athletic than Geelan's and she could get out of the hold but refrains.

"Don't be stupid, Jonas."

"Be quiet."

"You don't want to throw away a twenty-year career," she says gently. "You'd be ruined, and relations with London screwed for a generation."

"I can't be seen to leak this information," he whispers. "The file access is all on my security profile."

"I don't need to whole file, I just need to look at them and copy certain things," she whispers back.

They stand locked in the position for a few seconds, then he relaxes his hold on her.

"Just copies," he mutters, his eyes showing defeat.

They find the other location and drop the drives into a reader terminal in one corner of the archive. She scans the content she needs and takes pictures with her phone from the terminal screen then they replace the devices in their shelf positions, and he escorts her to reception.

"Thank you, Jonas." He says nothing and swipes his key card on the exit gate to let her out. She walks through the revolving doors and makes her way out into the street.

*

It is Linny's turn to make dinner and she is in the kitchen when Stephen arrives home to Highgate by 6:30pm. He changes his clothes and joins her while she cooks.

"Very interesting case I'm on, Stephen," she says. "Fraud in a London firm; one of the men turns out to have links to the security services and has potentially received information from them."

"Are you allowed to tell me any names?"

"Sorry, I'm not."

They eat in the dining room, which sits on one corner of the house and provides a view over the Heath. When she had seen the house twenty years before, she had known it was the place she wanted to live with him. Over dinner, they talk about holidays. They both like travel and get away three times a year. After a while, there is a pause in their conversation.

"Do you wish we'd had children, Linny?"

She thinks for a moment before she answers.

"When you and I talked about it and decided that we both wanted careers, I had made up my mind. For me, children would have meant five years out of work at least in those days. I know it's all supposed to be different now and you can go back after a week and get childcare, but I wouldn't have been that sort of mother. I would never have wanted to go back."

"Yes, you would have been like that," he says quietly.

"What about you?" she asks. "Regretting the decision now?"

"No." he says vaguely, then realises how it sounded. "Sometimes, I suppose. When I have a long day at work. Something to take my mind off spying."

"For me," she says. "It has always been about the two of us. From the moment I met you, I wanted to spend the rest of my life with only you. I always knew that."

He smiles at her.

"Children wouldn't have changed that," she adds. "But I still want to spend my time on this planet with you, for as long as we have. We can grow old in this house together. Travel the world and come back to see this view and walk the Heath with each other. That's what love is, Stephen."

The price for Linny's happiness is that he continues in MI6 and continues to leak information that will send British agents to their death. The Russians would kill him if he stays in the job but stops leaking. He needs to decide quickly and can feel that the window when he has the luxury of self-determination is very slowly closing. All the options are full of pain for everyone involved. His mind shifts to the arsenic capsule upstairs, hidden behind the bathroom cabinet and he can feel a shiver run through his body as he watches his happy wife.

*

Geraldine dislikes hospitals. It has nothing to do with the smell of disinfectant, it is more that she doesn't like the rules that are enforced on her for no reason whenever she visits one. On the outside, she knows, she is seen as a timid and organised woman, but inside there is a rebel waiting to get out.

Stuart is asleep when she arrives by his bedside. She sits and waits, taking the chance to look at his face for longer than she has done before. She wonders if he is as kind as he seems; she has had boyfriends over the years, but none ended up being kind to her. Some had been gentle, but kind and gentle aren't the same thing. Her presence or something else entirely prompts Stuart to open his eyes and see her sitting there. They watch each other for a second, neither with any agenda.

"Thank you for coming," he says "Did you take the day off?"

"I didn't tell anyone I was coming here, I wasn't sure if you..."

They let the incomplete sentence say more than the complete one would have done.

"What did they say about your infection?"

"It's not unusual to get an infection after an operation."

"You had an operation?"

"They had to inspect the stab wound," he says.

"What happened? Why were you there?"

"I was just shopping and stopped for a drink then all hell let loose."

"Do you know who stabbed you?"

"He just passed me in the street. But it was the shooting that I was running from."

"I don't understand," she says.

"There was an old man who was shot, then I was stabbed."

"Because you were a witness?"

"I don't know that either," he says.

"Is it to do with work?"

"Maybe, has anyone said anything in the office?"

"Nothing, they won't even talk about it, I tried to ask but was told not to ask again."

"I don't know then," he says with finality.

"I'm not going to stop asking, Stuart." Her passion rises. "You could still be at risk. I don't want you to be hurt."

He smiles at her honesty.

*

The Novotel in Brussels sits on the Rue de la Vierge Noire. Gabby registers under a cover name, goes to her room and sleeps all afternoon. She wakes at 6pm, takes a cab to the east of the city and finds a little French restaurant in a back street. When she emerges, the pavements are wet but the night is clear, and she decides to walk back to the hotel to clear her head. The vast bulk of the Cathedral of St Michael and St Gudula is silhouetted against the darkening sky as she crosses the giant courtyard that runs along the length of the building. From one corner of the square comes the whine of a moped, distant at first then ever nearer. Gabrielle notices it when it is forty feet away, coming straight towards her. The bike is ten feet away now with two people on it, the rear passenger has a baseball bat hanging down beside him. The bike is suddenly next to her; the man lifts the bat and swings at her legs. She dodges and runs towards the cathedral; the bike circles and they come again, faster this time. She pulls out her hand gun and raises it; the driver sees it and swerves away. The bike skids on the cobbles and the whole thing slides sideways. The two riders roll, the bat man gets up and faces her. Gun versus bat, she knows which she'd rather have. The second man draws out a knife from his back pocket and comes for her too. She doesn't want to fire as it will attract too much attention.

The man swings at her body and hits her in the ribs, she bends with the impact but has no time to recover. She can see the knife glint in the moonlight as it comes down on her shoulder. She kicks the guy with the bat in the back of the leg and he falls to his knees, she takes a step back and kicks the bat away. She takes a second step and lands a kick to his crotch, he falls with a congealed thud. The knifeman runs at her, she pushes the blade up and away to the right, twists his arm back and spins him to the ground. She pushes the barrel of her Smith & Wesson to his face.

"Who sent you?" she says in French. He groans. "I will kill you if needs be." Her voice is dead calm. "Who was it?"

"Ulrich," says the man.

"Tell Ulrich, I'm not scared," she says and pushes his head down into the wet cobbles. Gabby gets up, darts across the square and up to the main street. She hails a cab and sinks back into the softness of the seat. The lights of the Belgian night flash passed the window lighting minuscule specs of water which glint on the glass as the cab runs up to speed.

In the security of her hotel room, she lays on the bed. Sebastian Ulrich she knows; ex-Russian military, he made a billion from the sale of state assets after Perestroika, now he is one of the big players in arms sales to the Middle East and has connections to illegal migration into Europe. A nasty man, he personally shot his number two after the guy did a deal without Ulrich knowing about it. Her question is, why would Ulrich want her dead? She flicks back through her memories and where her path and Ulrich's could have crossed. She has never met him but his tentacles of crime spread far and wide across the continent and she may have unconsciously upset a plan of his. She will need to find out, as having a contract out on her from Ulrich will mean that other assassins will come calling. The two at the cathedral were amateurs, but Ulrich has the money to fund some of the best. Her mind is racing and keeps her awake. After too long, her brain finally lets her fall asleep but only once she has decided that her next step must be to find Ulrich before he finds her.

*

CHAPTER SIX

The flight is delayed at Zurich airport and Catherine becomes increasingly annoyed at the Heathrow holding pattern as she circles Docklands for the third time. She emerges from Terminal 3 and hails a taxi. It is 11am.

She selects a number from her phone. The line rings then switches to voicemail.

"Richard? I'm in London later today, flying in about five this afternoon. How about dinner? My treat. Meet you at your place." She hangs up and the car heads off into the London traffic.

*

The walk from the tube station to the MI6 offices has changed little in twenty years. The doorman at Vauxhall Cross nods to acknowledge Laughton's status as he breezes in through security. He ascends the stairs, opens the door to his large office, and goes to his desk where a tray of tea and toast is already waiting for him.

Martine has left a pile of papers on the right-hand side, neatly marked with different coloured stickers according the priority and security sensitivity of the content. He will miss the routine, he will miss Martine, and he will miss being so relied upon. In his stomach, he starts to feel slightly sick. Laughton doesn't want to end up in some tiny godforsaken flat on the outskirts of Moscow. To Russian eyes he is useful but not important; just another one of the people who has changed sides seeking truth or glory.

The door from Martine's office opens gently and she sweeps in.

"Sir?"

"Good morning, Martine. How are you?"

She is taken aback, her boss has never asked her how she is, in all the years they have worked together. She knows everything about him, how he likes his tea, when he doesn't want to be interrupted and the date of his wife's birthday; but he has never asked about herself before. She likes the formality of their relationship and gets great comfort from her detached efficiency.

"I am well, thank you, sir."

"How was your journey, this morning?" he continues.

"Fine, thank you."

"Where do you live, Martine?"

"Ealing," she replies. "By the park."

"I know it," he says. They breathe in unison across the void between them.

"Anything else, sir?"

Laughton is suddenly consciously aware of two forces pulling apart his normality, the desire to escape on one hand and the comfort of his daily life on the other. Each tempting him to move or stay, each pushing him to evaluate what is important.

"Do you enjoy your job, Martine?"

"Of course."

"Could you ever imagine a time when you did another job?"

"I can't, sir. Is that likely?" Her face screws up in an unusually frank show of emotion.

"No, of course not," he says quietly.

"I'm glad, sir," she says, but he has drifted back into his world again and the weight of familiarity lifts from Martine's shoulders. After a few seconds, she walks back to her office.

*

The cab drops Gabby off at a car showroom on the southern outskirts of Brussels that specialises in convertibles. She looks round the lot until a salesman comes out.

"Puis-je vous aider, Mademoiselle?"

"I'm interested in this Z4," she replies. "How much is it?"

"That's a very powerful car, Madam."

"I know. How much is it?"

"What is your budget, Madam?"

"Do you want to sell it?" She is getting mildly frustrated.

"Of course."

"Price?"

"Twenty thousand Euros," he says bluntly.

"I'll take it," she replies curtly. "I'll pay cash and I want to drive it away now."

"I'm afraid that's not poss...," he starts to say.

Gabby moves swiftly across the two metres between them, grabs his arm, twists it back on itself and puts her face an inch from his.

"I'm taking it now," she says slowly.

The man struggles but she has him held in the self-defence movement 12C in the MI6 handbook. He can't move.

Oui, Madame." She releases him. "Let me get the paperwork," he says and scurries off to the office at the back of the lot, and Gabby follows him.

"Do you have a driving licence, Madame?"

"Just give me the keys."

"I need to do the paperwork."

She takes a bundle of cash from her inside jacket pocket.

"This is twenty thousand Euros," she says. "And here's another five for you personally. I'm going to give you this and you're going to give me the keys. Then you're going to fill in the paperwork with whatever name and details you want to because I could make some name up and tell you, but I'll let you do that."

The man stands in silence.

"Keys?" says Gabby. He says nothing. "Keys!" she says more loudly.

He goes to a wall safe, taps in a code and opens the door. He removes a set of keys and hands them to her.

"If these aren't the right ones, I will be back directly," she says and walks out of the office.

The Z4 burst into life, she breathes out and presses the button to open the automatic roof. As it starts to pull back and reveal the deep blue of the sky, she pulls out on to the main road and heads south.

*

The houses in Park Street slumber gracefully as Catherine walks up the steps to the wide front door. She surveys the panel of door bells with name cards neatly printed underneath and choses one randomly. Two rings and the person answers.

"Mr Clarke?" says Catherine. "Westminster Council here, we wanted to talk to you about the road works that are due to start next week. The road is going to be one-way for a fortnight and I wanted to explain it to you."

"Oh really?" says the voice. "You'd better come up, fourth floor. Bloody road works."

The door buzzes, Catherine pushes it open, makes her way to the first floor and finds Flat 5. She enters silently and closes the door behind her. She pulls out a pair of gossamer thin plastic gloves from her bag and slides them on.

She surveys each room, moving quickly and efficiently, searching for anything untoward. Finding evidence of a woman in a room is not difficult: hair, jewellery, perfume. She works her way from the bedroom through the bathroom to the kitchen. Nothing; but she isn't convinced. She had run a voice trace on Richard's voicemail messages over the last two weeks and he has been showing 45% of stress in his voice. Normal life gives a reading of 20%. Rich is not telling her everything and women have always been his weakness. Catherine had seen the intel sweep of him that was carried out when they started dating, a standard MI6 practice for any personal relationship. He had been married for four years and had two affairs in that time before his wife chucked him out over the third misdemeanour. The Service's comms sweep was comprehensive; GCHQ had run email, text and instant message tracers across all platforms. Catherine knows more about Richard then he does.

Just as she is starting to think that the visit is going to yield no evidence, she realises she hasn't checked the dustbins. She goes down the back stairs and through a rear door to a small yard beyond. The bin bags are in a cage to one side, waiting for collection later in the week. She opens the cage and starts rooting through the five bags that are stacked up. The first glance into the top of each one tells her immediately whether it is from a man's or a woman's flat. The fourth bag is male, she opens it and empties it on the floor of the cage. Kitchen rubbish, plastic bags, a pizza box and a bag from a bin in the bathroom. She opens the bathroom bag and adds the contents to the pile of detritus. She sifts through a toothpaste tube, a razor and at last her heart bounces, there in the bag is what she needs but hoped she wouldn't find; a condom. She wraps her plastic glove back round it and puts it in her pocket. Next stop, the MI6 genetics lab in Marylebone. If there are cells from the woman on that condom, she will find her.

*

CHAPTER SEVEN

At lunchtime, Laughton suddenly announces to Martine that he is taking the afternoon off and can she please cancel his appointments for the rest of the day. She bristles at the idea but she is getting used to this new era of eccentricities.

He takes the District Line to Richmond and walks across the High Street to The Green. It is a Tuesday in September and there is no trace of a breeze on the grassy space before him. One hundred-year-old houses gaggle together on the periphery, like chattering old ladies staring out across time. He chooses a bench and sits down.

Laughton thinks about the years that he has lived two lives and how he longs to be able to tell Linny what he really is. After all this time, he wonders whether he really still believes in Communism. He is the first to admit that the experiment failed, the dreams of 1917 and then the 1950s Cambridge elite to create a society of equals had collapsed under the weight of human vanity. The need to be something more important that your contemporaries couldn't be shut away for long. An equal society seems to him further away now than when he had first met Ivan.

He saw the end of the Berlin Wall in his last years at school, and the time since then as Russia struggled with its new-found role in the world. He saw former KGB officers become billionaires from the sale of state assets, and he started to question the motivation of those in the party who sought so much personal power. He remembers sitting in Oxford, the day after he was first contacted by Ivan, and feeling excited by the idea of being part of a political movement that would make better lives for thousands, possibly millions, of working people. But that's not how it worked out.

"Petrov." Ivan is suddenly standing immediately behind him and he jumps. "Nervous?"

"Not particularly," replies Laughton. "Not unless you continue to creep about."

"How have you been?"

"My mind hasn't changed, if that's what you mean."

"I expected nothing less," says Ivan. They sit in silence for a moment.

"I spoke to Moscow."

"What did they say?"

"They are considering your request," says Ivan coldly.

"Nothing else?" asks Laughton.

"They were critical of my handling of you," replies Ivan. "They said I should have known you were unhappy but I had no idea. You kept it from me very well."

"The weakness of dealing with spies, I suppose," says Laughton.

"I have been called back to visit Moscow next week to explain," says Ivan.

"I didn't think it would reflect on you."

"Sadly, it does, comrade."

They both think of what might happen to them now that this chain of connected events has started. The blue touch paper has been lit but they can't stand back, they must take the full force of what is inevitably coming.

In the same moment, it becomes blindingly obvious to them both that their fates are intrinsically linked. Without realising it, they have become mutually dependent on each other. For Laughton, this is another man whose life he has become responsible for; for Ivan, his ticket to a long and happy life has been torn up at the gate.

Laughton is also acutely aware that while he may survive the next weeks and months, Ivan's life expectancy is much more likely to be shorter.

After several minutes, Ivan breaks the silence.

"I have details of your final job, Petrov," he says.

"Go on."

"One of your field agents has upset one of our friends," says Ivan. "Moscow wants her terminated."

"Which agent?" asks Laughton.

"Blackhawk," replies Ivan.

"Ah, the rebel," says Laughton. "What did she do?"

"She killed a friend of ours. Things like that are not forgotten."

"What do you want from me?" asks Laughton.

"All the information you have on her; contacts, friends, family, all known addresses and aliases."

"I need a guarantee from you, Ivan," says Laughton. "A guarantee that this will be the last job, then I want to be left alone to get on with my life. I want to stay in MI6 and continue on in my job. I want all the evidence of my leaks to be destroyed and a commitment to never contact me again from the moment I give you this information. Can Moscow agree to that?"

"I will have to ask, Petrov," says Ivan.

"I will not provide you with any more information until I have that commitment," says Laughton. "But I do trust you, Ivan. If you say that this is all possible then I know you will be telling the truth."

"We have come to respect each other over the years."

"What will you do?" says Laughton.

"I will go to Moscow next week and see what they have to say."

"And after that?"

"I think I will opt to retire if that is an option," says Ivan. "My sister lives in Vladivostok, and it is beautiful at this time of year, the sea, Petrov, you have to see the Sea of Japan from the Russian coast to know what life really is about."

"It sounds wonderful," says Laughton. They sit and enjoy each other's companionship for what could be their last minutes together.

"I have to go," says Laughton.

He gets up and holds out his hand to the Russian. Ivan stands, starts to shake hands then hugs Stephen. They know that the future is not in their control. This arrangement, the passing of secrets between the two men that has gone on for so long, is not something that they can alter without consequences. They are merely pawns in a game of lies, truth and death.

Laughton turns and walks back across the Green towards the town and away from his friend.

*

It is early evening by the time Gabrielle arrives in Nice. The evening sun washes the buildings and the foreshore with a golden light. She drives down Quai Lunel and surveys the yachts that are moored alongside the dock. One of those is Sebastian Ulrich's. She needs to find a way to get on it and talk to him.

She turns right along the Promenade des Anglais and parks behind the Palais de la Méditerranée hotel. It is a vast building with huge French windows that give a view of the ocean. An original façade and a shiny hotel and casino behind the mask. A place where people who know Ulrich would stay.

Gabrielle needs to be one of the set that he and his friends would naturally socialise with, so, as well as the hotel, she needs clothes and shoes to create the right image.

She registers and asks the staff to bring up some evening dresses to her room later. Gabby walks out in to the French sunlight, along the Promenade then turns off left up into the back streets. She finds a small chemist shop, buys a bag full of products, and heads back to the hotel. She empties the purchases onto her bed in the room; blonde hair dye, fake tan, make up and false eye lashes. She goes to the bathroom, dyes her hair and puts on the tan. She looks at herself in the full-length mirror in the bedroom. It will do.

A knock on the door is the porter with three dresses, she chooses the blue Chanel. She clicks open a compartment on her suitcase and removes six sets of contact lenses. She chooses blue and puts them in. With her new hair and tan, she looks distinctly different from her normal self. Even if Ulrich has seen her picture, this will put him off the scent. She picks up her sunglasses, calls reception for a car, and goes down to the lobby.

The car drops her off at the port. She chooses a bar on the harbour, sits on a high stool in the centre of the place and orders champagne. She needs to be seen, which feels ironic given that she has spent three days hiding from everyone. She researched the yachts and knows Ulrich and his henchmen by sight. The bar is his favourite landside retreat before he boards.

Ulrich arrives at 9. He is surrounded by two burly minders, two other men and two young women. The party has reserved a table at one end of the room overlooking the port. Gabrielle knows the two men with Ulrich - Dima Lebedev and Larry Robinson, both well-known names in the criminal fraternity around the Mediterranean. They order drinks and Gabby watches the group dynamics. Ulrich is the prime focus but the two other men are of similar standing in the group and there is a respect amongst the three men. The women display a different dynamic but they are not there to only pander to the men and they hold their own authority.

She needs to get introduced to the group. After half an hour, Robinson gets up to go to the bathroom. This is her chance. She waits until he reappears, takes her champagne in one hand and makes directly for him. Robinson is heading for a gap between the tables, Gabby cuts him off, knocks into him and the glass spills on her dress.

"What the..." she starts to say.

"I'm sorry, it was my fault," says Robinson.

"Bloody champagne ruins silk," she mutters.

"A cloth over her, quickly," he calls across the bar. A waiter approaches and they all try to help. After a minute, the stain is less marked.

"That looks better," says Robinson.

"Yes, it does, thank you," says Gabby. She looks at him directly for the first time and smiles. He is dark with kind eyes and a scar on one eyebrow.

"Will you be ok?" he says.

"I think so."

"Are you here with someone?"

"No, a vacation on my own. Getting away from a frantic life and unreliable men."

"I am here with some friends." He points to Ulrich's party. "Let me say sorry with a new glass of champagne, if you will join us?"

Gabby pauses, careful not to seem too keen.

"I am fine, thank you," she says. "I don't want to intrude."

"You wouldn't be," he says, then adds in a whisper. "To be honest, I have only met some of them earlier today."

They laugh. He smiles at her and holds up his arm inviting her.

"Alright then," she says. "That would be lovely."

"What's your name by the way?"

"Charlotte." They walk over to the group.

"This is Charlotte everyone, and this is Sebastian, Lily, Sasha and Dima," says Robinson. "Come and sit here." He indicates a chair between his and Ulrich's.

The group talk for an hour about nothing of consequence. Ulrich watches her but doesn't engage her directly in conversation. The women seem envious, assessing the new girl. At just before 10:30pm, Ulrich indicates it is time to go.

"We have a party tonight, Charlotte, you would be very welcome."

"Is it far?" says Gabby. The others laugh. "Did I say something funny?"

"It is just over there," says Ulrich pointing towards the yachts moored in the port. "I have a little boat."

"I see," she says. "Then, great, I'd love to come along."

They all get up and make their way from the bar along the quay. Ulrich stops at a 120ft, three-floor super yacht moored alongside.

"This is my baby," he says. "Welcome aboard."

He leads them to a bar on the first level with cocktails and a barman. The captain and crew are in uniform and Ulrich signals for the craft to move out. Two more men and a woman arrive late just as the crew is casting off. As the sun starts its descent, the MV Quarrel moves away from the dock and into open water.

*

The open plan office on the first floor of the British Embassy in Berlin has the ambience of a library in the Home Counties on a quiet day. Geraldine's hands are sweaty; she has been building up to the conversation she is about to have for twenty-four hours, since she left Stuart in the hospital.

Melanie pops her head around the door. "Chief will see you now." Geraldine gets up and follows the assistant up the grand curved staircase to the second floor, through the doors marked Strictly No Admittance, and along the thickly carpeted corridor that leads to the offices of the MI6 operation embedded within the Embassy.

Melanie knocks, a muffled voice from within calls them to enter.

"Geraldine Tyche to see you, sir."

"Thank you, Mel. Tea, Geraldine?"

"Please."

"Two teas please, Mel." The assistant walks out and closes the door behind her.

"Come and sit over here," says Marcus Murphy, Head of MI6 Berlin Station. He directs her to two sofas at one end of his office. They sit. He is a stocky man with big excited eyes and a flabby jawline that he continually strokes with his hands.

"Always good to hear from the civilian staff and chat about how things are."

She smiles, unsure if he has finished any preamble that he might have prepared. Her short brunette bob sits evenly across her shoulders and her grey-green eyes show nothing of her soul.

She is right to wait, Marcus restarts his theorising. "You know, one of the things, the key things, to success in the Service is to listen to people," he continues. "I'm very much a people person, always have been. I can remember I was reprimanded for being too much a people person as a young officer like yourself."

Geraldine likes that he referred to her a young as it's not how she always feels.

"What's on your mind, Geraldine?"

Mel arrives with the tea. Once the door closes again, Geraldine stops her breath for a second, then begins. "I wanted to talk to you about Stuart Palmer, sir."

"Palmer?"

"He was attacked the other week."

"Oh yes." Murphy becomes more guarded in his demeanour. "Tragedy."

"I am concerned about what happened."

"We all are, Geraldine."

"Do you know why anyone would stab him?"

"Sadly not."

"Are you concerned that a member of the Embassy staff has been attacked in the street?" she says.

"Naturally, Geraldine. I am concerned about Palmer. I have a team looking into it."

"Have they found anything?"

"Not as yet." he says. "Can I ask why you're interested?

"Stuart is a friend of mine."

"More than a friend perhaps?"

Geraldine is not about to discuss her private life with Murphy. She pauses for the right words, not wanting to reveal too much but also not wanting to say something that isn't true.

"A close friend, certainly," she says quietly.

"I see," says Murphy and she feels naked in front of him.

"What do you do, Geraldine? Here in the Embassy?"

"I work in commercial relations, sir. We liaise with British businesses wanting to operate in Germany."

"But what about you? What is your role?"

"I provide a research service, sir."

"Researching the businesses?"

"Yes, providing reports to the Commercial Committee to allow them to decide how to support the companies."

Murphy is watching her talk and assessing her potential.

"How long have you been here?"

"In Berlin? Three years. I was in Brussels for five years before that."

"Tell you what, Geraldine, I think *you* can help *me*."

"Can I?"

"I have some plans for young Palmer and you might be just the girl to help those plans along."

"Oh?"

"How do you feel about working with us spooks from this side of the Embassy?"

"I don't know."

"Have a think. You can help your close friend and provide a great service to Her Majesty's Government to boot. Can't say more right now. Let me talk to some of the chaps and we'll come up with a plan for you. How does that sound?"

Geraldine is taken aback, she had only wanted to ask about Stuart's safety.

"If I can be of help, of course."

"Good. I'll be in touch." He gets up and waits expectantly for her to follow suit. She does.

Blackman holds out his hand and she shakes it. "Welcome to the wild west," he says.

Geraldine walks back out to the thickly carpeted corridor and downstairs to her desk.

*

CHAPTER EIGHT

The MV Quarrel cuts through the azure Mediterranean, heading south-east away from the French coast. Seagulls flock off the back of the boat chasing the swell and churn of the disturbed water.

Gabrielle decides that attack is the best form of defence and heads directly for Ulrich once they are all on board and the boat has navigated out passed the point of no return where the ship's captain is free from the strictures of the harbour authorities.

"You're not like other women I meet," says Ulrich as she pours a glass of champagne for them both.

"Is that good?"

He is smooth; he doesn't respond. He knows enough about humankind and disloyalty to tread carefully over new ground that could be mined.

"What are they like? The other women?" asks Gabrielle.

"More enthusiastic to get to know me," he says.

"Maybe it's you that needs to be enthusiastic," she says.

He laughs, honestly. Sasha starts to walk over towards them and he shakes his head almost imperceptibly; she turns and goes back to the others. Gabrielle wonders if her own senses are over developed as an action like that is as obvious as if he had written a sign and hung it up for all to see. It confirms her assumption that she must make the most of every second in his company to learn about her prey.

"What do you do, Sebastian?"

"Run my businesses."

"Doing what?"

"Commerce, trading between the people who make and the people who buy."

"A middle man?" she says. "How did you get into it all? Was your father in this business?"

He stops, not knowing how to answer the question. She knows that he killed his own father five years before over a drug smuggling disagreement.

"No," he says quietly. "My father wasn't in this business."

She gives him a minute to recover without him realising it. They both look out to the waves and the sun bleaching the horizon.

They talk on, her being pushy, him gradually realising that she is a force to be reckoned with.

"Can I show you around?" he says after three drinks. She nods and he drags the bottle of Louis Roederer Champagne from the ice bucket next to him. They drop down to the lower deck and around the aft section of the boat.

"Look here we have jet-skis. Have you been on one? You'd like them."

"I love speed, you're right," she says, touching his hand. They continue around the deck and end up at the prow.

"What made you buy a yacht, Sebastian?"

"Escape."

"To where," she says deliberately not asking the obvious other question.

"As far as I can go," he says. "That's always been my ambition. Never stop."

"It's all about the destination for you, then, not the journey?" she asks.

He takes a swig from the glass. The length of time between her asking and him answering is getting longer as she gets more personal with her questions.

"You're very interested in what I do, Charlotte."

"You're interesting," she replies. Ulrich is gradually tensing, she can tell, but it doesn't faze her. "Self-made millionaire, boy made good, great story."

"Are you a journalist?" She shakes her head.

"What do you do?" he says.

"I change things, for the better."

"Don't we all." He takes her hand and down the stairs to the lower deck seating area. "More champagne?"

"I'm fine."

He pours the drink anyway, she moves her glass away and he pours it on the carpet.

"I did say I didn't want any."

Ulrich is not used to being treated like an equal. "Come and sit with me," he murmurs and grabs her wrist, but she pulls away.

"I'll stand thanks."

He ignores her and reaches out again. She turns and punches him cleanly in the stomach, winding him. He tries to lunge for her but misses and falls. She turns to walk back up to the rest of the group but he keeps coming and crashes into her body at full speed. They fall back onto the sofa behind her, she pulls one hand across his face, fingers out, catching his eyes sockets and nose. He cries out in pain. She pushes him off her and adds her leg to give him extra momentum. He turns and smashes his wine glass on the table then slashes the serrated edge through the air. The razor sharp remains of the glass come within a centimetre of her face. She grabs his arm and hits his hand hard with all her force, the glass falls away to the floor. The full impact of the pain reaches his brain and he pulls his arm back, it gives her time to grab the champagne bottle and bring it sideways against his skull, he falls back momentarily dazed, the bottle crashing against the bulkhead.

She reckons she has one minute before someone sees them. She hurries out and down the far side of the boat where no one is socialising, then Gabby hears a shout from behind her as she reaches the aft section. One of the guests has found Ulrich; she rips the cover off one of the jet-skis, grabs her dress and tears off most of the skirt, then yanks the jet-ski up and pushes it with her full body strength towards the water. She can hear shouts coming from the core of the boat, but she keeps pushing. The jet-ski crashes through the cowling along the back of the yacht; she jumps on it in mid-air, starts the engine and it hits the water with a bang. The craft sinks low into the swell, then the water swirls down and round the machine and it leaps with power. She opens the throttle but doesn't let herself look back until she is fifty yards away. Ulrich's bodyguard is ripping the cover from the second jet-ski and is on her tail.

The two jet-skis bounce through the warm water of the Mediterranean. Flecks of moonlight jump up from the spray as Gabby pushes her craft as fast as it will go. Somehow the bodyguard is gaining on her, she twists on the throttle to get more thrust but it is up against the end stop. Thirty yards of clear water separate them now. The land is approaching fast; Ulrich's captain had not gone far out to sea despite the feeling on board of setting sail for the wide blue yonder. She looks back again and sees the man balancing an Uzi on his left forearm while steering with his right. She is expecting to sustain fire and it comes quicker than she thought. Bullets spray either side of her as the guy grapples with gaining control of the gun and the ski. She knows he'll have a better aim next time as she mulls over her options in the two seconds she has of breathing space.

The bodyguard is twenty yards from her, he masters the art of steering and firing and the Uzi spews metal out across the water. This time he hits the back of the jet-ski but misses her. Closer than last time and she doesn't want a next time just to test her theory. Her hands are getting cold and her body is aching from the incessant bouncing of the ski over the waves. She tries to manoeuvre on a course that straddles the up and down of the tidal flow, but it's not the direction she needs to go and has to cut a diagonal slash through the water against the tide, still pounding her back with each rise and fall.

Gabby can see the white cliffs of Cap Ferrat clearly now through the black of the night. She leans into the turn and carves a vast arc across the sea, heading back west towards the coast of Saint Jean. The bodyguard follows her path. The rocks of the southernmost tip of Cap Ferrat yawn before her out of the water. She needs a landing place and knows that the Club Dauphin that sits high up on the coast, provides a path for tourists from the hotel to the water's edge. She slows to get her bearings, the guy is on top of her; each second counts, now more than ever. He steers straight towards her jet-ski and the two craft collide, Gabrielle is knocked sideways, off her seat and only her grip on the handlebars keeps her from the wetness. Her ski yaws over at a frightening angle, at the limits of its buoyancy; Gabby's body slips, her feet crash into the sea, then the engine revs as the water outlet rises and gasps for air, then disgorges a column of water up into the night. The bodyguard is momentarily caught off balance as his jet-ski takes the brunt of the impact. It takes all of Gabrielle's strength to haul her wet body up out of the water and throw one leg across the seat to regain her balance. She twists her wrist and the craft booms into life, pushing it down into the foam. The bodyguard's craft is caught in the eddy and he spins away momentarily out of control. She pushes on to the cliffs, sees a break on the shore and drives straight for the tiny stretch of sand that interrupts one section of the rocky coastline. The jet-ski rises on the impact with the land, not in her control but going in the right direction. It skids sideways, she jumps out of the impending crash and the jet-ski bounces to a halt on the beach. The bodyguard has regained his composure and is heading for her across the water. She pulls her jet-ski back around and points it towards the sea, rips a tattered length of her dress and ties it around the throttle full on. She turns the craft in the water, removes the fuel cap and depresses the start button. It roars into life and heads out towards the approaching bodyguard; it rams him full on. The two craft rise up in the air, the man above the swirling machines. There is a second of silence then a thunderous ripping of the night sky as the jet-skis explode together creating a balloon of fire against the silent glow of the moon. Gabrielle turns and runs up through the rocks to the club; she reaches the pool where a handful of guests are enjoying the night and collapses into a chair by the bar, her hair wet and her dress in tatters.

"Madam? Can I get you a drink?" It is a barman, professionally silent in his movements. He doesn't cast any look over her appearance.

"Margarita, double the tequila."

"Madam." He disappears as he appeared, without noise.

*

The amber light from the morning sun floods Sir Bernard Macintosh's office. He sits at his desk reading a document headed Top Secret, a label reserved for only the most sensitive documents that pass through the hands of the British security services. His glasses are perched on the end of his nose, a habit he adopted early on in his career, partly due to his failing eyesight and partly to help his youthful looks gain some more gravitas. His hair has been black in the past but now has a dusting of grey. He has the demeanour of a reliable uncle, a friendly, wise man who has the time to listen when others may not.

He finishes reading the report and puts the file back down on his desk. He still deals largely in paper, despite the growing pressure to have everything on screens. His brain still treats real words written on real paper to be more accurate than anything held electronically on a database. He knows that this doesn't make sense but he can't get passed thirty years of working in this way. Not that he doesn't understand technology, he is the first to use the 'boys and girls of the mystic arts' as he calls tech branch, and he knows that the job of security can't be done without a growing dependence on servers, clouds and mice.

His mind is interrupted by a knock on the door; it is his secretary, Lawrence. It is only ever his secretary Lawrence.

"Ms Peretz, sir, from Investigations."

"Thank you, Lawrence. Ms. Peretz, shall we sit over here?" Sir Bernard leads the woman from the Crows to his sofas set under the large window in the centre of his three-bay office.

"I have my report on the Stranraer termination, Sir Bernard."

"Right."

"I thought you'd like a verbal outline of my findings," she says methodically.

"Yes, yes, go ahead."

She picks up her tablet computer. "As you know, Stranraer was one of most experienced snipers, he had been in the Service for ten years and came from the Special Reconnaissance Regiment. He was active in Iraq with SRR as part of Task Force Black Knight and after that Operation Illois in Afghanistan. With us, he has completed 124 target ops."

"You can't get much more experience than that," says Sir Bernard.

"On the day in question, he received a CT72 at 02:14, originally from Blackhawk and allocated by London Ops Central Control to Stranraer," reports Peretz. "He confirmed and flew out of RAF

Brize Norton at 07:24, arriving Berlin 09:58 Berlin time. He vacated the Berlin airbase in the company of Blackhawk at approximately 10:45."

She looks up from her notes. Sir Bernard says nothing.

"They were then off comms until Blackhawk contacted London Centre at 19:07," she continues. "After that Blackhawk went off-grid protocol OP15."

"How did we know of the Stranraer termination?" asks Sir Bernard.

Ela flicks through several screens then reads from the device. "It was posted by GISS to London Centre at 18:03."

"The Belgian Security Service?"

"Yes."

Sir Bernard frowns. "That's odd," he says. "Why them?"

"They discovered the body, Sir Bernard."

"Are you saying that the first thing we heard of the death of one of our own staff on one of our own ops, was from another country's security service?"

"That's right, sir." She shifts uncomfortably.

"Not good enough." He's getting frustrated now.

"My team have interviewed all of the people involved with the Stranraer death except agent Blackhawk."

"And why not her?"

"We have not been able to get in touch, I'm afraid," says the woman.

"Has she not called in on comms?" asks Sir Bernard.

"Only once since that day, sir, apparently from Barcelona."

"Why was she there?"

"She wasn't, she had bounced her comms. We think she was in Amsterdam but we can't be sure."

"She doesn't want to be found then. Do we take that as a guilty plea?"

"Impossible to say, sir."

"Even so, if it sounds like a duck, Ms Peretz. Arrange with my secretary to get all of the key people in a room latest tomorrow, I need a comprehensive view so we can identify a plan to rectify this."

"Sir."

"You, me, Laughton, any contacts that Blackhawk has spoken to in the Service since Stranraer need to be there. I need a full profile of her known contacts, aliases, everything."

"Sir."

Ela Peretz gathers her things and hastily makes for the door, as she does so Lawrence appears with tea and cake.

"No time for cake, Ms. Peretz," calls Sir Bernard, and she hurries away.

*

Catherine lies awake and looks up at the patterns of light and shade on the ceiling. Her phone shows 2:17am on the table beside the bed. Rich breathes heavily next to her; he is on his stomach with one leg lying across hers. The evening had been tricky for her. She is used to being able to address any problem immediately but she isn't in a position to do that just yet and it is gnawing at her stomach. Part of the reason for her choosing this career is the control that it gives her, at least with targets that she is given by London Centre.

In her twenties, she had no idea what she wanted to do. She had joined the naval officer cadets to travel the world more than anything. Part of basic training was the use of weapons and she had excelled on armaments. She had come top of her group and was taken aside before the training was over and offered accelerated personal tuition by the Special Boat Service instructors. She had moved to the security services after two years as part of the elite assassin C9 Branch within MI6; officially they don't exist.

Problems in her personal life though are different; she can't act so cleanly. She knows that she could lean over with one hand right now and end Rich's life, she has the skills and training to simply kill him. That power doesn't frighten her, it's essential to do her job, but it is only a job to her, a job that she happens to be very good at.

Catherine considers her next moves. The Marylebone testing lab are over-loaded and when she dropped off the condom for genetic analysis with them they could only promise 48 hours before a result. This leaves her with two days to keep pretending to Rich that he's kosher which she doesn't relish. Acting has never been her forte.

She also needs a plan for what she'll do when she gets the DNA identified from the lab. She just wants to find out who the woman is, then she'll decide what to do. Even though Catherine feels that she urgently needs to get away, she decides there's nothing she can do yet, and snuggles in closer to Rich's body heat.

*

CHAPTER NINE

As Geraldine walks into his office, Marcus Murphy is on the phone, his short frame bouncing on one leg then the other. With his free hand he manages to indicate to her both that he won't be long and to take a seat.

"Yes, that's the plan, Sir Stephen," he says in answer to a question from the caller. "I'm seeing her now in fact." He looks across at Geraldine and raises his eyebrows to connect her to his words.

"OK, sure. Talk then. Yup, bye." He finishes the call. "Ms. Tyche, good of you to drop by."

"You wanted to see me, sir?"

"Indeed. The other day I mentioned a plan we are cooking up on the dark side here that features you and Mr Palmer."

She nods hesitantly.

"I have spoken to my colleagues and I want to share our ideas with you," continues Murphy. "Truth is, young Palmer got involved with an op of ours without knowing it. Mistaken identity you see. He happened to be in the wrong place at the wrong time."

"When he was stabbed?"

"The background to this started last week. Palmer witnessed a murder within the criminal fraternity here in Berlin. We weren't involved, but it seems that the killers thought that your good friend was an active field agent and that he had witnessed their misdemeanour."

"He told me about the man being shot," she says quietly.

"Did he? Nasty business." Murphy walks from his desk to the window and looks out, still talking. "The people concerned are part of a network across Europe run by a man called Sebastian Ulrich. I won't go into details but safe to say his mother's probably not too proud of him."

Murphy looks at her, she doesn't know what the expected reaction is, so nods and shakes her head simultaneously.

"Ulrich has increased his potential in Berlin in the last three or four weeks. He is running his operation from France but the Berlin cell is particularly violent, made up of men who are well known to us. What we have been doing is breaking into their operations and attempting disruption from the inside."

Geraldine is feeling uncomfortable as even though she doesn't know about the security work in a British embassy, she does know that you only get briefed about something like this if you're going to get involved.

"Do you know what a drop point is by any chance?" asks Murphy suddenly.

"A place where documents can be left," she says succinctly.

Murphy is impressed by her awareness.

"Quite, you'll know that we have dead drops which are unmanned, and drop points which are people," says Murphy. "Our drop points apparently live normal lives until they are needed as part of an operation. Let me tell you about the plan I have for you and Mr Palmer." He sits down opposite her and starts to explain what he needs her and Stuart to do.

*

The Mett Bar is quieter than usual. Hans picks up empty coffee cups and glasses from previous customers and stacks them on the bar. The door swings open and a man who Hans doesn't know takes a table by the front window. Hans gives him a couple of minutes then approaches.

"Hallo, was kann ich dir bringen?"

"I'm not here for coffee," says the man. Hans's training kicks in without him or the guy realising it. American accent, Washington as an adult with a hint of Seattle from his youth. Hair dark, closely cropped; eyes alert, blue, one slightly off centre; hands tanned, he holds them together for reassurance, Hans thinks.

"What were you after?" says Hans putting on heavily German accented English.

"You can drop the act, Gordon."

"Who are you?" says Hans.

"CIA."

"And I'm supposed to believe that because...?"

The guy reaches into his jacket pocket and produces an ID. Hans inspects it and it seems real; his name is James McKinney.

"I'm looking for a colleague of yours."

"Official business?" asks Hans.

"Maybe."

"Tell me," says Hans, sitting down on the other side of the small, round table.

"Gabrielle Lane," says McKinney. "We're keen to know her whereabouts." Hans's poker face remains static.

"You'll know that I have no operational information passed to me in this role," says Hans.

"Sure, I know that's what it says on your job description," says McKinney. "But we know how it works in the real world don't we, Gordon?"

"Do we?"

"We know she was here. We know she called on you three days ago and the two of you chatted away like old friends."

It's Hans's turn to say, "Maybe."

"You don't need to confirm or deny it, Gordon, we know that already. What we don't know is where she went after your cosy tête-à-tête."

"When you say, we, James, you mean the CIA is looking for a British civil servant, and the only way to find out where she is, is to ask a barman in Berlin?"

"We know she's off-grid."

"This is an official CIA op, James, is it? You know I can check that."

"You won't find it in our operational logs," says McKinney.

"Interesting," says Hans.

McKinney's eyes narrow. "What are you hiding?"

"Tell you what, I'll feed your enquiry into my official channels and you can collect the answer from Langley."

"That ain't gonna work I'm afraid."

"You surprise me."

"Let's not make this difficult for ourselves, Gordon. You just tell me where she's gone and I walk out of here all friendly like."

"I hope that's not a threat, Mr McKinney."

McKinney smiles with one side of his mouth. Hans predicts his next move in the half second before McKinney's hand moves around the right side of his body to his handgun. Hans slams his hand down on McKinney's arm with all his force. McKinney's hand crashes on to the metal table causing a hard echo on the walls of the Mett Bar. Hans pulls his other arm up and across McKinney's body, removes the gun from its holster under the American's arm and pushes it into the man's gut.

"Nice and slow, McKinney," says Hans. "Stand up for me."

McKinney waits a full second, considering his options, then slowly stands.

"Walk to the bar." They reach the long straight wooden counter that runs the length of the room. Hans reaches over and pulls out a plastic tie grip from under the bar and ties it around McKinney's two wrists, then dumps him on a nearby chair.

Hans dials a number into his phone. "Catharsis? I have a parcel for collection, location Epsilon 14." He listens to the response. "It says it has DC address on it but I'm not so sure that is the right." He rings off.

McKinney sits staring into the distance.

"Going to tell me who you are before my cavalry arrive, McKinney?" says Hans.

"You got any water?" says McKinney. Hans collect a cup from behind the bar, fills it and comes back round to where McKinney is sitting. He lifts the cup to his lips and the guy drinks slowly. The next thing Hans feels is a stinging in his left leg and the warm spout of blood coming from a gash in his thigh. He bends with the pain, McKinney slashes the knife along the skin then pushes Hans away off balance. He sprawls across two tables sending chairs sliding across the surface of the floor. McKinney kicks Hans in the stomach and the Englishman's body jerks with the impact. He stands over the bloodied man for a second.

"If we don't find her, we will come back and talk to you again, Gordon. That's a promise." He turns and walks hurriedly out of the premises one minute before the parcel collectors pull up outside the bar.

*

Laughton walks along the 6th floor corridor of the MI6 Vauxhall Cross Building on the south side of the Thames. He is feeling tired and can't explain it to himself. The Ivan meeting has been preying on his mind for 24 hours. He can't shake off the feeling that he has put himself in a position where others are starting to shape his life, a life he has so forensically created and controlled over the last decades. The mysterious contacts in Moscow are a worry to him. He has never met any of them but knows that they have changed over the years. The people who told Ivan to recruit Laughton at Oxford are all no longer working for the SVR, the replacement to the Soviet-era KGB. But decisions are being made about him by new people, somewhere in the faceless grey offices of the First Directorate Headquarters in Yasenevo, an hour out of Moscow on the long, lonely road to Kaluga.

He stops at a door marked 'Churchill Conference Room' and goes through. Inside the room are people from an array of departments from both MI6 and MI5. Sir Bernard is sitting at the head of a long rectangular table reading a paper file in front of him while people mill about getting tea and finding seats. Laughton takes a chair next to his boss.

"This is an extraordinary situation, Stephen. You know I have never had a field agent go off grid like this since Bagatelle in 2004, do you remember?" says Sir Bernard.

"I do remember," he says. The truth of the last twenty years is starting to pound away in Stephen's head and it won't go away. Bagatelle had been the agent Pamela Faulks. She had been stationed in Austria, overseeing turned agents from the smaller countries of the old Soviet Union. Her role was to get them to cross over to MI6 and either defect or be re-launched as double agents. Faulks disappeared from her station in the British Embassy in Vienna on a cold, dark November night in 2004, never to be seen again until her body was dragged up from the lower reaches of the Danube a fortnight later. Agent Bagatelle was just one of the British agents who Laughton had sent to the wolves during his illustrious career.

"Ladies and Gentlemen, please take your seats," says Sir Bernard. "We are here to discuss and identify an ops plan to manage agent Blackhawk. All of you know her in some way, or have been in touch with her in the last five days. In the next two hours we will build up a profile of her to inform our plan to locate her and bring her back under section control. You'll know Sir Stephen Laughton here on my left. Laughton runs Ops Europe and so is Blackhawk's Head of Section."

Laughton smiles weakly.

"We'll go through the events of the last five days chronologically," continues Sir Bernard. "Let me introduce Ela Peretz from Investigations who can start the ball rolling. Ela?"

"We have compiled an all known data file on Blackhawk which is Eyes Only for Sir Bernard and Sir Stephen," she begins, looking in turn at the two most senior men in the room. "For this meeting, I will take you through the operational events leading up to the Stranraer death."

She goes through the details as she had done the day before for Sir Bernard. Then Cabinetmaker from London Centre Control relates the conversation he had with Gabrielle when she was in the London safe house and porting her network to Spain.

As Cab finishes, the door at the far end of the room opens and Marjorie Allardice walks in. The faces in the room turn simultaneously to look at the late comer. Marjorie finds a chair and sits.

"Welcome," says Sir Bernard. "This is Agent Exeter, she worked in 6 and has now crossed the Rubicon to our friends in Thames House. Your timing is excellent, Exeter, as I wanted to run through a psychological profile of Blackhawk and I know you are a close friend. I think you worked together in Alpha Ops?"

"Yes, that's right, Sir Bernard." Says Marjorie, who has an ability to speak intimately but simultaneously to the whole room. "Apologies, I could only come for the second hour of this."

"One second," says Sir Bernard. "Just before Exeter shares her thoughts, I meant to introduce you to Agent Riverside." He indicates a tall, sandy-haired man in his late thirties sitting at the far end of the table. "Riverside is an experienced agent. He will be leading our recovery op to bring in Blackhawk. This session is vital for him to formulate the details of how that can be done."

Riverside looks around at the people in the room with a faint smile.

"Exeter, if you would?" says Sir Bernard.

"Gabrielle Lane is a loner," begins Marjorie. "She always has been, it's not the Service that has made her one. We met on her first day in 6 and even then she wasn't the sort to make friends easily. It comes from a fundamental distrust of people. Her father died when she was a girl and her teenage brain hard-wired a self-dependency into her soul."

She stops for any reactions. There are none and so she continues. "Gabby is also unpredictable. She doesn't believe in doing the thing that is expected of her, it's almost as though her first option is to go against the rules, but actually she's more sophisticated than that. She'll comply with the rules as long as they suit her, but go her own way when they don't. She's difficult to manage; several of her senior managers found her nearly impossible to deal with, but that says as much about them as it does about Gabby. But she is also a completer-finisher; she won't stop until she has what she wants, but not in a selfish way, she is driven by her desire to do the right thing. The operations she has been involved with are always a success, and any consequent deaths are always justified in her mind."

"What do you think she will do next?" It's Ela Peretz from the Crows.

"She doesn't feel trapped, she never feels trapped. She feels as though only she knows the truth and that no one she meets will be worthy of her trust. So, she'll have a plan to sort out whatever she feels is the problem."

"And that is?" asks Sir Bernard.

"She believes there's a mole in 6 across our European network. The Stranraer death could only have happened with a leak of his kill location. Gabby only registered the location on the network the previously evening, so it's someone who has full access to the ops data as it flows in real time."

"Someone in Ops Branch then?" Laughton says as his pulse rises.

"That's the most likely, then the individual leaks would seem like ordinary mission comms."

"That's a serious accusation, Exeter," says Sir Bernard. "Peretz, did your team find any leak potential?"

"We didn't but we weren't looking for that," says Ela. "We were just recording the steps from Blackhawk logging the CT72 to Stranraer's termination being registered with London Centre."

Eyes turns to Sir Bernard; his own eyes flit between the people around the table. "We need to move quickly on this, ladies and gentlemen," he says. "Riverside, any initial thoughts?"

"I have an idea that should be attractive for her to meet me."

"Go on," says Laughton. Marjorie is listening intently.

"As Exeter said, Blackhawk is a problem solver, driven to get to the bottom of things, but she holds her own view and doesn't accept the official line unless she can personally validate it." There are nods at these words.

"I suggest I offer a meeting to help find Stranraer's killer, implying I know the mole and can help her with her cause."

"Would that work, Exeter?" It's Laughton.

"Yes, her world is her world, you have to understand that and be relevant to her," says Marjorie.

"Is there any way to get a message to her, Laughton?" asks Sir Bernard, turning to Sir Stephen. "Some sort of back channel?"

"She has some trusted people on her network," says Laughton. Marjorie shifts in her seat. "Agent Hans is one of her closest, we'll see if he can get a message to her."

"Alright," says Sir Bernard. "Where will you meet her, Riverside?"

"Neutral territory, Switzerland."

"When do you go?" asks Laughton.

"Immediately," says Riverside. Laughton's brain spins.

"Anything else, anyone?" Sir Bernard looks around the table, no one speaks. "I'll need a daily update, Riverside for me and Laughton, eyes only."

"Sir."

Sir Bernard stands up and walks from the room. Laughton tries to remain outwardly calm. In his mind he is trying to recall what exactly he was doing around the time of Stranraer death.

*

CHAPTER TEN

The light cascades in to the room, rolling in from the water beyond; a slight breeze billows the curtains at the window. Gabrielle wakes and inspects her body for damage. Her legs have a dozen tiny cuts, made red with salt water from the ride. Her feet are injured too, a minor wound on her left ankle and a bigger one on her right foot which has spread black and yellow across the bones. Otherwise, she escaped relatively unhurt.

Two thoughts tumble across her mind, firstly that Ulrich will be redoubling his efforts to find her now; followed by the contrary idea that he may not have linked the woman on his boat last night with contract he has out to kill her. If he hasn't realised, she will make the most of his poor lateral thinking. Either way round, he knows her face now and she will need to remain hidden from view or disguised. She showers, re-dyes her hair to dark and goes down to breakfast.

The message from Jim arrives in her phone as she finishes her meal. She answers the call and walks out into the French morning. As she speaks to him she crosses the Promenade des Anglais and walks along the seafront. She is between a smattering of people and couples on the pebble beach and a thin stream of cars travelling the roadway by her side.

"I managed to set the data file running overnight, Gab."

"Great. Did it take long?"

"About five hours. There's a big spike on two nodes that will interest you."

"Oh?"

"Yes, you said you needed to know where most of the messaging activity came from in the time bands that we spoke about," he says.

"What did you find?"

"These nodes have significantly larger rates than the others." Gabby thinks back to which node labels match to which people from the real data.

"Which are the high-volume nodes, Jim?"

"Nodes 16 and 43. The rest show some activity but nothing like these."

"That's exactly what I needed," she says. They chat pleasantries for a minute or two, but her clockwork mind has already started to turn.

She turns and makes directly for the hotel. Her heart is pounding in her chest as the lift rises to her floor. She runs to her room, fumbles the key card and it falls to the floor. She grabs it, slides it across the lock and the light goes green. She goes straight to her suitcase, presses a combination of the numbers on the keypad and a compartment clicks open on one side of the bag. Gabby lifts out a mini tablet and powers it up. She flicks through screens and reaches a page with the nodal codes displayed against real users in the data that Jim analysed. Her fingers trace down the third column. "Node 16," she says out loud. "Let's see..." She again tracks the information along. She catches her breath. "Can't be." She retraces the line but it comes to the same name. The words sit on the screen, glowing steadily back at her from the display; node 16 is Marjorie Allardice.

For a second, Gabrielle can't think. "Marjorie?" she says over and over in her mind then concludes it must be wrong. Marjorie is MI5 and they don't have access to information from 6 as part of their daily routine. Requests for access have to be made on a case by case basis to London Centre.

Node 43 is only listed as somewhere in the British Embassy in Berlin. That isn't a surprise as they have a role to be aware of operations in their patch, even those controlled directly by London.

She wonders if the data she downloaded using Lady Allardice's computer had become corrupted. The MI6 mainframe could have scrambling servers in place that damage any data grabbed off-grid. She will have to confirm with Marjorie that 5 have no interest in the Stranraer killing. It is frustrating as it delays her progress to trace the mole but it has to be done.

*

Riverside descends the back staircase from the reception area of the British Embassy in Berlin and goes in through the heavy door that leads to some of the areas of the building that are not generally on tours when dignitaries come to visit. The secure comms room is first on the left with green and red lights outside, both currently unlit. The archives store is next with a half-glazed door revealing rows with dark shelves of paperwork. The medical room is last on the right. It is starkly bright and efficient. A white-coated doctor sits behind a desk at one end.

"Can I help?"

"I'm here to see Hans," says Riverside showing his ID.

"Second bed on the right," says the doctor despite the ward having only one man in it.

Riverside walks on and stops at the foot of the bed. Hans is lying with his eyes closed, his thigh heavily bandaged from the stab wound and a drip in his arm fed by a tube from a bottle of clear liquid.

"Gordon?" Hans opens his eyes.

"We haven't met," says Hans.

"Riverside. Can we talk?" He sits on the bed next to the lying man. "I'm trying to contact Blackhawk."

"You and many others it seems."

"Others have been here?"

"The guy who did this," says Hans touching his bandage. "Said exactly the same."

"Was he MI6?"

"Said he was CIA but he wasn't."

"Recognise him?"

"Nope."

"What did he say?" asks Riverside.

"Almost the same words as you coincidentally."

"How did you get the wound?"

"I said I didn't know where she is."

"And do you?"

"I'll have to disappoint you, Riverside."

He pauses and considers whether Hans is being totally open with him. "How well do you know Gabby?"

"She's a friend."

"We don't have friends in this job," says Riverside with more personal remorse than he intended. Hans watches his visitor.

"Can you get a message to her?" asks Riverside.

"What's the message?"

"Meet me in the Gstaad Alpina Hotel at noon in two days. You know it?"

"I know it."

"Can you do that?"

"I'll explore the possibility."

"You got a dead drop for her somewhere? I can drop a message if you can't walk out of here."

"I can walk, Riverside, it's just a scratch. Why do you want to meet her?"

"I have some information about a leak which I think she'll be interested in as it is about her friend Stranraer."

"A leak? Shouldn't you be going to your Head of Section with that information?" says Hans.

"I'm on your side, Gordon. I know the ramifications of a broken network as well as you do. Our bosses may be involved, we don't know. But I do know that certain people are batting for both sides in the ops team."

"You think we have a broken network?" asks Gordon.

"I know you think the same."

"Where's the leak?"

"Eyes and ears only I'm afraid."

"Why her?"

"I know enough about her to know that she'll have a plan to fix it," says Riverside.

"You need to go," says Hans and he closes his eyes.

Riverside smiles but only to himself and gets up from the bed. "Thank you, Gordon." He walks back the way he came.

*

Her court robes and wig hang on a Victorian coat stand near the large mahogany door that leads to the main corridor of the chambers of Milson Laughton Hendry, barristers at law. Caroline Laughton QC sits with four very large ring binders on the desk in front of her. She has known Greg Milson and Rebecca Hendry since university and they worked together in chambers as juniors before going their separate ways in their late twenties to follow their chosen legal branches then re-met and formed a chambers seven years later. By then, Linny knew that criminal law and fraud are the things that make the hairs stand up on the back of her neck. The buzz doesn't fade each time she starts a trial. When she chose to do law as her degree she had a vision of battling for justice, being a guardian of the poor and needy. The reality of being a barrister, in her mind, is that it is as much about assimilating a huge volume of information in a very short period of time as being the defender of the impoverished. In fact, most people who get as far as needing a barrister aren't the poor and needy, she has discovered; they are the already rich, those who have the wherewithal to launch a legal case to prove something is true or to avoid something that is true. A phrase that she heard as an 18-year-old undergraduate scampers across her mind, "half the time, all the people in court are lying, otherwise there's no case to defend."

Her current client is David McAllister and she doesn't trust him. He is accused of obtaining and passing on information from the British security services under the cover of his private security business. She wonders if he is part of the honest half or the lying half, but either way he is paying her to convince a judge he's the former.

McAllister has told her that he has contacts in the British security services, which she needs to confirm before the case starts in court. For this reason, the court will be closed; no public will be allowed and the session is confidential to all those who take part. Any personnel of MI5 or MI6 who are involved will appear on video link and anonymously. She has had a few cases that link back to national security over the last decade but this is the largest.

She turns the page of the file on the desk. The defence that she has put together is based on the conversations she has had with McAllister over the last three weeks as well as the extensive research and collation of data that her clerks have done to create the folders. She is due in court in two weeks and there is a particular area that she still needs to understand before standing up in front of a judge.

McAllister said he openly received information from MI6 and that the criminal accusations are nothing more than the legal and justifiable covering up of the security work, so that the interaction with McAllister remains invisible to foreign powers. Effectively, McAllister's position is that he acts as a private extension to British Secret Intelligence Service.

She reads a page in the file dated six months ago. It is a copy of a message that McAllister says he received. It mentions the operational detail of one of his projects and it is clear from the document that MI6 are asking for the work. There are no names on the sheet apart from McAllister's. The words say that the detailed instructions for the work will be conveyed to him in a packet of papers and that they will be sent by a contact who is inside MI6. Linny is at a loss to know how she will validate that information and she starts an email to her clerk to approach the UK Government Cabinet Office and start a formal request for court evidence from the MI6 contact.

She turns the pages and reads more about the arrangements. After twelve sheets of paper the instructions end. At the bottom of the final page, there is a name that she hasn't seen before. This person seems key to proving McAllister's side of the story. She adds a further paragraph to her email, "…The enquiry needs to focus on finding the source of the information given to our client and we have evidence that the contact is called…" She checks the folder to get the name right. "…the contact is called Petrov."

*

CHAPTER ELEVEN

Zurich Airport glints jewel-like as Catherine's plane hits the tarmac and the reverse thrusters power up to bring the craft to a walking pace for the approach to the gate. She guides her Jaguar out of the car park and on to her flat in the centre of the city. She had toyed with the idea of waiting in London for the Marylebone results to arrive but gave up on that idea as she sat at breakfast with Richard and realised she would lose her temper with him before two days were up, and she can't predict what she will do when that happens.

She throws her bag down on her bed, goes to the kitchen to make coffee, and slides her balcony doors open to let the autumn air seep in. Catherine has always been fascinated by the difference in the summer and winter in Switzerland, who would have thought that a thick blanket of white would change the personality of the place utterly. In summer, just another central European state with mountains and bratwurst; in winter a playground for the rich, bad skiers and child snowboard prodigies. Catherine tells her friends she enjoys the summer but actually the winter speaks more clearly to the cold, hard heart inside her.

She collects her laptop from the bedroom and sits, legs up, across two chairs on the balcony. The sun glides out from whiteness and lights her face. She checks her emails and she can feel her body respond as she sees there is one from Marylebone, fortunately early. She clicks on the mail which contains several pages of technical and biological detail about the sampling process. But it is the last paragraph that yields the information she needs; the genetic ID of the sample. Marylebone only provide analytical services and not DNA matching to individuals. Catherine copies the long identifier from the sample to her desktop then opens up the MI6 network, then on through the security layer into Oberon. A genetic match in the system takes longer than face matching and she sets it going, then makes lunch.

The screen pings a completed tone and Catherine leans over from her Waldorf Salad to see the results. On the results screen, there is a single word 'Classified'. She scrolls for more and the message says that the owner of the DNA is a member of the security services. Catherine does not have sufficient approvals to see the name of the person in the sample. She screws up her nose. Rich is not MI6, she met him outside work, so the chance of him knowing anyone in the agency is tiny, let alone sleeping with them. She considers if this is misinformation, deliberately planted by London Centre to cover up something, then her brain sways the other way and she thinks that her bosses aren't interested in who her boyfriend sleeps with. But as is usually the case, she thinks, the truth lies not at the extreme ends of possibility but somewhere in the mix. Rich sleeping around could be a security risk or that is how the higher ups could see it.

There is only one place locally to get passed the Oberon security levels and view more sensitive data, and that is to talk to the spooks who are resident in the British Consulate in Zurich. She grabs her things and bangs out of the door leaving her laptop and food. Twenty minutes later she is striding into the Consulate. She shows her ID and goes to the third floor.

"Bradley," she says as she stands in the doorway. Bradley Stewart is a middle-ranking MI6 officer, but the highest you get in a British Consulate. His eyes are sad and his hair is a mass of dark brown.

"Hi," he says, brushing his fringe back from his forehead. "Long time no see, Kate."

"Was passing, Bradley and thought, you know I haven't seen you for ages. How's things?"

"Busy, you know. We've had a few stakeouts and cases, not like your high-profile ones but big for us." She smiles at him and they chat for fifteen minutes.

"There's something that I have never understood though, Bradley," she says in the flow of the conversation.

"What's that?"

"You know Oberon and how it is not always that great?"

"Tell me about it, I had to get on to tech branch about their data."

"I had this job the other week and I went in to Oberon to get DNA information and it just said classified! Crazy!"

"What was it, because I might be able to get in," he says as she inches him along.

"The job's done now but..." she begins.

"No, go on, it's stupid that you can't get in when you're sent a job." She pulls out her phone and finds the genetic ID.

"Here." She hands him the phone, he turns to his computer on the desk next to him and types in the identifier. "I needed the genetics to confirm the kill target," she says then realises it is her guilt talking.

"It's quicker here too than over the open internet," he says. A result comes back within half a minute, but the same as before, with only 'Classified' displayed.

"See?" she says.

"I can get round that," says Bradley. "It takes a couple of days though."

"Great, that's really kind of you, Brad."

*

Stuart sits in a wheelchair by a large open window in the day room of the Alexianer Saint Hedwig Hospital in central Berlin. A green and red blanket rests on his knees and an open book sits in his lap. His hands lay palms upwards either side of the book.

He has been reading, but now he looks into the middle distance at the parkland outside.

"Hello," says Geraldine from behind him. He turns his head and his eyes track her round as she arrives and sits down opposite him on a chair.

"Hello," he says.

"Good book?"

"This?"

"What is it?"

"Far From the Madding Crowd."

"I love that," she says "A woman fighting for happiness." He smiles at her.

"Is that you?" he asks. She looks away, not being able to cope with the intensity of the moment and is driven to change the subject.

"I spoke to the Chief," she says.

"Murphy?"

"Yes, he asked to see me. Well, at first I went to see him."

"What about?" says Stuart.

"You."

"What about me?"

"Remember I said I thought they weren't doing enough as you'd been attacked?"

"What did he say?"

"He asked to see me again and they have a plan for us."

"For us?" says Stuart.

"Yes, they want us to help them out." She waits for his reaction before fully committing to a smile, then it drifts away.

"What do you mean?"

"They want us to be a document drop point and pose as a couple and live in a flat."

"Why?"

"Let me tell you the whole plan," she says and relates the mistaken identity that Murphy had briefed her on and how the Berlin criminal fraternity think he is a field agent who witnessed the murder.

"The gang is planning various activities over the next few weeks, but the spooks had someone on the inside and they found a weak link, a young man whose brother was killed and now wants out. He is willing to provide information to us about the gang's activities but they need a way for him to drop his information without the gang knowing; so the drop can't be some hole in the wall or station locker like they normally use. Murphy suggested that we take in the information from him."

No words come to his mouth although plenty flood his head. This is a side of Geraldine that he has never imagined; quiet little Geraldine.

"What do you think?" she says searching his face for anything.

"Is it dangerous?"

"No, it's just waiting for this chap to turn up."

"What did you say?" asks Stuart.

"I said I'd talk to you. It's a way to help, and it's exciting isn't it?" Her eyes widen but his don't.

For an hour, they talk about the plan. Minute by minute, inch by inch, sentence by sentence, Geraldine moves his view from a definite no to a maybe. She talks about the good they will be doing, that is won't be for long, and how she feels safe with him near her.

A nurse approaches and tells them that visiting time is over. Geraldine gets up and stands over him. "I'll come back tomorrow to see how you are," she almost whispers.

They say their goodbyes and he sees the smile in her eyes. She turns and walks away and Stuart watches her go until she disappears through the swing doors at the far end of the corridor.

*

The windows are open and the sea breeze plays between outside and inside. Gabrielle sits in her hotel room, wearing a summer dress due to the warmth of the day. On the tablet computer in front of her is everything she knows, or has found out in the last two hours, about Marjorie Allardice. While Gabby does not believe the data is right about Marjorie being Node 16, she can't afford to take chances and has been trained to always be suspicious. The personal profile on the screen is largely as she thought it would be apart from one key fact. Marjorie's father is alive and well and living in Jamaica. Gabby finds this hard to fathom. She and Marjorie once had a long conversation in a pub in Soho in London about how Marjorie would have to move from MI6 to 5 due to her mother needing support as her husband had been killed in an accident. Yet in the deep dark reaches of the MI6 database, Gabby found a file marked Top Secret that did not have its encryption settings turned on as it should have. The file was about Project Dolos and the arrangements that were put in place eight years ago. While the objectives of Dolos were not in the file, the fact that they needed to fictionalise the death of Marjorie's father was included, but without explanation. Another new piece of information for Gabby is that Marjorie has a code name, Exeter. This means that she has been on field operations duty at some stage. Gabby had thought of her as an Ops Control boffin until now and they don't need code names. A code name isn't a game changer, she thinks, sometimes they are allocated for a single operation and never removed.

One thing is clear, Gabby urgently needs to talk to Marjorie. She would prefer face to face but that is out of the question until Gabby has neutralised Ulrich. As that thought crossed her mind, she realises it is the first time her objective has been crystallised in her head. She must neutralise Sebastian Ulrich or the killers will keep coming for her. Neutralise doesn't mean kill necessarily, it may mean destabilise his business empire so that he abandons the contract on her life; but if it has to be death, then that will be his fate.

Her laptop pings a notification. She stabs in the decrypt code and it shows a message that Drop Point 23G has a new upload. Gabby goes to the machine's barrier application, then accesses 23G remotely. One message sits in the inbox from Hans. She opens it.

"Old girl, Riverside requests the pleasure of your company in the bar at 12 Noon on Thursday, wants to talk about Stranraer," plus a location using the MI6 unique global grid system. Gabby translates the location so it can be read by civilian mapping software and it shows the Alpina Hotel in Gstaad. She knows that Hans will not be sending her into a trap if he thinks there is danger but she doesn't know if he has been compromised. She checks the letter code that she and Hans set up for their messages, based on where certain character combinations sit in the message. She counts along, records the letters then uses a grid decoder to verify. She applies the rules and the count is 17, one of the secure numbers that tells her Hans is not setting a trap, as far as he is aware.

She knows she cannot resist the invitation and decides to travel up the next day to scout the area before the meeting. Her push to solve the mole problem could be sending her into what could be all above board or another test of her nerves and fight, but that's the job.

*

CHAPTER TWELVE

Gabrielle is up early. She drops down the back stairs of the hotel and trips out to the parking garage. She fires up the engine of her Z4 and noses it out into the early morning, through the near deserted streets of Nice and onto the autoroute that takes her east. The glistening Mediterranean lays passive in the bright day, the blue water turning to white as the sea hits the horizon. Her route to Switzerland hugs the coast until Genoa, then pushes inland, across the green pastureland of Italy's Piedmont Region before going over the Swiss border. Once on the Autostrada, she gentle squeezes the accelerator of the car and the machine responds with a burst of impetus that speeds her through the September air.

She had needed to know more background information before meeting Riverside and had researched about him on Oberon into the early hours to understand why he might want to meet. He has been in 6 for only four years, transferring from the British listening service GCHQ and moving straight into a senior role in Delta Branch, the anti-terrorism specialists within MI6. He has been on a dozen operations as a field agent with Delta, all highly successful, and all within the European and Middle East territories. There was no mention of his real name on the record which is normal for field operations, but there was a list of his aliases and the passport numbers for each cover name he uses, all of which she had noted down. Gabby knows that there will be a few things not fully recorded in his profile. Where an agent works on eyes-only operations involving foreign governments or senior figures in government or royalty, then the MI6 records become scant, even non-existent. It is par for the course; she knows that there are some of her own past operations that simply do not exist on her record, or anywhere on any database or in any paper file.

She turns the car off the Route E27 and tracks east again up through the twisting roads of the Alpine slopes. She has booked a hotel for tonight to allow her to get a feel for the town layout and the meeting place. She turns off the main road a mile out of Gstaad and onto a side road. Gabrielle drives around behind a tall bank of grass that blocks the view from the main highway and opens the secure compartment in her suitcase. She pulls out two wigs, one blonde and one auburn and tries on both. She feels the red-head is a more fitting Gstaad choice. She gets back on the road and parks up outside her hotel, then checks-in speaking only German and with sunglasses firmly in place. She asks for a room overlooking the main valley and has carefully plotted sightlines to give her a view of the Alpina Hotel. She unlocks the door to the room and goes straight to the windows; the Alpina lies just below her and the view from the room gives a vantage point across the whole of the back of the place.

There is nothing more to do until nightfall and she orders room service then sleeps heavily in the king-sized bed and Egyptian cotton.

Gabrielle had set her alarm for 1am. The light buzz starts from the far distance of her consciousness and kicks through the layers of sleep into her head. She wakes suddenly, inhaling a gasp of air and looking all around; then stops and breathes out as her mind catches up. She rolls out of bed and ties her hair up into a bun, dons black leggings and top, and covers her face with military night ops camouflage. Gabby opens one of the windows of her room, locks a tech branch rope calliper to the window frame, presses a combination of buttons on her phone and a nylon rope spews from the calliper to the ground below. She grabs the hand slide and skims silently down the cord, then presses a button on her phone again and the rope re-reels into the calliper, ready for her return.

She runs like the wind across the lawns of her hotel, then drops down to a high-walled roadway that delineates the two set of grounds. Gabrielle clambers up the other side using foot holds in the stones. She reaches the top and ducks down behind the hotel's private helicopter that is used to ferry guests to the mountains during the winter. She runs across the grass to an outside door that leads from the bar to the pool. She picks to lock, slips inside and along the bottom corridor. She hacked the hotel's security system the night before and knows the alarm code which she hammers into the flashing box behind the bar, just inside the 30 seconds she has before the main alarm triggers.

Gabby pulls out her tablet on which a floor plan of the Alpina glows in the night. She runs along the corridors, following the map, and arrives at the final turn before the reception area. She stops and stands by the corner, selects the camera app on the machine and pulls the camera head up and out of the main body of the adapted MI6 tablet. The extension allows her to push the camera around the corner and see if the reception is still manned. A single night receptionist is there but it is only a minute before the woman walks off to the office behind the desk to collect something. Gabby scurries to the desk, clicks the mouse and scans the guest list for any of Riverside's aliases. On the third page, she sees Dr Michael Hill in room 251, it is one of Riverside's cover names. She darts away as the receptionist re-emerges from the office behind. The woman wonders for a second why the guest list is showing on the screen, then shrugs, closes the list and resumes her place at the desk.

Gabby finds the staircase, arrives at the 2nd floor and hurries to near room 251. She takes an adapted key card from her a pocket in her leggings and pushes it into the lock of the room next door. She plugs her phone into the key card and runs an app, the light on the door goes green after 2 seconds. She pulls out the card and noiselessly goes inside. A woman is sleeping alone in the bed inside the room. Gabby knows there is a connecting door between rooms to create suites and unlocks the connecting door, then gently pushes it open. There is no sign of anyone in the room; Riverside is either yet to arrive or the room booking is a decoy. Either way, she continues with her plan and takes listening devices out of her pocket and fits them around the room. She tests they're working on her tablet, then goes back out to the corridor, through a side door, and across the grass to her own hotel. She calls the calliper from her phone and the rope descends as she approaches; Gabby latches her hand on the cord and it lifts her back up through the night air to her window.

*

At 11am the next morning, an auburn-haired Gabrielle leaves her hotel by the front door, and drives down the access road that skirts the town centre of Gstaad and brings her to the front of the Alpina Hotel. She parks, goes in through the front door and disappears into the maze of corridors beyond. She arrives at the same bar from last night that overlooks the pool and gardens, orders coffee and sits by the window with a good view over the area outside, as well as visibility of the various entrance doors from the body of the hotel. She waits, aware of every movement from every person both inside and outside. Civilians behave in certain predictable ways, while military and security service personnel all have an air about them; imperceptible to the untrained eye, but a flashing neon sign to anyone who had been through the training camps for British forces and spies across the world.

The barman is a young man, she estimates 25. He constantly moves behind the bar; serving, clearing away, getting bottles out or sorting something when no customers are demanding his attention. She studies his movements. If he is an agent then he is very good at it as he isn't giving away any tell-tale signs. A woman sits three tables away from Gabby reading a magazine. She is more nervous, Gabby can tell, but not to the extent that it sets off any warning signals. The hands of the gold and glass clock behind the bar turn on through the hour. At five to twelve, a sandy-haired man appears from the main corridor, orders a coffee at the bar, turns and walks directly towards her.

"Gabrielle?" he says. She raises her eyebrows and he sits. "Thank you for coming."

She is guarded but not tense.

"I wanted to talk about Stranraer," he says, watching for any movement in her face muscles.

"I've heard it is lovely in the summer," she says.

"I know Mac was a friend of yours." She says nothing, but scans every element of his demeanour.

"I may have information about how he ended up..." says Riverside. "Well, we know how he ended up."

"What information?"

"How the location was leaked."

"Was it?" says Gabby.

"Can we stop playing games? We are both experienced field ops and know what happened."

"What do you want, Riverside?"

"To help you find the mole," he says a little too earnestly.

"How would you do that?" she says, looking directly at him, urging him to reveal more.

"I have evidence that someone inside the security services actively shared the Mac location with outsiders."

"What's your evidence?"

"Message traces from the night in question." It sounds similar to the Jim Cartright data, she thinks. Could they have detected her mask environment on Fi's computer? Or got to Jim? If they have, Riverside is bluffing; or he is genuine and has acquired the data himself; or he has been fed false data without his knowledge.

"Did you bring it with you?" she asks. He reaches inside his jacket and produces a hard drive which he places between them on the table. She doesn't look at it but her eyes are locked on to his, as they will betray him if anything will.

"Take it," he says. She waits for three seconds but it seems like ten. She reaches for the drive and stows it in the side pocket of her leggings. "Get back in touch when you have looked at it." He gets up to go.

"Why?" she says as he stands.

"I don't like leakers any more than you do. I read your file, you're willing to do almost anything in the field, but it's always justified. You're not some aimless outsider. I believe what you believe."

He turns and walks back the way he came. As he reaches exactly half way between Gabby and the doorway, the whole side window next to her explodes inwards; the ten-foot sheet of glass tumbles in pieces like a waterfall into the room. She scrambles out from the glass shower and runs for the door. Riverside has been caught in the blast and lies on the floor but is moving. His hands bleed red from the impact of flying window fragments. From the far end of the pool in the garden, she can see a man in a gasmask advancing towards them brandishing an Uzi.

The woman with the magazine is lying still in a pool of her own haemoglobin. Gabby has no time to check her; she draws her Smith & Wesson and takes a position at the end of the bar. The guy is still advancing, walking hard with intent in his gait. She doesn't want to shoot him in public with civilian witnesses, so waits until he reaches the doorway. He stops and pushes the door wide.

"Put your gun down," she says. She can't see this eyes through the mask. "I'm not asking twice." He is still and silent, then slowly starts to raise his weapon. She has no choice and fires her gun, it discharges into his chest; he is knocked backwards and falls through the doorframe, but he is not killed due to his bulletproof vest. It gives her enough time to run to where he lays prone on the floor but she over-estimated his injuries, and he tries to grab her ankle as she stands there. She kicks her foot into his ribcage, his grip loosens and she jumps over him to the outside then runs at full pace across the grassland. As she reaches the helipad, a second man in a gasmask appears from the undergrowth and gives chase. She swerves way, down the side of the hotel and back to the front entrance.

She presses her car key fob as she runs and it unlocks the Z4; she turns the key, skids on the gravel and out of the gateway of the hotel. She looks back and can see the men ripping the cover off the helicopter, one gets into the pilot's seat and the other jumps in beside him. She steers the sports car out of the town and south-east towards the peaks. After two minutes she hears the steady drumbeat of the helicopter's rotors behind her. She pushes the car faster but at the next bend, her back wheels drift round and slip dangerously close to the sheer drop beyond.

The helicopter is fifty yards away now; she pushes the car further upward into the hills and the road gets narrower and more twisting. The helicopter flies out in front of her, turns and takes a low run straight for her. As it passes overhead, the injured man in the passenger seat leans out with his automatic weapon and sprays the ground around her. Bullets rip into the passenger seat of her car, then the aircraft turns again and comes back for a second buzz. Another burst of gunfire disgorges from the gunman overhead but is wide and creates min dust storms on the ground around her car.

Gabrielle expertly guides the Z4 along the road, taking the twists and turns in her stride. With no notice, the tarmac ends and the route becomes a dirt track; and she knows that she is running out of time before the road reaches the top of the mountain. The helicopter pilot has realised this too and spins out ahead of her looking for a landing place. Her car beats along the final straight, narrow ridge as she nears the top. She can't see where the route goes as she accelerates towards what looks like a fence across her path. Gabby is fifty yards from the fence before she realises it marks the end of the usable highway. She slams on the brakes, the car spins in the dirt and ends up sideways against the end stop. The helicopter has failed to find a landing place and the pilot brings it to a hover thirty feet above her head. The passenger gunman leans out, the pilot dips the machine and bullets spray around her. She jumps out and rolls under the vehicle. The helicopter drops dangerously low and the gunman jumps and rolls out his impact with the ground.

The man gets up and holds his gun with two hands showing his military training, the steady beat of the blades is only just above their heads and a thick cloud of mud, branches and leaves spins between them, whipped up by the rotors. He has to push against the downdraft to move forwards, she rolls out from her hiding place and releases a bullet which hits the target in his leg. He turns and fires a dozen rounds at her, as soon as his finger comes off the trigger, she runs at him, fires twice, once in the upper body, once in the head. He collapses where he stands, she knows he is dead without looking, she aims up to the helicopter and releases three rounds, but the pilot has seen what happened and pulls the craft up and away out of her range, it circles once while he considers his options, then he peels off to the North and away.

She checks the dead man; no ID. She pulls off his gasmask but doesn't recognise him. Gabby is unhurt but the car has bullet holes in it. She raises an anonymous call to the local police about the body, stows the hard drive from Riverside beneath her seat, then turns around and accelerates back down the trail.

*

CHAPTER THIRTEEN

The unusually hot September sun bounces off the restaurant tables in the grounds of the Grand Hotel du Cap-Ferrat. Sebastian Ulrich walks out from the main building, a purple bruise evident around one eye. He sits at a table with a sea-view where Larry Robinson is already eating lunch.

"How is it?" says Robinson, nodding at the bruise.

"It's nothing."

"What was she on, that girl?" Robinson smirks under his sunglasses.

"She was crazy," mumbles Ulrich as a waiter appears and takes his order.

"We need to talk about this pick up," says Robinson.

"You've got the information, Larry."

"I only got the outline; my guys need times and dock numbers.

"They'll get it."

"How much gear?"

"Twenty mill." Robinson whistles. "Coke and Molly."

"When?"

"Two days."

"I need some guarantees this time, Ulrich."

"For what?"

"That you're not going to end up with most of the haul and I get fucking nothing," Robinson starts to raise his voice. "I got a million of gear last time and paid two for it. That ain't happening this time."

"Keep your cool, Larry."

"You keep your end of the bargain and I'll keep mine, but if you screw me over, my guys will come calling."

"Don't threaten me, Larry. This is my operation."

"Get me those details," he sneers and returns to devour his food.

A bodyguard comes up to Ulrich and hands him a folded piece of paper which he opens and reads. "Son of a bitch," he says to no one.

"What is it?" asks Robinson.

"A job that I paid good money for."

"Didn't come off?"

"Nah."

"Is that to do with our delivery?"

"Nothing to do with it," says Ulrich decisively.

"What then?"

"A contract I have out."

"They didn't kill him?" says Robinson, mid-chew.

"Her actually."

"Another girl causing you problems, Ulrich, you losing your grip?"

"Fuck you," says Ulrich.

"If you can't control the ladies, can you control this trade coming in?" Robinson is laughing.

Ulrich gets up grabs Robinson's hair on the back of his head and tries to shove his face down into his plate of food. The attacked man reaches behind him and pulls out a knife from his belt, then lunges at Ulrich but he swerves and avoids the blade. Ulrich grabs his hand and forces it down on the table. The pair are locked in position, both scowling at the other. Other guests look over at the sight of the two men fighting and the maître d'hôtel approaches them.

"Gentlemen, I must ask you for some restraint."

Ulrich releases his grip, waves a hand dismissively at Robinson and sits back down. His food arrives and he starts to eat. After a couple of minutes, they are both calmer.

"You got more jobs we can do, man?" says Robinson.

"What you got in mind?"

"Drugs, security, girls; that's what my guys are good at."

"What about guns?" says Ulrich, making a sudden look at Robinson to see his reaction.

"Not done any," replies Robinson. "What sort of scale you talking?"

"Big. I need a team to oversee transit of arms from the Russian border through Ukraine and Turkey to Syria."

"I dunno, man, that's war zone stuff. My guys ain't got the experience."

"Up to you if you don't want to hit the big time," says Ulrich.

"I already got the big time, don't you worry about that, but I'm choosy on what I get involved with. Gun-running needs a whole deck of security around it."

"I can go with others who have more balls, don't sweat, man."

"I got balls, Ulrich," he says with anger in his voice, then drops the level of emotion. "I don't know if I want more jobs with your guys anyway given last time."

Ulrich shrugs and continues to eat.

*

The curtains are drawn in Room 251 of the Gstaad Alpina Hotel. The in-house doctor packs up his bag and leaves Michael Hill to rest after being caught in the incident earlier in the day. The Swiss police had been cursory in their interview with him and Riverside wonders if they know he is a member of the British security services. There are cuts on his body where flying glass fragments flaked his skin and released blood, but nothing life-threatening. He remembers two years ago he was nearly killed in Afghanistan on a black ops mission that officially didn't happen. He moves his leg and can feel some pain below one knee.

His work phone rings beside him and he starts to roll over to pick it up but a shot of pain hits his leg. He manages to grab the device and falls back down on the bed to relieve the pain. He rests the phone on his chest, picks up the call and switches on the loudspeaker.

"Riverside? It's Laughton. I'm interested to know how it went."

"Successfully," says Riverside, but his voice gives away a less perfect reality which Laughton has heard many times in the voices of field agents.

"Did something go wrong?"

"I incurred some injuries."

"Did the two of you fight?"

"Two enemy combatants attacked us. One civilian dead, two injured. I have minor cuts nothing more."

"Who were they?" asks Laughton.

"No idea."

"You didn't kill them?"

"Escaped."

"What about Blackhawk?"

"She got away but they could have killed her."

"Are you confirming an agent down?"

"Negative," says Riverside. "I have no intel."

"What's our next step?" says Laughton.

"If she's not dead, I'll have to wait for her to respond once she has seen what's on the hard drive."

"And if she is dead?"

"We'll deal with that if it happens," says Riverside.

There is a pause. "You need to make sure this works," says Laughton.

"I'm aware of what is riding on it, Sir Stephen."

"This is more than just bringing in a rogue agent."

"Go on."

"We suspect that Blackhawk is a mole and that she is laying a trail using people she knows will leak, to create a fictional narrative that she is chasing the mole herself. It's the perfect cover."

"Clever if that's true."

"She is our most likely candidate, Riverside."

"What evidence do you have? Has she leaked before?"

"That's all eyes only I'm afraid," says Laughton. "But safe to say that there are several agent terminations in the last year that have been the result of information that she has leaked."

"I didn't know," says Riverside.

"That is why we put our best man on it – you."

"I'll do all I can, Sir Stephen, but she is a very sophisticated agent, there's no guarantee our plans will be successful."

"I realise that, but this is as serious as it gets," says Laughton. Riverside notices that Sir Stephen is being unusually directive. His field training tells him that there is more to this than he is being told. Up to this moment, Riverside had thought his objective was to bring Gabby back to London for debrief until the powers that be feel happy that she is manageable; now the operation is taking on a much more sinister line. Riverside will have to rethink how the whole plan works.

"I'll be in touch, sir," he says and rings off.

In her car on the way back to France, Gabby switches off the radio that has been tuned into the listening device in Riverside's room.

*

The flat selected by the spooks for Geraldine and Stuart is on the first floor of a 1970s block on the southern outskirts of Berlin. A development of two hundred apartments, all the same, once the cutting edge of architectural panache, now leaking, greying containers of people. Where there had been grass on that spring day in 1972 when the mayor opened them, there is asphalt; where there had been flowers in planters, there are seats with paving slab tops; where there had been light and ambition, there is dark and dampness. Inside the flats, aluminium frames support floor to ceiling glass panels so there appear to be no walls along the back half of the place. Too big for double glazing, the smear of condensation clings to the glass for five months of the calendar.

Geraldine unwraps the flowers she bought earlier and arranges them in a vase in the middle of the kitchen table. She has tried to make it as homely as possible inside the flat, creating something that even her mother would have commended her for. The doorbell rings and she looks at herself in the hallway mirror before opening the front door.

"Welcome home," she says. Stuart is standing in the porch wearing the same clothes as on the day he was stabbed. He steps over the threshold and she takes his coat.

He walks in to the main room, then trudges around every part of every room before going to the sitting room window and surveying the outside. Geraldine watches him take it all in.

"I was given some money by Murphy to get you some new clothes, they're in the bedroom," she says pointing. He goes to change and emerges ten minutes later.

"Very nice," she says. "I've made some tea."

They sit either side of the small, square table in the kitchen. She pours him tea and cuts him cake.

"How do you feel?" she asks.

"Still trying to understand how my quiet life has turned in to this."

"Are you scared?"

"Not any more. I was after the stabbing, but I know we're doing the right thing and the Chief will look after us."

"Did you ever find out who poisoned you?" she says.

"How did you know about that?"

"One of the nurses mentioned it."

"A mistake was made that's all. No one tried to poison me," he says.

"The nurses thought it was deliberate."

"That's not right," he says as adamantly as she has ever heard him speak.

After a moment, the discomfort fades away into the air and they talk more. They talk about the hospital, they talk about working at the Embassy, his holidays as a child and why she doesn't like prunes. The light of the day casts a moving background to their chatter, and time ticks by without either of them realising it. She laughs and he is captivated, no one has given him this much attention in his life.

"What about this chap who is going to going to give us the information?" says Stuart.

"He is called Alexander," she says. "We don't know when he is going to do it, but they'll tell us beforehand."

"What is the information?"

"I don't know, something about what this gang is going to do, I guess."

"How long will it be?" says Stuart.

"A few days I think," she says.

He smiles at her.

*

Linny pushes open the door to the Villa Bianca restaurant in Hampstead and is shown to a table. She pulls the tie out of her ponytail and lets her chestnut hair falls about her shoulders. Stephen arrives ten minutes later.

"Good day, darling?" she says looking deep into his eyes so she knows what he will say before he does.

Stephen pauses to give due consideration to her question, and carefully selects the right word. "Difficult," he says.

"Anything you can talk about?"

"It just seems as though there are a number of things going on that are acting in concert and not for the good of the Service," he begins. "Too many fingers in pies, too many enquiries, too many people asking questions who have nothing to do with the area in question."

"Are they asking you?"

"That's my concern, I'm getting the distinct impression that I'm being kept out of it."

"Haven't you told me many times that the Service only works effectively as information is on a need-to-know basis?" she says watching the man she loves.

"That's true, but something's different this time. There are operations in Europe that I should have been briefed on but I know that I haven't been."

"What do you think it means?"

"Black ops maybe or eyes only, but at my level I should at least be aware."

"They value you, Stephen, I know they do," she says. "You'd soon know if they had lost faith."

"Would I?"

"Of course, you're one of their most experienced senior operations people. Think of what you've done in the years you've been there? Think of the people you have protected, the secrets you have kept from enemy hands? You should be proud."

"Linny?"

"Mmm?" she murmurs as she looks at the menu.

"What if I told you that there are secrets that I have kept from you?" She looks up at him. For a moment, the years fall away and she can see the innocence and passion of the younger man who she first met. His dreams and ambitions that had driven him on in those days.

"As you always say, my darling, most of what you do, you can't tell me about anyway." She reaches across the table and touches his fingers. "Do you know what you're having? I'm starving."

His sense of isolation clicks on another notch as outside, in the dark, it starts to rain in the street.

At the end of the meal, the waiter places coffees on the table and Linny spoons one sugar into her cup.

"How's your case?" says Stephen.

"Getting a bit hairy. My client's defence rests on the confirmation of information from a source with the security services."

"That won't happen."

"Really?" She wonders at his sudden bluntness. "I had an MI5 chap give a witness statement a couple of years ago, anonymously of course via video link."

"There's a feeling in the Service that we let too many people give evidence over the last decade. It damaged us internally."

"But it's justice, surely?" she says.

"There are some things that we get involved with that are hard to explain to civilians. Things that people are better not knowing."

"You and your old boys' games! It's endearing but the Cold War is over."

"Whoever told you that?" he says looking directly at her. "Countries still needs protecting."

She lets the pace of the conversation drop, a trick she has learnt over the course of their many discussions about MI6. The air gap allows them both to breathe and halt a rolling juggernaut before it runs away out of control. She knows that he is right in part, but she also knows that he is old school when it comes to MI6 justifying itself. In his eyes, she knows, they should be able to do anything in the name of protection. The world has moved on and she can see that he has struggled to do that, but it is true that some secrets are best left unsaid. It reminds her of her affairs and how she could never break his heart by ever telling him about them, despite them being such a vital part of who she is.

*

CHAPTER FOURTEEN

The morning slides onto the beaches of the south coast of France, children and seagulls play in the lightest of breezes as it glides from west to east towards the sunlight. Gabrielle's head is spinning with options and ideas after the experiences in Gstaad. She rises early and eats her breakfast hurriedly, without taking in the sea view or the yachts battling the waves half way to the horizon.

She asks the man at reception if they hire scooters, which they do. She books one to use immediately and glides out from the centre of the town toward Cap Ferrat, in her pocket is her auburn wig just in case she needs to be invisible. Gabby speeds through the lanes that criss-cross the land around the Hotel which sits squarely in the centre of the headland. She slows to a crawl and descends the Avenue de la Corniche which skirts the southern border of the hotel grounds. She stops along a straight stretch with on one else in sight, pushes the scooter into the undergrowth and walks around to the lower entrance that leads to the hotel. A long, grand path stretches from the road to the main body of the place. She dons her wig and walks up the hill. She is wearing a Balmain top and trousers and Gucci sunglasses to blend in with the surroundings.

As she gets nearer to the main building, she can see three café and bistro areas which she scouts on the lookout for Ulrich or his associates. There is no one there she recognises and decides to broaden her search and go inside the building. The bar is empty at this time in the morning except for two old German men reading their newspapers. They look up and she smiles at both of them but they do not react. Her search inside yields no members of the gang and she goes outside again to redouble her efforts. She is nearly regretting arriving so early, as Ulrich may be a late riser, when she sees Dima Lebedev by the pool on a lounger with Lily from the night on the yacht. They are talking intimately, watched over by a large guy who stands motionless behind his shades. Gabby recognises him from the party and knows that she needs to avoid his gaze.

She returns to the hotel and finds the kitchen entrance where waiting staff are emerging like bees from a hive, but taking sweetness out instead of bringing nectar in. She pushes a green baize door and walks along the corridor inside that runs between the bottle store and the kitchen service area. She methodically tries each door until she finds what she needs. The kitchen staff lockers are in a room painted entirely white. Sets of chef and waiting staff clothing are neatly stacked in cubby holes at one end, she rifles the piles and finds what she needs then changes into a black skirt and white shirt and ties her auburn hair back. She retraces her steps up the corridor, circles back to the service area, takes a waiting tray of drinks from the hatchway, and makes for Lebedev. By the time she arrives, Lily has gone and

155

Larry Robinson has joined Lebedev on the next lounger. They are chatting, and she stands as near as she can to them with her drinks as though waiting for her customer, while straining to hear their conversation.

"How many guys you got on this gig tomorrow night?" says Robinson.

"Four maybe five," says Lebedev. "Why?"

"You trust Ulrich?"

"Sure. He's been good to me, and you. You concerned, brother?"

"He screwed me last time, I paid over the odds."

"Increase your distribution prices, Larry, it's just business. Buy low, sell high."

"I have an uneasy feeling," says Robinson. "Has he given you the details?"

"Meet at the Villeneuve-Loubet marina but I don't know when yet."

"I got nothing from him."

"Chill man, he'll tell us," reassures Lebedev.

"You doing this gun-running he's on about?"

"Too big for me," says Lebedev. "I got my clubs along the coast I don't need more cash flow. You doing it?"

"I don't know, sounds like high-risk."

"Worth a couple of mill profit I reckon," says Lebedev.

"Yeah? Ulrich got buyers?"

"All sorted. The job is just security."

Lily and Sasha from the yacht walk up to the men and divert their attention from crime. Gabby has heard enough and got far more insight from that conversation than she could have hoped for. She walks down the long path to the lower entrance of the hotel, ditches the tray and drinks and reclaims her scooter. She speeds along the coast road and stops half way between Cap Ferrat and Nice. Far below her, the thrashing sea pounds the rocks of the French coast and breaks into whiteness before retreating and returning. She pulls out her phone and goes into encrypt, then onto 23G and leaves a message for Hans asking him to join her urgently. This is an opportunity she can't miss.

*

The door to Martine's office opens and she walks up to Laughton's desk with an armful of papers.

"How are you, Martine?"

"Well."

"Do you have family?" asks Laughton. Martine's heart sinks as she prepares for another personal life onslaught.

"My father is alive, sir, but my mother died. I have a brother in Staffordshire."

"When did your mother die?"

"Last year, sir."

"You didn't mention it," he says looking for something in her face but not finding it.

"I like to keep myself to myself, sir."

"How is your father?"

"Coping."

"Does he miss her?"

"Every day, sir," she says as she looks at the floor.

"Can I do anything, Martine?"

"For my father?"

"I just thought…"

Her face displays an emotion he is unsure of.

"I have influence, I thought, I could help, in some way," he says, but not even convincing himself.

"Can I ask, sir?" she says.

"Go on."

"How are *you*? You seem to be different recently."

He wants to say that there is no one on the earth who he can talk to and the loneliness of his life is becoming unbearable. In the Venn Diagram of his existence Martine occupies the unique position of knowing about MI6, knowing about Linny, being trustworthy and having an intelligent advice-giving mind. No one else has all of those things. If he could tell her about Moscow too, she would know it all. It isn't sexual attraction, he doesn't want to take her to a hotel on the south coast for the weekend; he just wants to pour out his heart to someone who both knows and cares. He teeters on the brink of saying it all in that second of time and space that lingers between them in that moment. Then the moment has gone. and his emotion ebbs.

"I am a little tired," he says.

"I'll get you some tea, sir." She walks back out to her office and Laughton watches her leave.

He turns to read the pile of papers that she brought in. The first folder is a routine report from research branch on the rise of local criminals in the ex-soviet states that now have independence. The second is an operations report about Gibraltar and the various suspicions that the MI6 station have in Madrid about security. The third folder is another research report, he opens the cover and his heart misses a beat. It is the eyes-only Blackhawk profile file that Sir Bernard commissioned from the Crows.

He can feel the blood in his veins and the acid in his gut. His palms are hot, he notices, as he opens the cover. Everything is in there, Ela Peretz has done the work personally and she is one of the best investigators in the Service, destined for higher office. He doesn't read the content, but closes the manila file and picks up his briefcase. Laughton's hand stops mid-way between desk and bag, his fingers around the folder. He has never questioned an individual leak before but this time it seems different. Maybe it is because he knows Gabby and her death will feel much more his personal responsibility; maybe it is the feeling that the net is closing in on himself and it is making him more risk averse; or maybe it is because he is scared, for the first time in his adult life.

*

Gabby gets back to her hotel by mid-morning. One woman tries to ask her for a drink, mistaking her for a waitress, but she ignores the request and goes straight to her room before she ditches the skirt and shirt and orders coffee on room service. Gabrielle opens her laptop and plugs in the hard drive from Riverside. The military grade security on her laptop auto scans the drive for viruses but finds none. She examines the structure of the external drive; it is British security services standard issue, 5TB, dual encrypted with minor and major unlocks keys. She can't see the content of the drive remotely so transfers the data to her laptop. Once across, she runs a strike analysis but finds nothing. She collects the minor key from the internet address given on the MI6 network and clicks to unlock.

The data files unwrap in chronological order, each with an animated opening sequence as the decrypt works through the code blocks. Seventeen files are displayed once the decrypt has finished. She goes through them one by one, they appear to be messages on the network that fill in some of the blanks from the Jim Cartright analysis of traffic flows. The senders and receivers are not shown, but the messages are. Some are conversations about Martin Teileter's Berlin cell and how central Franz Keneely is important to MI6; others discuss Ulrich and how he is being tracked using deep cover in his operations; another group talk about Klingerfeld, Mac's target the day he died, and Mac's kill location. As Gabby clicks on to the final page, she can feel her body react and a cold shiver run up and over her head. The message is one from London to Berlin and it says that the Klingerfeld job has to be a guaranteed failure, under no circumstances must Klingerfeld be killed. Why then, was a kill order sent out to the opposite effect? The bigger question in Gabby's mind is though, why is Riverside sharing this information with her? These questions are all valid but she doesn't know the answer to any of them yet.

*

Sir Stephen Laughton passes through the security gates of the MI6 Vauxhall Cross building and out into the evening air. A stiff wind has played around with the trees for two days and it has not given up yet. As he going out, Marjorie is coming in the other way.

"Hello, Sir Stephen."

"Miss Allardice, what brings you to our hallowed international shores?"

"A meeting."

A quizzical half-smile appears on his face. "I won't pry," he says. "How is your mother?"

"Embarrassingly well in fact. She often talks of you, Sir Stephen."

"Does she?"

"I have been regaled with the full and detailed history of 6 from the day she started and you appear at the end. I think you worked together in her last couple of years?"

"Yes, I was a young buck, fresh down from Oxford and she gave me the benefit of her many years of experience," says Laughton.

"Can I ask, did you hear any more from your Riverside op?" says Marjorie.

"The first step went well, I understand. They met and he started to build trust between them."

"Do you know how he did that?"

"I don't, it was eyes only for Sir Bernard, I'm afraid."

"Did he give her information?" asks Marjorie.

"Possibly, he did," says Sir Stephen. "Although I don't know what. How will she react do you think?"

"Cynically."

"You know her better than anyone."

"She won't be taken in. If he gave her something genuine then he'll build trust, but if it's fake then she'll see right through it."

"I can keep you across how it goes if you would like?" he says. "You have security clearance for Top Secret ops so you would know as much as me."

"Thank you, I'd appreciate it. Sorry, I need to rush," she says. They part ways, both wondering if any of the conversation had been genuine.

Laughton crosses under the Vauxhall railway arches, walks south-east down Harleyford Road and passed The Beehive pub. He starts to see the bulk of the Oval Cricket Ground ahead, and enters the site at the Hollioake Gate. The place is deserted. Laughton climbs the staircase in the bowels of place and emerges from the dark backroom area into the light of the arena. He never stops being in awe of this view and stands for a second just taking in the sight, then walks to section 9 and takes a seat. Ivan appears at pitch level and slowly makes his way up the stand toward the spy. It is only when the Russian is within twenty feet of him that Laughton see that he has a bruise on his face that runs across one eye.

"My God, man," exclaims Sir Stephen. "Did they do this to you?" Ivan does not answer but sits in the next seat but one to Laughton. They do not speak for a minute as Laughton is mute but flabbergasted.

"Our friends in Moscow," begins Ivan. "Are not minded to let you stop your work helping the mother country."

Sir Stephen considers the response.

"What are the consequences if I stop anyway?"

The Russian looks at his friend directly for the first time since he arrived.

"I'm sure you and I can answer that question equally well, Petrov."

"I could get us protection," says Laughton.

"They would find us in the end, comrade. Not tomorrow or next week, but next year or in five years' time.

"I can arrange for a new identity for you."

"Why would the British security services want to give a Russian spy a new identity?"

"You could come over, tell us what you know."

"Be a traitor, Petrov?" says Ivan quietly. "I could never do that. I have spent all of my life loving Russia. I owe her everything I have, everything I am. All of my memories of living in our two countries are due to what Russia gave me."

"Look at the two of us, Ivan. I don't want to continue to be a traitor and you won't become one!" Laughton chuckles and Ivan joins in. The sound of their laughter echoes along the terraces of the arena, along the gangways and up to the sky, free to go where it wants.

"What are we going to do?" says Laughton after half a minute.

"Face the consequences, Petrov. Like we have been doing for decades. Take responsibility."

Laughton changes tack. "Do you run any other assets, Ivan?"

"I can't tell you that."

Laughton looks at the man, trying to find an answer in his time-worn face.

"You don't do you?" says Laughton. "I'm your only asset. Or the only one left. They've let you run me only because it has worked all of these years but the others have stopped, or died, or been killed by your friends in Moscow, haven't they? This is your final test, isn't it? The last reason they have for not killing you."

The Russian's eyes talk a thousand words.

"I'm not going to let you die, Ivan."

"Then you must continue."

"I'll find another way."

"What about the intelligence on your Agent Blackhawk?"

"If you remember the deal was that I only provide the information if I can stop."

"Do you have a plan, Petrov?"

"I don't yet," says Laughton. "But tell them that you and I are working through our arrangements and the information will be with them in the next week. We're not going to let them beat us, Ivan." Laughton feels more alive than he has done in weeks. His friend looks on at his boyish panache but doesn't feel any less worried than he did when he arrived.

*

CHAPTER FIFTEEN

Tourists and locals flow constantly in and out of the doors to Nice Côte d'Azur airport as Gabby leans against her car reading a copy of Le Monde. The midday air hangs heavy around the coastline and she watches the comings and goings, second guessing the people and their histories as they move from the artifice of the airport lighting into the French sunshine.

She thinks about Riverside and how much she can trust him. It doesn't make sense that he has given her what seems to be genuine intel on illicit activity inside 6 if he is trying to ensnare her, although you do put real cheese in a mouse trap or it doesn't work. What does he know that she doesn't? There are two options in her mind, either he is genuine and wants to help, or it is an elaborate plot hatched by the mole to remove anyone who can potentially reveal their identity. Gabby has built her life on never trusting anyone so it's easy for her to know the right path ahead. If anyone had had faith in her at any time during her life, then the choice would be much more difficult.

Hans is wearing a bright green shirt and light grey trousers. She sees him and starts to walk so that their paths gradually get closer. He spots her and stops, they do not signal to each other but she turns and he follows. Gabby gets into her car, drives it to the exit road and Hans jumps in before she hits the gas and accelerates back towards Nice. They find a small Italian restaurant in the streets above the old town and take a table inside at the back.

"Thanks for coming," she says after they order. The waiter pours two glasses of Sauvignon.

"My pleasure, life in a Berlin bar gets a tad mundane."

She laughs and takes a swig of her wine.

"What do we need to do?"

"Tonight," she begins. "A cache of drugs will arrive at the marina just along the coast from here. We need to disrupt it."

"Because?"

"It is being organised by the man who has a contract out on my life and who was responsible for your knifeman. We need to undermine his powerbase so that he realises he's not going to win the war."

"War?" says Hans. "Strong words, Gab."

"That's what it feels like. Two attempts on my life in six days and the guy in your bar. It's an organised and credible threat."

"This is Sebastian Ulrich, right?" says Hans. She nods.

"What do you know, Gordon?"

"Only what's on Oberon."

"Why did you mention him, though? It could have been a number of people."

"I know he has a Berlin cell because I've been getting intel as part of my role in the Mett Bar; and Ulrich is the only one who has both a network of scale in cities across Europe and is based in the South of France.

Gabby wonders if his analysis has been briefed to him.

"What did you do with the USB I gave you, by the way?"

"Safely hidden in Berlin, Gab." He senses her nervousness.

They talk on over lunch then go to the hotel to prepare. She has booked him the room next door and they both sleep briefly in the afternoon but not at the same time.

He knocks on her door and she opens it.

"Ready?" he says.

"Almost, come in." She goes in to the bathroom.

"So, you getting near to the mole, Gab?" Hans calls from the bedroom.

"Not really."

"What's your latest idea?"

"I've got various bits of intel," she says emerging from the bathroom. "Some files from Brussels that I acquired, data on traffic nodes the night that Mac dies, and Riverside gave me some comms tracers."

"Does it point to anyone?" asks Hans.

"Not consistently."

"We can go through it if you like?"

"Sure, in the morning. When you flying back?"

"I can stay a few days and help you, I'm off duties because of my leg."

"You in pain then? she asks.

"Nope, I over-egged it a bit. I'm in no rush to get back to the Mett Bar."

"I'm getting that impression."

"Not enough going on, or not that goes through me. I might leave."

"What would you do?"

"No idea, civil servant somewhere?" says Hans.

"Weren't you in the Army?"

"Guards Short Service Commission, after uni."

"Good?"

"I'm a bit too much of a hippy," says Hans. "They had too many rules."

"So you went in to the civil service? Very logical." She smiles. "Can't the Honourable Rathbones offer you something? Hasn't daddy got a business you could run?"

"Fuck, right, off," says Hans.

"Just saying." She holds her hands up in playful surrender. "There must be a few doors that you could push open easily though?"

"Not sure the minor gentrified class is like that anymore," he says. "A few decades ago I could have walked in to Sotheby's or White's Club and been offered some lucrative job that I wasn't qualified for."

They smile at the idea.

"You went to private school though," he says. "Your family must have done alright. What does your father do?"

Her face drops. "I don't talk about my family," she says.

"What, never?" says Hans still rolling on with the momentum of the conversation then realising that the rolling has come to a sudden standstill.

"Did something happen?" he says.

"Dad's dead."

The moment gels like aspic in the room. She turns away to the open window, half steps out to the balcony and looks unblinking at the horizon and the never-ending sea.

"I didn't mean to drag anything up, Gab."

"Forget it," she says. "I try to."

"If you ever want to talk about it..."

"I don't do that, Gordon. That's why I'm in this job. I'm isolated for a reason, so no one can ever get to me. Anything else wouldn't work."

"It must be tough inside that shell of yours."

"You have no idea."

He looks at the floor then back up at her.

"Time to go," she says softly. They pack up and head out to the rendezvous point.

*

Mostly white boats of all sizes bob on the tide in the marina at Villeneuve-Loubet, and cursory clouds sit across a distant claret and sapphire sky above them.

Gabrielle parks her Z4 in the back streets. She is wearing trousers and a light jacket with flats, her Smith & Wesson in a holster under one arm. She carries an Aspinal brown midi tote handbag over her shoulder with four flash bombs inside. They walk to the marina, find a bar that overlooks the main moorings and order a Margarita and a Negroni. They chat and both keep a lookout for any of the characters in Ulrich's gang. Gabby went through photographs and profiles of the players with Hans over lunch.

Dusk runs in smoothly across the Mediterranean and the lights around the marina gradually shine out to create a playground for the rich. Men and women walk from the boats and hotels and create a hub-bub that rises across the hulls and ropes of the waterfront. Hans is the first to see Lebedev.

"Gab, is that...?" he says touching her arm. She looks in the direction he indicates and her eyes widen in the affirmative. They watch the man. He has a pre-booked table in a bar next to theirs. Lebedev sits down and within minutes is joined by Robinson. The men talk and order several drinks over the next couple of hours. As Gabby and Hans are starting to wonder if the whole thing has been a waste of time, Robinson and Lebedev finish up their last drinks and walk off towards the far side of the marina. Gabby and Hans follow through the crowd. Robinson particularly is looking around nervously every few minutes and she is sure he looks directly at her but he doesn't react. She and Hans dodge and swerve through the people, all of whom seem to coming in the opposite direction. The crowd seems never ending and Gabby loses sight of the men. She looks across at Hans who puts up his open palms to the sky to show he doesn't know any more than she does. Gabby is getting worried that they have lost their quarries, then right at the moment when she is about to turn back, she sees the criminals skirting the outside of the moorings and heading down the long west side of the docks away from the bustle and into a deserted stretch of quayside. The men reach a jetty at the far end that sits at the mouth of the harbour. Two berths have been left empty and Lebedev talks to three men sitting on a bench at that part of the dock. Gabby and Hans drop out of sight behind a boat showroom that sits on the very edge of an area of delineated moorings, and wait for movement. She pulls out a second handgun from her bag and silently taps Hans on the shoulder.

"You may need this," she whispers. "Show me what the Guards taught you." He looks into her eyes with kindness, but says nothing and takes the weapon and a spare clip of bullets.

The minutes go by. As the day cools, the pools of light under each lamp around the marina buzz less as the insects die off at the end of their single days of existence.

Gradually, across the open water, the rhythmic beat of a boat's engine skates in from the distance. The noise gets closer, then cuts dead. A 50ft boat drifts in from the half-darkness and glides on the tide over the last few feet to the mooring.

"All good?" They can hear Lebedev talking to the pilot of the craft, who gives a thumbs up.

The boatmen throw ropes ashore and others tie off the cords to nearby bollards. Robinson is the first on board and disappears below deck. He comes up seconds later and gives Lebedev a big smile.

"Where's Ulrich?" says Robinson.

"He's not coming."

"You taking the piss?"

"We can handle it, Larry."

"Fuck him," says Robinson.

Lebedev starts to direct the men to unload. As packages come up from below, Gabby hears a vehicle heading along the marina towards them. She drops her head down to remain hidden and Hans follows suit. A van appears from around the corner of the final building and stops next to the boat. Two men get out and open the back up to start receiving the goods. Gabby reaches into her bag and pulls out a flash bomb, sets it live and rolls it across the concrete to just under the front of the van.

The bomb explodes into the night and lifts the front of the van off the ground, the men start to shout, drop their packages and draw weapons. Gabby throws a second bomb, this time at the back of the van. The vehicle lurches with the impact of the blast and fire engulfs the rear doors.

"Now," she says to Hans. They each run at speed to the opposite far ends of their hiding place and start rapid fire into the van. The gang cannot see their assailants due to the flood lights across the roof of the showroom. Lebedev runs along the quay to the front of the boat and fires off rounds in the direction of Gabby but without being able to see her. Hans circles around the far side of the mooring and draws the fire of Robinson and his men. Gradually, step by step, while under fire from two gunmen, Gabby moves toward the boat. She reaches the water's edge and has run out of cover. In the two seconds that the bullets coming from the gang intensify, she computes timings. She falls back behind a brick store that sits at the far end of the dock and waits.

The third blast comes within a minute. Hans has unleashed a flash bomb into the back of the boat, raw flames spew up, swamping the deck and running at speed to flare up around the wheel. Two men caught coming up the stairs from below deck are caught in the fire, one jumps overboard and the other falls back down the stairwell. As Lebedev and his men turn their attention to the fire on board, Gabby takes the final incendiary and throws it on the front deck of the boat. It explodes with ferocity, taking the upper portion of the front windows with it and creating an inferno. Gabrielle skirts round away from the burning craft and back down the outside of the marina buildings. She finds an opening and watches the flames for a second then realises she can't see Hans. The plan was that they both retreat after the fourth bomb but there is no sign of her colleague.

Her mind flicks through the options. She darts out from her cover to the boats moored nearer to the town and drops down behind one. She jumps into a small motor boat that is hanging off the back of one of the craft and silently lowers it into the water. Gabby pilots the boat out toward the burning, keeping as close as she can to the larger yachts so that the gang can't see her coming. She is two boats away from the fire and can see Lebedev and Robinson desperately trying to recover any boxes of drugs from the hold. She can't see Hans and ties her motor boat alongside a yacht, then clambers up the side. She keeps low and creeps nearer to the gang. As she reaches the aft deck, she sees Hans. He has a red stain on his shirt and is lying behind three large crates by the dockside, but he is moving.

A car speeds along the roadway of the marina and skids to a halt near the van that has all but burnt out. More gang members fall out and start to help putting out the fire. Gabby jumps across to landside, runs to the crates and drops down next to Hans.

"Gordon?" she says. "How bad?"

"Not serious," he says. "Bullet skimmed my ribs, bloody painful though."

She puts an arm around him and lifts him up, together they crouch down and move as fast as his wound allows. She gets the two of them into the motorboat, opens up the throttle and speeds away across the cool water. They look back at the smoke and flames billowing up into the night sky. The shell of the craft is utterly destroyed. As Gabby turns away and heads east, a loud shudder breaks the air and a fire ball rises where the boat had once been. They can see people scurrying along the dock from the town to see what has happened in their marina. She looks at Hans and can see the fire reflected in his eyes as he watches their handiwork disappear into the darkness.

She steers the tiny boat back towards Nice, hugging the coastline. They slip through the water around the airport perimeter and into the bay that surrounds the old town. They run the craft up onto the Plage de Carras and abandon it, then walk back through the deserted streets, Hans without one shoe that was lost somewhere on the quayside. Her face is blackened but her eyes are shining brightly.

*

CHAPTER SIXTEEN

The air cuts thick along the deeply-carpeted top corridor of the British Embassy in Berlin. Marcus Murphy knows that the need for secrecy is at the heart of everything they do 'this side' of the diplomatic presence in Europe's most important economy.

He has always been completely open with his staff that they all live or die on the basis of their reliability, literally so in some cases. If London trusts an MI6 country operation to get things done effectively then everything in the garden is rosy; the ambassador is given more responsibilities, the MI6 local station chief is heralded with promotion and knighthoods often beckon in later years. But cock it up and a silence descends. You won't hear of your demise, but you'll sense it. You'll notice conversations stop as you walk into rooms in Vauxhall Cross, memos of import will not be sent out with you on the distribution list. Becoming the Mayor of Coventry, as it is known inside MI6. Murphy has no intention of putting himself in that position.

He walks back to his office from the conference room where he has just been interviewed for the second time by the Crows about the Stranraer termination. He doesn't understand why the enquiry is going on for so long, usually, even though tragic, deaths in the field are to be expected and are dealt with promptly. But this one seems to have a rolling momentum which makes him feel uncomfortable. Unexplained behaviours in the Service are always due to some internal enquiry or other, covert or otherwise.

Something is nagging at his brain, and it tapped away in his head throughout the Crows interview. They're experts on people lying, of course, and probably knew he was being less than open. He didn't lie to them exactly, but they did trigger thoughts in his head which he didn't immediately voice.

It isn't like him to be paranoid, he thinks; his easy, relaxed bonhomie takes him everywhere he wants to go. But he should know why Stranraer was killed. It is his patch and the only measure of competence from London's perspective is your awareness of what is going on in your geography. You have to be the fount of all knowledge or someone else will be.

The truth is that he has become bored of Berlin. Two years is enough in any posting and even though Berlin is still an 8 or a 9 on the scale of desirable jobs, he knows he is ready for something more. Ever since he entered the diplomatic service he has wanted to go to Washington. It still holds a kudos like no other British embassy. Moscow is another posting he craves. Those two are very different MI6 operations of course but stimulating and a passport to a senior role in London by the time he gets to his 50s.

He sits in a large leather chair behind his larger rosewood desk and types in his password to the desktop computer in front of him. He scrolls through the Berlin activity logs on the day Stranraer died but nothing obvious leaps out at him. He checks the server traffic and drills down into any spikes of activity. One spike shows up and he traces the routing data. The source inside the Embassy is unregistered on Oberon, and he runs a trace programme to decipher any barrier applications that the spike user could have used. He transfers the data to his local machine and loads it into the reporting tools; the display starts to build the result, piece by piece, until the true destination of the spike traffic is evident. The machine flips open a map of the Embassy and the traffic mappings are shown at each desk in the place. Due to the data volume, the spike is the last to load, it builds as Marcus watches. On the display, he can see quite plainly that the spike came from the office on the first floor, outside of the MI6 operational suite. The spike was from Stuart Palmer's desk.

*

The brightness of the room wakes Sebastian Ulrich. He puts a pillow under his head and lies in the king size bed in the most expensive room in the Grand Hotel du Cap Ferrat. Sasha lies asleep next to him, the covers half across her body, her golden limbs outlined against the white sheets; an empty champagne bottle and the remains of cocaine lines are scattered near the bed where they lay. He reaches for his phone, taps through the various messages received and answers some of them. The cell in Paris have a problem with a dealer who is refusing to pay; in Moscow the arms shipment is near ready to move; and in Berlin they have killed the nightclub owner who had been caught talking to the police.

There is a knock on the door. Ulrich gets up to tell the maid that they should not be disturbed; he is naked but he doesn't bother to put anything on as a show of his power. He reaches for the handle and turns it.

The door is pushed open from behind and hits him in the face. In the second when his eyes are closed from the impact, he feels a fist hit his jaw and the force carry him backwards through the air. He crashes on to the floor ten feet away.

"You fucking double crosser," says Robinson, and kicks the man in the groin while he is down. Ulrich writhes in pain. Robinson continues his assault, leaning over and punching him in the face. Ulrich is getting his bearings and starts to fight back. He rolls over and gets up, still winching from the groin pain. He runs at Robinson and they fall together, punching and gouging. Sasha wakes, runs around them to the bathroom and locks herself in.

They fight hard using the years of practice they have both had protecting their criminal patches. Ulrich is stronger but Robinson is bigger. They crash down onto the glass table in the centre of the room and it showers the carpet with smithereens. There is blood now, across Robinson's face and in cuts across Ulrich's body. Robinson produces a knife from the back of his waistband. They stand, arms and legs apart, facing each other.

"Come on, what are you waiting for?" says Robinson between heavy breaths.

"What the fuck this is about?"

"Like you don't know. Where were you last night? We got screwed."

"You failed again, Larry?"

Robinson lashes out across the space between them but misses his target. "If you had been there and not fucking some tart, you'd know we got attacked, man. Fire bombs, the whole lot, some gang shooting us up."

"What about the gear?" says Ulrich.

"Destroyed. There was a fire."

"You fucking idiot."

"Don't put this on me, they were your contacts supplying that load, they've screwed us," screams Robinson.

"No one would destroy the gear would they if they were nicking it? Think, Larry," says Ulrich. "Whoever it was just wanted to screw us over. It was your job to keep the local cops sweet, you didn't do that and now they've got their own back."

"As usual with you," says Robinson. "It's never your fault when it goes wrong but you get all the praise when it works out. You bloody set us up, Ulrich." He is spitting every word now.

Robinson lunges and brings the blade down with force to within an inch of Ulrich's skin. Ulrich grabs the arm and twists the hand, Robinson turns with all his strength and brings the blade round to face his opponent. The two men push their bodies to force the weapon one way or the other. Ulrich fails first, the knife turns in Robinson's hand and, in a second, pushes down into Ulrich's flesh. The blood oozes up through the wound, slow at first then quicker. Robinson pulls out the knife and Ulrich falls away, his wound spouting red gore across the bedclothes. Robinson turns away, wipes the blade on the bedclothes, and walks purposefully out of the room. Ulrich is left shaking on the floor.

"Sasha!" he screams with his full voice and the woman appears from the bathroom. "I need a doctor." His voice is weaker.

Sasha runs out of the bathroom and kneels down next to him. In his voice, she can suddenly hear fear for the first time in the 18 months she has been with him.

"Sebby, what have they done to you?"

He winces with pain as she touches his skin. "Get the sheet, push down on the wound, quickly!" She tears the bedclothes and applies pressure to his shoulder. After three minutes she gets her phone and dials for an ambulance. She is crying as she saves his life; his eyes fluttering between closed and open as the blood spreads up and out across the cotton. She pushes down with her body weight harder and prays to a God she doesn't believe in.

*

Gabby sits on her balcony overlooking the sea with the hotel's room service breakfast tray in front of her. She messaged Hans five minutes ago and he pushes the door to her room and saunters in.

"How are you feeling?" she says.

He lifts up his t-shirt and shows her the bandage around his stomach. "A bit sore but it missed me, thank God. I enjoyed it, though." He sinks into the chair opposite her.

"Were you ever in the field?" she says.

"The Mett Bar is the field, thank you very much, although not in the way you mean. But, I did realise that I want to see more stuff like last night."

They eat breakfast and talk about their jobs and dreams.

"What about this data you got?" he asks as they finish the meal.

"I'll get it." She collects the Jim and the Riverside data from her bag, and adds an envelope to the pile, then sits back down.

"This is the traffic flow data," she says, handing Hans paper printouts of the data from Jim. You can see there are high nodal points in the flows. This is across the period between me calling in the kill location for Mac, and his termination being registered on the network. That's about 20 hours."

Hans looks at the papers. So, Nodes 16 and 43 are...?" he says.

"London and Berlin."

"Got IDs?"

"Not yet," she lies.

"How are you going to find them?" he asks.

"I need to match the nodal list with the data from Oberon."

"What else?" he says.

"This." She hands him some of the Riverside data on her tablet. "Messages from the network for the same time period."

"No names," he says as he flicks through the screens. "Not conclusive yet, Gabby."

"Then there's this." She holds up the envelope, opens the flap, extracts three photographs and lays them on the table between them.

"What are these?" asks Hans.

"GISS photos from an operation they mounted on the same day."

"Doing what?" says Hans.

"Good question. I don't know the answer to that, but they were in the building opposite Mac. In this first image, you can see them at the kill site and there is Mac's body." She holds a picture up and points to it for Hans. "That photo has a time stamp of 15:58:16. Now this second picture shows the GISS team in the opposite building and you can see the kill site in the image. It's time-stamped as 15:45:34. Thirteen minutes earlier."

"And?"

She holds up the second picture. "No Mac," she says. Hans takes the print and looks at it intently, up close.

"Weird," he says under his breath. "What time did you leave him?"

"Three fifteen," she says.

"And what time did they called in the agent termination to London?"

"4:28"

"Doesn't make sense," says Hans.

"Agreed. Then there's this picture, taken at 16:03:50." She holds up the final print. "Guess what?"

Hans shakes his head with a down-turned mouth.

"No Mac," she says. "Just a bloody pool on the concrete floor."

"The GISS moved him? Why would they?"

"Maybe he didn't die immediately and they got medics to him," says Gabby. "But, what's rule number one with a gun-shot wound?"

"Don't move the body."

She raises her eyebrows. "So, what have we got?" she begins. "A GISS team who seem to have killed a British assassin then removed his body and who had no good reason for being on-site in the first place. We have a bunch of emails and messages that indicate the kill order needed to fail; and we have some traffic data that indicates someone in London was talking a lot to someone in Berlin in the period of time between the kill location going on to Oberon and Mac's death."

"And that tells you what?" says Hans.

"For all the world, it looks like London set up the kill order then got the Belgian Security Service to scupper it as a black op."

"When they could have just cancelled the order?"

"Yup."

"I can't think of another set of circumstances that make all that data ring true," says Hans, leaning his head back on his hands.

"There's another question," says Gabby. Hans turns his eyes to her expectantly. "Why would Riverside give me the messages?"

"What did you think when you met him?" asks Hans. "Genuine?"

"Is anyone?"

"Was he at least genuine about giving you this information? He said to me he wanted to stop the leak."

"He said the same to me," she says. "I believe that is the ops job he has been given, but it's not possible to assess his honesty."

"Does he know the mole?"

"I don't think so, or he would have moved on it. He's an experienced field ops agent."

They stop and let their brains absorb the questions before moving on.

"So, what's next?" says Hans.

"I need to confirm who is Node 16 and our friend Riverside is expecting me to go back to him."

"Can I help?" asks Hans.

"You'll be more useful back in Berlin," she replies.

"OK," says Hans, then he pauses. "You do trust me, Gabby?"

She considers the question honestly as she looks at him.

"I do, Gordon. Welcome to a very exclusive club." They smile at each other.

*

Geraldine is up at dawn. She showers and dresses and makes tea, then puts on her coat and goes out of the front door to the walkway that runs the length of the housing block that contains the flat. She walks down to a children's play area and sits on a swing, then reaches into her bag for a packet of cigarettes. The flame from the lighter flares in the cold morning; highlighting her face with a stark yellow stain. She draws heavily on the tobacco and blows a cloud into the sky of half smoke and half condensed air. There is no one about at that time in the morning. She has always relished the hours after people have gone to bed and before they rise. To her, this is the real world, unsullied by others, some sort of fundamental truth.

Out of the early morning misty haze in the open space between blocks, the outline of a man gradually becomes more defined. She watches his progress as he walks towards her. He wears a white mackintosh and has a woollen hat pulled down too far so that it hides his eyebrows.

"They said you'd come," she says without emotion.

"And here I am."

"Are you checking up on me?"

"Not at all," says the man.

"Nothing has happened."

"It will."

"When?" Her frustration is genuine.

"Soon enough. It's only been a day."

"Every minute counts, you know that."

She takes another long pull on her cigarette. The smoke creates a halo around her in the coldness, dispersing slowly at first then at speed as it is caught by the biting wind that whips around the wall at the end of the playground.

"You need anything?" he says.

"Not from you."

"You only need to say and I'll be ready, now or afterwards."

"I won't need you afterwards, Ned."

"I only want to help."

"You can't, you have never helped. You have always destroyed, always ended things. I don't want to go on ending things my whole life. Life should be about creating not destroying."

"It wasn't up to me," he says so quietly that the words shatter and spread, so she doesn't hear them but knows he has said something.

"You need to take responsibility," she says.

"I want to be responsible for you."

Geraldine laughs. "You don't get it, Ned."

"Tell me then, show me."

"You need to be responsible for your ideas, your thoughts, your plans," she spits out the words from the years of sadness behind her. "Own them, do them, when they go wrong stand up and say, yes I did that and it didn't work out, but I'll learn and do it differently next time."

"What do you want me to do?"

"Just be here when I call, Ned." She turns away from him and blows out a cloud of smoke.

Without more words, he turns and walks back into the dawn, she turns to look but he is no longer there.

*

Stuart sleeps for most of the day and Geraldine footles around the house, tries to read, watches the television and makes food for herself as Stuart isn't hungry. After lunch she suggests a walk and they talk quietly all the way round about nothing in particular. The flat, for all its faults, is warm, and he stands in the kitchen, leaning against the units, while she cooks a Shepherd's Pie. Geraldine used some of the money from Murphy to buy wine, and they get through a whole bottle without realising it. By the time the sun has gone down, they are full of food and warmth.

"How did you decide that you wanted to be a civil servant?" asks Stuart, swirling half a glass of Pinot Noir by the base.

"Seemed natural," says Geraldine. "It's what mum and dad did."

"Where?"

"Mum was in the Home Office at Queen Anne's Gate," she says. "She was a clerk and ended up head of a clerical team. Then she moved to Marsham Street when they all did, and retired in '08."

"What about your dad?"

"Dad was in the Department of Transport, he got up to Deputy Assistant Director."

"Impressive."

"What are they like?"

She looks at the room. Her eyes flicking across the odd combination of pictures that had been purchased by the Foreign Office procurement branch, the same set in all safe houses. He waits, watching her contemplate.

"Kind," she says. "Always kind. I had a happy childhood, not adventurous, but happy."

"Do you see them much?"

"When I can. I don't often get back to the UK."

"Why?" His attention is held utterly in the story.

She shakes her head. "Don't know. I should go back more. I don't want to be a burden to them."

"Why would you be?"

She doesn't answer but looks down at the carpet in the sitting room. She leans forward to pick up her wine glass but fumbles and it spills red across the surface.

"I'll get a cloth," he says and runs out, then returns and kneels to mop the liquid.

"Let me," she says and puts her hand on the cloth. They both hold it, neither letting go. Their eyes rise to each other's view. There is no emotion between them in that instant, then she lifts her hand to his cheek and feels the warmth of his skin. He puts his hand over hers on his face, then leans in and kisses her gently on the lips.

*

CHAPTER SEVENTEEN

Caroline decides to walk the last leg of the journey to the Cabinet Office and takes the tube to Green Park, then cuts down the broad path that runs from Piccadilly to The Mall. She walks fast, not due to any lateness, but because that is what she always has done; going somewhere quickly, throughout her life.

She walks across St James Park and heads for The Park Bridge to cross to the southern side of the water. She thinks about her current case and wonders how likely it is to be successful. The security services are famously reticent when it comes to appearing in court, she knows that from twenty years of hearing Stephen stop mid-sentence when he knows he has reached the limits of what she can know. She has always told herself that she doesn't mind his secrecy, it's more than a job to him, it's part of his whole being, without it he's not the same man. Caroline had known that from the outset and it seemed exciting at first to have a boyfriend with a job she couldn't talk about. She was very strict with herself for years, but five years ago she told her closest girlfriend in the Ivy Brasserie in Wimbledon on a cold Thursday in February after Stephen had been particularly annoying and dangled information in front of her but then said he couldn't go in to details.

Linny rehearses in her mind what she needs to talk about at the meeting she is going to. Her client, McAllister, told her in great detail about the work that his staff carried out, but his tone changed when she asked about his sources inside MI6. Not only did he say that he couldn't tell her, but also that the information was not relevant to his case. She had to put it to him that the case against him would stand or fall on the security services confirming what he had told her, and what they would tell the judge. Courts are all about evidence, she had underlined to him; if there's no compelling evidence about something then it never happened, it's as simple as that.

Caroline reaches the end of the park and turns left along Birdcage walk. She will push the Cabinet Office for evidence of the information supplied to McAllister, whether he wants it or not. Now she has agreed to take the case, she needs to be seen to put a strong argument together, even if her client is reluctant. The whole focus is the contact called Petrov. Her tactic, she has decided, is to ask for an interview with that source first and if the Cabinet Office refuse, then she will ask for an enquiry, if necessary through a judicial review. She isn't going to let them get away with ignoring her request. If that means consequences for this Petrov character as they are involved in something untoward, then so be it. She is sick of the security services hiding behind their anonymity when they overstep the mark and stray into illegal activity.

On arrival, Linny is led through a maze of corridors. All civil service buildings have a similar atmosphere she thinks, as she follows a small man with a large hat down corridor B6. He stops and opens one of the huge oak doors that mark out each fifty feet along the walls for as far as she can see. They go in to the meeting room. It is quiet, as though sound-proofed; dead air with nowhere to escape to. The man leaves her with a promise of chasing up, and she sits at one end of a table built for twenty. Her brain is all ready to go, on the start line, honed by her court experience. She sits back and pushes one shoe off her heel, enough to give the slightest release of tension and the minutest relaxation in her muscles. The awareness scares her, and she sits up, pulls her shoe back on and pulls her blue suit jacket across her body. She stands and looks out of the window onto Great George Street and can hear Big Ben chiming the quarter hour from across Parliament Square.

Behind her, the door suddenly opens.

"Ms Laughton?" He is in his forties, dark hair, tanned. A nice house in Reigate, she thinks. His face is smooth like his demeanour and two eyelashes on his right eye are pure white. They shake hands and he suggests they pull two chairs together away from the table as he is not a great believer in formality.

"How can I help?" he says in a way that reminds her of a marketing manager of a mobile phone company. She explains the case that she will be bringing to court in the next fortnight and the need for his help to liaise with the security services. He starts the usual spiel about the importance of anonymity and secrecy for the spooks. Linny tells him that she knows all about that as she married one. He laughs but not with his soul.

"What do you need?" he says.

"My client received information from the Secret Intelligence Service," she begins. "It was part of his contract to provide security for them as part of an integrated programme of work over eighteen months."

"Where was this?"

"Slovenia."

"What was the nature of your client's work?"

"The contract defines it as security services, in practice, he was providing additional manpower for British intelligence."

"Do we know what the manpower actually did?" He is cool, but intense.

"Not spying, if that's what you mean," she says with a slight smile which he returns. "Personal security guards mostly, he employs ex-military personnel."

"All vetted I assume?"

"Of course," she says.

"And what about this contact you say he has in the security services – Petrov?"

"That's the name he was given."

"I can't confirm if there is someone in either MI5 or the SIS with that name, I'm afraid."

"I understand the policy of denial that the security services use," she says. "I don't need to know their real name, I just need a video link interview with me, one to one; and a live black-screen video feed in the court to give their evidence."

"What is the information that was passed to your client?" The man is becoming more closed, she perceives.

"Just the details of operations that his team would need to be involved with."

"You're saying that details of SIS operations were given to your client?" he says.

"Yes."

He stops his flow, having got to the end point of whatever process he was following for the discussion. She watches his face as he turns his eyes away, down and to the right.

"I'll have to come back to you," he says eventually.

"When? The court date is set for the 16th."

"I can't commit to a date, your timescales may have to change."

She starts to protest but he holds up his palm. She adds, "I don't want to go to judicial review," and watches his reaction. He flicks his eyes up to meet hers.

"I'm sure that won't be necessary," he smiles weakly. "Let me show you out."

*

The message from Marjorie agreeing to talk comes through in the morning as Gabrielle is driving back from the airport having dropped off Hans on his way back to Berlin. She hasn't particularly been looking forward to the conversation as she can't work out a legitimate rationale for Marjorie to be a spike node of activity in Jim's data.

She grabs the tablet from her room and books a meeting room at the reception desk in the business suite on the third floor. There are five rooms, she has booked a small one and swipes the door access. The room has a table for six and is over-lit with stark down-lighters. There is a large screen at one end. Gabby opens the cupboard that contains all of the display equipment, pushes her hand into the cable looms and pulls out a fistful of wires. She traces them back to the wall box, finds the network leads and plugs in her tablet to the network. She runs her porting application to block her location, and pushes the tablet into the cupboard so it will sit there and divert the network during the call. Then she selects video conference software on the control panel and calls London.

Her friend answers immediately, at first without video switched on and after sounds of doors closing, Marjorie's face appears. They greet each other and talk inconsequentially for a minute.

"Anyway, where are you?" says Marjorie.

"Back in Berlin, just planning my next move." Marjorie's eyes look away from the camera for a second which tells Gabby that the MI5 network is returning 'location unknown' to the screens in front of Marjorie.

"Did you want to chat about something, Gab?"

"I do. You know we were talking about Stranraer?"

"Your friend who was killed?"

"Yup. Well, I did some digging and your name came up." Gabrielle had expected an uneasy silence but there isn't one.

"My name is always coming up!" says Marjorie with a laugh in her voice that seems real. "What particularly?"

"The night before he was killed, after I had put the location into Oberon, I have a trace of comms activity on the network."

"Right."

"Two people were particularly active that night and into the next day. One was in Berlin, and the other was you."

"That happens a lot as I'm leading live ops in the 5 control, so there are always dozens of messages. They are probably all mapped back to my user ID on the system as I'm the officer responsible."

"Was there a live overnight op on that date?" asks Gabby.

"I don't know off hand and I'd need approval to share that with you."

"Why would the messages be going from 5 Control to Berlin? Your ops are all in the UK, surely?"

"Yes of course we're domestic, but there are often players involved from outside of the UK. It could be that the Embassy in Berlin has an interest in one of our ops, for instance."

"Do you know Murphy in Berlin?" asks Gabrielle.

"Berlin Station Chief for 6? I've met him once or twice," says Marjorie. "Why? Do you think he's involved?"

"Don't know, but as the comms have a spike in Berlin too."

"Why don't you ask him?"

"I intend to."

"Off the record, Gab." Marjorie says. "We have no official interest in anything with a German flavour right now." She is getting somewhere at last.

"Can I put words into your mouth?" says Gabby. "Nothing official doesn't discount unofficial?"

"I can only confirm our official ops, of course."

"And those unofficial ops could involve Vauxhall Cross?"

"I couldn't confirm that."

"Any guidance on who else wouldn't know about unofficial ops?"

"Ask in Berlin." Gabby looks at Marjorie on the screen, there is not a flicker of movement in her face.

"A pity that you haven't got any information then," says Gabby. "Good to see you. Love to your mother."

"Talk soon, Gab." The woman from MI5 gives the smallest of waves as the video image fades on the television.

"Thank you, Marjorie," says Gabby to herself.

She packs up, disconnects the network proxy divert and goes to the restaurant for lunch. She takes a seat by the window overlooking the Promenade des Anglais and studies the menu. After ordering, she thinks about Marjorie and whether her friend had given her anything useful or was this some sort of trap. The one thing that Gabrielle can't work out is why Marjorie has fabricated her father's death. He must have done something that required the need for a 17J Order - the creation of a new fictional life for someone who needs to disappear. But her father wasn't in the Service, so did Marjorie do something? It doesn't make sense given the information Gabby has, so her brain moves on to thinking about Riverside. The information he provided wasn't a game changer for her; it told her that there were people talking about Berlin ops on the 6 network, but that's not news. Whenever there is any planning or a live operation, various branches get involved and will message each other. So, why did he provide those specific message to her? In Gabby's view, every single action is motivated by someone getting a benefit; the question here is, who benefits from his actions? Riverside's stated belief in being driven to find the mole seems legitimate, but why come to her? If he has evidence, then the easiest route to find the mole is to just escalate the data. While she is concentrating, she doesn't notice a man come up to her table, and takes a second to realise he's talking to her.

"Hi."

"Can I help?" she says.

"I wanted to ask. I've seen you eating alone a few times here and wanted to know if you wanted to have dinner?" He's handsome, she thinks, and smiles at him.

"I'm fine, thank you."

"A drink? Tonight? What harm could it do?" She looks at him; forties, American, blue eyes. She considers maintaining her barriers, but then thinks that she might enjoy the company of someone who doesn't want to talk about spying.

"OK," she says.

"Great, I'll meet you in the bar, at 9?"

"Sure. I'm Charlotte, what's your name?"

"James McKinney."

*

CHAPTER EIGHTEEN

Catherine has been restless for two days. More than anything, she wants to find Rich's lover but London gave her a number of jobs to do and she hasn't been able to get the time.

She feels that her work has started to become monotonous over the last few weeks. The same loop of repetition: kill order received, do some preparation and carry out the job; then hang around for days waiting to be called on again. She needs more stimulus than this.

She sets an enquiry running on Oberon about London operations that mention Rich, his flat address or his work, and makes supper while it runs through the algorithm. By the time she has finished her food, a list of ops is displayed on one of the two enormous screens which she insisted on having for her night-time online gaming sessions. Killing in a virtual world to take her mind off the reality of killing in real life. Kate scans the operations list in the results but nothing is directly relevant. The results are too broad and include anyone called Richard who has been mentioned in reports across London, and any operations which involve the immediate vicinity around his flat and work addresses.

She is starting to feel vaguely ridiculous with this search and knows that the chase to find who her boyfriend slept with is futile. She just needs to dump him and forget him, the opportunity for revenge will never come up anyway.

A message notification pops up in the top corner of one screen and she clicks to open it. It's a message from Riverside, an agent who she worked with a couple of years ago; he is on an op and needs C9 backup. Can she come to Berlin so that he can brief her? He has cleared her allocation with London and asked for her personally because he knows she is good from when they worked together.

This is an opportunity to go somewhere different and do something different at least for a few days. It will take her mind off the stupid jealous chase for an unknown woman. She replies that she'll be in Berlin tomorrow, then opens Call of Duty on her machine and plays until the early hours, killing into the night.

*

The Mett Bar has been quiet, even for a Tuesday. Hans sits on a tall stool with his feet up on the bar and flicks through his social media again to keep his brain awake as the sun climbs to midday. Two men sit around a table at the far end of the place discussing German football, and an old lady at another table reads a copy of Stern magazine. The door opens almost as if it has been blown by the wind. Riverside walks in and sits at the end of the bar. Hans feels his muscles tighten.

"Hans," he says with a slight upward nod. The barman descends from his perch and walks down to him.

"How did your meeting go?" says Hans.

"I think you know," says Riverside. Hans shakes his head.

"Did she turn up?"

"She did, as did two guests."

"A party? Always good to catch up with old friends." Hans smiles innocently.

"Did you tell anyone about our rendezvous, Gordon?"

"Are you accusing me of leaking secret information?"

"Someone did," says Riverside not moving his gaze from Gordon's face.

"I don't break the rules."

"Only you and I knew."

"Must have been you then, Robert" says Gordon with a half-smile.

"How do you know my name?"

"We can all hack Oberon, old chap," says Hans.

"How do you communicate with her, Gordon?"

"On a need to know basis, that's for sure."

"I need to know."

"Didn't she give you her address when you met up?"

"We can stand here all day being stupid."

"Something you're used to?" says Hans.

Riverside springs into life and brings his hand up to Gordon's throat, his fingers spread and press together just enough to stop his breath momentarily; then they relax. Hans coughs but contains it. He steps back away from the bar.

"Is that standard protocol when talking to a colleague where you come from?"

"You know where she is, Gordon, and I have a job to do."

"I don't know where she is, and I'm not sure I'd tell you anyway now you've had your hands around my throat."

"Why the loyalty? She could be the mole." Riverside is getting annoyed now.

"She's done nothing wrong, and I'm against heavy-handed internal operations that damage too many people and don't solve the problem," says Hans.

"I'm going to find her, you know I am. If you've looked me up on Oberon, you know I don't give up."

"This is not the way to solve it."

"What is?"

"Let me talk to her," says Gordon. "I can convince her to come in and then we can all sit down like adults and decide what to do. But she's not your mole, she's trying to find the mole. Look, I can tell you what she suspects, that there's been some suspicious comms between London and Berlin; she doesn't know who, but that's the focus of it. We've lost three agents in the field in a month, which means the leaks are regular and well-informed. It's not Gabby, and also, it's not one person. Two nodes communicating to each other." Gordon intentionally omits the GISS photos evidence as he doesn't trust the man in front of him.

Riverside considers the words he has heard and Hans walks off to collect glasses from tables to give the man some brain space. Riverside's eyes land on Gordon's jacket hanging on a peg behind the bar. He slowly gets up from his stool and walks around the end of the bar, pulls the coat off the hook and goes through the pockets. He stuffs a fist into one pocket and pulls out a bar of chocolate and coins. As he does so, an airline ticket falls out and floats to the floor. He picks it up and unfolds it. The ticket is from Nice Côte d'Azur to Berlin, dated yesterday. He slips it into his pocket.

"Let me think about what you've said, Hans," he says as the man returns with a tray of empties. "Thanks that was a useful chat."

*

The coolness of the day cascades through the open window above and behind Ela Peretz's desk. She shivers momentarily, pulls her jacket across her shoulders and turns her head to the other window at the side of her. The leaves on the trees outside are ninety nine percent green but one in a hundred is yellow, the sign of a coming cold snap. They're the weakest leaves, the ones not prepared for the gathering storm. That's how she sees her job, finding the yellow leaves.

She scrolls the page on her tablet and re-reads the statements from the witnesses on the Stranraer case. They are all consistent, maybe too consistent. Consistency means one of two things in her experience, they're all relating their views about real events and are telling the truth; or they have all agreed a story to tell and think that consistency is the best way for lies to look real. The truth is never the same from everyone, even those who witness the same event. Five people seeing a road accident will all have slight variances in their memories of what happened. Their natural biases and predispositions will colour the way they see things and the way they recall. What they notice will be different. It's her job to assess whether witness variations are natural, or fabricated.

Ela's mobile rings, it is Lawrence from Sir Bernard's office calling her for the meeting they are going to with the Cabinet Office. She collects her things and throws them in to her Mulberry Bayswater bag, a luxury that she bought for herself for her last birthday.

Despite Sir Bernard's seniority, he is travelling to the Cabinet Office rather than making them come to him; a power trick that the CO often use, she knows, to reinforce their closeness to No.10, politically as well as geographically. Sir Bernard's Jaguar Sentinel idles just outside the rear door to Vauxhall Cross. Ela arrives on the ground floor and pushes out into the September day. She would normally walk but Sir Bernard believes that how you arrive is a significant part of your presence, as he tells her in the ten-minute journey along the river, passed Thames House and around Parliament Square.

They pull up into the secure entrance off Whitehall and are shown to a lift that takes them to the third floor. Ela likes Vauxhall Cross as it feels like a modern office, the Cabinet Office feels to her like something from an era long gone. She gets the tradition, but Victoriana doesn't talk to her soul. They are escorted through an outer office into the inner sanctum of the Second Permanent Secretary of the Cabinet Office, Sir Stuart Dunn. Sir Bernard and Dunn are old friends and have worked together on numerous high-profile security operations.

Dunn outlines the matter that has come up. A barrister has raised a request for a witness statement from a member of MI6, Dunn already asked Ela's investigations department to research the case and in particular, to find information on the source in 6 called Petrov. There appears to be no such person, relates Dunn, hence this meeting today to discuss and identify where we go from here. Ela goes through the searches that her department have carried out looking for Petrov. They have run multiple, cross-tabulated searches for real names, aliases, cover names and operation code names but nothing has come up. There was an Operation Petrol in 1984 and one agent has a passported alias of Peter Rover, but nothing apart from those.

They discuss the information that was passed to the third-party contractor who is represented by the barrister who is requesting access. The level of concern rises palpably in the room as they review the details of the secret operations in Slovenia that were supplemented with outside mercenaries. Dunn wants to know whether it is standard practice for the SIS to hand out state secrets to commercial companies, which Sir Bernard vehemently denies and talks for five minutes non-stop on the rigour of the practices adopted in the European Operations Directorate.

Ela and Sir Bernard are sent away with a Cabinet Office flea in their ear. Dunn makes it perfectly clear that this is potentially explosive and looks like a leak of information. He reinforces that they need to find the Petrov character urgently. They retreat to the comfort of the Jaguar that has been waiting for them.

"There, Ms Peretz, you saw a wonderful example of a Cabinet Office power play," says Sir Bernard as they sit waiting to get out into the flow of traffic along Whitehall.

"They're right though, aren't they?" she says.

"That it looks like a leak? Yes," says Sir Bernard. "This could be an ugly one; I've seen this sort of thing before, where a small enquiry becomes a big snowball."

"What do we do?"

"Petrov is obviously a cover name," says Sir Bernard. "I suggest you talk to our sister security services in Europe and run some searches in their databases too, maybe they have come across the name."

She types on to her tablet.

"Do we know if any lives were lost in these Slovenia operations?" he asks. She flicks through documents on her screen and reads hurriedly.

"Yes," she says while still reading. Sir Bernard watches the crowds on Millbank as the car speeds up then stops as they negotiate the London traffic. "Yes, two lives lost, both agents of ours."

"When was this?"

"Seven months ago."

Sir Bernard is lost in his thoughts. His mind switches into damage limitation. If this has happened on his watch then he needs to be seen to move quickly now that the Cabinet Office is involved. Then he remembers the conversations on the Stranraer death and Blackhawk's belief in a mole. It is looking more and more likely that she may be right. What he needs to do urgently is to ensure that any mole is stopped dead in their tracks.

*

Robinson arrives at the top floor of the Skylounge roof top bar and is shown to a table overlooking the Notre-Dame de l'Assomption Basilica in Old Nice. He orders a Negroni Aperol and spends his time watching the women at the tables scattered across the space. Dima arrives ten minutes later, they order more drinks and talk about the events at the Villeneuve-Loubet marina the night before. Lebedev is more trusting of Ulrich than Robinson who hasn't shared the news of the fight in Ulrich's hotel room yet. But Lebedev can tell his friend is angry, more angry than he has seen him before.

"You need to chill, man," he says. "Ulrich is a bastard but ain't no way the attack was anything to do with him."

"I don't know," says Larry. "He's stepped over the line this time."

"It wasn't him, man. The more interesting question is, who was it?" He has Robinson's attention. "Who could have done it? There's only ever three possibilities for ambushes; the cops, competitors or someone inside the gang."

"It wasn't me," says Robinson.

"Nor me. What about your boys?"

"No way, they're all loyal," says Larry.

"Mine too," says Dima. "We got competitors? Sure. But have we got competitors with the balls to screw us over? I don't think so. You, me and Ulrich are respected. People know me because of my clubs and bars. What about you, Larry? You got someone trying to take over your patch?"

"Not me, man." Robinson takes a swig of his drink and raises his hand for another.

"So, what you think?" says Dima. "Who screwed us?"

"The cops didn't do that attack," says Robinson. "It was too clever, there were what, five or six of them? Those fire bombs were pro, man."

"So, who?"

"Mercenaries, I reckon."

"Working for who though? The gear went up in flames, no one wins."

They talk on into the evening, Robinson downing alcohol at twice the rate of Lebedev. He can't get passed his belief than Ulrich is behind it all.

"I got a plan, Dima."

"Yeah?"

"We top Ulrich," says Robinson. Lebedev's face shows no emotion. "What do you think?"

"Take his patch?" says Dima.

Robinson nods. "I knifed him today."

"You what?"

"Flesh wound, first thing. Now, I wanna finish the job."

"You gotta be careful, Larry."

"You in?"

Lebedev breaks the close intensity of their discussion and looks over the skyline and the setting sun. The scattered light draws long shadows of the church opposite that cut up into the sky and strike out across the deck of the bar where they sit. Dima doesn't think about the job of killing Sebastian, that is simple and he has killed so many that he doesn't need to think of it; but his mind runs through the consequences of what Robinson has proposed. Crime is a distrustful business, when an opportunity rears its ugly head, it is always worth considering the pros and cons.

"What's the deal?" he asks. "What split do you want of his businesses?"

"I hadn't thought," says Robinson.

"Think now, man, don't just be driven by revenge. Be driven by building up your portfolio. I'll take the clubs and the drugs businesses, you have the rest."

Larry nods. "The gun running?" asks Larry.

"And the migrants"

Robinson thinks for a second, but not in enough detail to give the options proper consideration. The air from the street glides across the table. "Let's do it," he says, looking at Dima.

The other man is more reticent and forces them to step through all of the things that need to be considered. Robinson's natural approach is emotional, wanting it all, and quickly. Lebedev is more circumspect and businesslike and he wants Larry to realise that it's not just one death, it's controlling the businesses after that. There will be lieutenants within Ulrich's organisation who won't like the takeover and will want a larger piece of the new operations, or will even fight to take it all. Dima has more experience of gang versus gang fighting, controlling geographic patches and defending the borders. Robinson's criminal activity has been more piecemeal, old school prostitution and small-time drug operations.

They eat then part after the meal. Robinson is going on to a club, but Lebedev wants to go back to the hotel in case Ulrich is causing waves after the knife fight. Dima drives back passed Mont Boron and Villefranche-sur-mer before turning on to the Cap Ferrat headland. Ulrich hasn't sent him a message today and he needs to know the state of Ulrich's mind. He'll want Robinson dead after the fight, that's for sure, and Dima has an opportunity to back both men, and guarantee being on the winning side, no matter what the outcome.

CHAPTER NINETEEN

Gabby orders room service and eats at 7pm. She showers and puts on a Galvan short red sequinned dress from the selection that the hotel staff brought her on the day she arrived.

They meet in the bar of the Palais de la Méditerranée Hotel and McKinney is charming. She is looking forward to not thinking about her job for one evening. They talk about holidays they have had, and Gabby impresses herself as she fills in the details of her fictional past from the bare bones of the 'Charlotte Baxter' cover story. He is in the vacation business; luxurious escapes for the very rich. Desolate islands, yachts, Michelin-starred restaurants and helicopter trips across the ocean to watch schools of Dolphins bubble and rise in the water. He can arrange for her to go on one, free of charge if she wants it; she says his life seems perfect, almost too perfect and he laughs with his eyes.

James wants to go to a casino and insists on driving to Monaco as it is so near. She is happy to ride the wave and they collect his car from the hotel garage. Half an hour later, they pull up at the front of the Place du Casino in his red Ferrari 458. The lights on the buildings and the chatter of the crowd create a crescendo of glamour that rolls out across the tiny city state and up into the purple sky. He hands his car keys to a waiting doorman who says, to Gabby's surprise, "Thank you, Mr McKinney."

He produces an Amex Black card to fund chips for them both. She learnt to gamble in the sixth form of her girls' boarding school with boys from the local village who had climbed the drainpipes of the Victoria mansion to be in their dormitory. How not to lose is one of the most useful skills that her education gave her; that and lying through her teeth.

The evening floats by, they win at blackjack and people around them take more interest after that, attracted by a success story. They move on to roulette and she can see that McKinney is enjoying the attention; he is in his element amongst the well-off. Occasionally he looks at her, but she isn't sure whether to connect or check up on her; but even so the spirit of the evening makes her forget entirely about the world of MI6.

Gabrielle doesn't notice Sebastian Ulrich arrive. Just before midnight, he stands at the grand front doors of the casino room while his coat is removed from his shoulders. He is shown to a table in the far corner that has been reserved. They know him here, respected or feared depending on whether you are on his payroll or not. A bandage is visible beneath his evening jacket and open-necked shirt, and Sasha sways beside him, thankful that he has taken her out on her birthday.

They order champagne and she is attentive of her damaged man but after a while she pulls at his hand to come and watch the tables. Ulrich doesn't want to and Sasha walks the room alone knowing she is being watched. James has just won from a split bet on two and five at roulette and he rakes the chips towards him while smiling at Gabby. In the second that Gabby sees Sasha arrive at the table, her brain shifts her unconsciously from a woman enjoying an evening out to a field agent of the British security services. Gabby holds out her champagne and a waiter offers a tray within ten seconds; she doesn't watch the tray but her eyes are fixed on Sasha who slinks around the backs of the players, looking at their faces, and not at the crowd that looks on. A tiny flick of her eyes and Gabby's and Sasha's eyes lock together across the crowd. Sasha knows immediately that this is the woman who attacked her boyfriend on his boat a few days ago. Gabby watches the woman's body change in its locomotion, the cogs in her brain are nearly visible as Sasha decides what she will do.

After a minute, Sasha continues her route around the room and aims her trajectory to end at Gabby. When she arrives, she smiles too convincingly.

"Charlotte isn't it?" she says with educated vowels.

"Sasha, how nice to see you."

"My boyfriend wasn't happy when you stole his jet-ski the other night."

"And I wasn't happy when he tried to grab me, so only fair all round," says Gabby turning her head towards the woman.

"He didn't do that."

"Known for his honesty, I guess?"

"Bitch," says Sasha and starts to move her arm to throw her drink in Gabby's face, but she is too quick for the woman, and shoots out a hand to pin down her wrist. Sasha struggles to regain movement of her arm but Gabby holds it tight.

"Let's not make a scene, Sasha," says Gabrielle, her voice a model of calm control.

"Get off me." Sasha raises her voice and people turn to see what the fuss is about. She pulls her arm away and walks off to Ulrich no doubt to report back. Gabby knows that she should get away before Ulrich is roused into any action. She skirts the room, kicks off her heels in one corner, and looks for Ulrich's table. Sasha is emotionally relating what has happened and Ulrich gets up and starts to push through the people towards the roulette table where James is still playing. Gabby plunges into the throng to head off Sebastian before her date gets involved.

Ulrich sees her when she is ten feet from him, he reaches inside his jacket pocket and pulls out a knife with an engraved handle. Those immediately near him see it and the crowd parts like Moses in the Red Sea, leaving Gabby and Ulrich facing each other. Gabrielle's mind flicks through her options; she can back off or engage the enemy, the two essential options in the field of battle. A soldier is taught the balance between the two, but Gabby lacks that balance and there is no real choice in her mind. She runs at him and brings her leading hand in low so Ulrich is forced to drop his knife hand in order to land a blow. Gabby knows this is the defensive position that all adversaries opt for given an attack from below. At the last second, as the knife is a foot from her skin, she shifts her body upwards and brings her trailing hand round to grab the knife and pull Ulrich's arm back beyond the limit of his skeleton's flexibility. There is a loud crack and his body spins where it stands, then he tumbles into a man standing too close to the fight. The knife bounces away across the casino carpet. Two security men are pushing through the crowds towards her; she jumps up on to a neighbouring roulette table, slips twice on the chips laid for betting, and bounds off from the other side. One guard catches up with her, she reaches wide and strikes him in the stomach, then pushes his head down into a blackjack table. The other guard is one her now, a stronger man, he manages to hold both of her wrists but leaves his groin unprotected which her foot pounds into with some force. He falls and she runs back around to the main doors but more guards come at her, one with a mace spray. He tries to get near but her training in Ontario gave her a perfect defence technique. She hits the can hard before he can press the button, the can slips and she grabs it, turns it and lets him have full throttle. Two more to go. The first is more violent than the others and she has to respond in kind; she bare knuckle punches him squarely in the face, once then again, his nose splits, she pounds her fist into him a third time and he turns away; she pushes her foot out and he falls into a blackjack table.

The final guy looks scared. She stops. "Just let me go passed if you don't want to get hurt," she says. He moves toward her.

"Your choice." She hits him in the stomach and he buckles. Gabby runs out across the foyer of the casino building and onto the driveway where they had arrived. McKinney appears from the crowd.

"This way Gabrielle," he shouts and runs to his car. She follows and clambers in as he pushes the accelerator and the machine skids away from the lights of the building and into the darkness.

They are silent in the car while he navigates the roads from the centre of Monaco. They speed through tunnels along the seafront, passed grand white villas and roaring blue water. At Saint Antoine, at the start of a large elevated section of the Route de la Moyenne Corniche, she asks him to pull over off the road as she feels sick and he guides the Ferrari onto the raw ground next to the carriageway. She steps out and stands at the top of a steep drop. She takes in the view of houses set in a rocky landscape for a minute, then returns to where he sits in the car. She opens the driver's door and he looks up. She brings a Glock 19 handgun up to his neck.

"I found this under the passenger seat," she says quietly. "I've checked that it's loaded and because you know that it is, I suggest you start telling me who you are."

"James McKinney," he says with equal measures of innocence and bafflement.

"And what's my name?"

"Charlotte. Look, what's this about."

"So why did you call me Gabrielle just now at the casino." A bead of sweat breaks its surface tension and starts the journey down the left side of his face.

"Hands on the wheel," she says. "Get out slowly keeping your palms up." McKinney stands. "On the floor." He lies down, she sits on him and pulls his arms up behind him so he can't move. He struggles and they rise up for a moment but she takes the butt of the Glock and hits him on the cranium. He falls back down.

"You going to say anything?" she says. "If not, what are we going to do now, Jimmy? You working for somebody?"

He pushes again, this time with more force, she is thrust up and off his back. She rolls off into the side of the car and loses her grasp of the gun, the Glock falls to the ground. McKinney is on his feet but twenty feet away, he starts to move toward the weapon; she pushes with all of her residual energy and scurries across six feet of dirt to where it lays. Her fingers touch it first and curl round the grip; she turns the muzzle and squeezes the trigger. For a full second, McKinney stands motionless, stuck in time, his eyes staring at her. Then gradually he collapses and falls onto the side fence. The wire strains under his weight, he is suspended over the drop, swinging in the air as blood stains out across his shirt to match his bowtie. The fence post to one side shifts in the earth, two more rocks from McKinney's dying body and the post wrenches out from the ground, the fence gives way and James McKinney falls soundlessly, bouncing off the rock face and into the void.

She stands and looks over the edge. Gabby's mind wants her to work out what happened tonight but she decides to do that back at the hotel. She walks to the Ferrari, drops down into the driver's seat and pulls back out on to road to Nice.

*

CHAPTER TWENTY

The sun is wrestling the clouds over Berlin. The windows of Murphy's office are witness to overnight raindrops that are now just a record of past events on the dry glass. He sits in an armchair in a pool of light in one corner, an iPad in front of him. The fact that Stuart Palmer was highly active on the MI6 network in the period of time before Stranraer's death has been bouncing around in his skull for the last twenty-four hours. He had not even heard of Palmer before news of his stabbing buzzed up from the light side of the Embassy. He had heard nothing formally from London and no spooks in Murphy's team knew about Palmer either. He is just a middle-ranking administrator doing something about trade.

Marcus needs to do something now that he has the traffic node data; he can't be seen to block it or be inactive. He flicks through Palmer's personal file, there really is nothing of consequence. No gaps in years when he might have been turned by some foreign power, no posh education where he might have been approached in the pubs of an English town by a man of opaque origin. Murphy is used to assessing people and his judgement is that either the data is wrong or Palmer is the most effective under-cover spy he has ever come across as his back story is so pristine. When he had agreed to put Geraldine and Stuart in the safe house as a drop point for Alexander Keneely, the push had come from London. Murphy was happy to go along with it, but it seems odd now in hindsight. Putting two untrained administrators in live field operations is high risk, but London had been adamant. Their rationale had been that Palmer was already considered to be field ops by Alexander and if they had told him to hand over his information to an administrator he would have been lost as a contact, and Murphy didn't have anyone else who was free or not deployed on a live op at the time. Blackhawk disappearing exactly at the moment that Alexander was ready to talk had been unfortunate timing but Murphy managed to recover the situation through comms to Alexander; texts seemingly from Blackhawk saying she had gone away to mourn the loss of her fictional boyfriend. Murphy's Comms Branch team had done a magnificent imitation of messages with the young man and now he is ready to become their active source.

This doesn't solve his Palmer problem. Murphy decides that the op can't be stopped as Alexander is due to be given the safe house address today and a win for Murphy in the current climate will be a boost for him. The killing of Stranraer on his territory still weighs on him, and more importantly as far as Murphy's perception is concerned, the death is a big black mark against him from London's perspective. There is nothing he can do immediately about Palmer, and he will deal with him after Alexander has handed over the information.

*

The stab wound from the attack a week before is itching and Hans tries not to scratch it, but his self-control collapses in the face of the discomfort and he presses circles into his skin around the wound. Two women come in from the street and order coffee and cake and he feels his phone vibrate five minutes later as he lays plates of Schwarzwaldetorte onto the table in front of them. The device displays a notification indicating that Gabby has left a message on 23G and he leans on the back wall of the bar as he logs in to the site. The message is direct and to the point, she is asking him to visit her flat in Berlin and upload the content of the USB stick that she left with him into the Oberon secure layer. Hans has access to normal Oberon in the Mett Bar so that he can make general enquiries of the system but the secure functionality is only available in embassies and consulates, or in secure comms rooms like the one at Gabby's flat. Also, not all MI6 personnel have clearance for the secure layer. He knows that Blackhawk has only standard Secret clearance, and Top Secret for the operations she is allocated onto, like all field ops personnel. Hans has Top Secret Plus clearance due to an operation near the Mett Bar three years ago when the BND and SIS had worked together to root out a cell of suicide bombers that would have devastated four sites in Berlin if it had not been infiltrated. Top Secret Plus also usefully gets him access to the Oberon secure layer.

After the lunchtime rush, he closes the Mett Bar and walks alongside the river then turns northwards towards the Moabit district of Berlin. It is mid-afternoon as he pushes open the door to her flat. He can immediately tell someone has been there; he has seen the place a few times before and usually Gabrielle keeps it neat and tidy. Now it is a mess, drawers hang out and their contents are strewn on the floor. In the kitchen, packets of pasta and cereal have been deposited liberally on the floor, and in the bedroom the duvet is in a large pile on the floor. All MI6 staff addresses are kept secret, as are safe houses and other operational buildings across the world. This isn't a random break-in; the TV and other saleable items are still in the apartment; rarely is anything random where the security services are concerned. A few candidates for the ransack flick through his mind; Murphy or London Centre may have ordered it after Gabby went off-grid; Riverside could be the culprit; or the guy who stabbed him in the Mett Bar may have found the address somehow and come looking for her.

Hans punches the keys on the TV remote and drops down to the comms room beneath the flat, his feet creating loud clanging echoes on the metal that bounce around the stairwell and join together in crescendo. He sits at the large screens in the room and logs into Oberon and in through the Meridian Gateway that separates Oberon from the secure layer. Gabby has been forensic in her instructions. Hans follows them to the letter and uploads the USB content, which is encrypted so he cannot see what it is. He then opens an eyes-only container in the secure layer and adds a 72-hour time lock. Finally, he addresses the container to Sir Bernard and copies the one-line message that Gabby left on 23G, "Here is your mole." Hans wipes the USB stick, backs out through Meridian and shuts down the session. Whatever was on the USB will be delivered to Sir Bernard under eyes only security protocol in three days' time and now the process has started, no one, not even Gabrielle, can stop it.

*

The Golvet restaurant sits eight floors up above Berlin on Potsdamer Strasse in the south-west of the city. Riverside arrives exactly at 9pm, as arranged, and asks for a table by the window. He orders a gin and tonic and watches the traffic negotiate the roads around the Park am Karlsbad then disappear into the urban sprawl beyond. His drink is half way down when he turns his head to see Catherine walking towards him through the forest of tables. He gets up and kisses her on both cheeks. She seems pleased to see him, he notices. They try not to reminisce at first then give in to the temptation and talk about their last op when they worked together in Italy. The Italian MI6, the AISE, requested resources from the UK to man a major crime operation. Riverside was the British Security Operations Lead and C9 were brought in to provide sniper cover on three occasions for raids on criminal hideouts. Catherine was commended for her work on the operation as she successfully wounded two of the top targets that the Italians were after. C9 was unusually present for three weeks on the same operation, and Catherine and Riverside talked when they were off-duty and shared drinks and food but hadn't taken it any further as he wasn't her type, which she told him directly one night to his apparent amusement.

"So, tell me about this op." she says after a while.

"We're bringing in a rogue agent. Blackhawk. You know her?"

"Nope. British?" He nods.

"She's off-grid, out of London control," he continues. "The order comes from the highest level, Sir Bernard Macintosh."

The waiter brings their starters and the social break allows the words to dissipate. She changes the subject and they talk about where their careers are going. Unlike people in jobs that don't involve lying and death, they both agree that they didn't quite realise the jobs they signed up for would remove any vestige of a private life. Riverside is single and ended his relationship with his girlfriend three months after joining 6. Catherine says nothing about her relationship as she is here to forget about all that.

"Can we finish that conversation on the op," he says later in the evening. She nods in agreement. "We're flying out tomorrow."

"Where?"

"You'll find out in the morning."

"Why did you want me on this?" she says.

"Two heads are better than one."

"To do what?"

"Find her."

"And?" says Catherine.

"Bring her in," he says with an unspoken obviously.

He gives himself thinking time between her stream of questions by moving a wedge of cheese onto a biscuit and biting into them. She moves her gaze to the window and the moonlit night outside that washes the German capital blue with darkness.

"How are you going to do that?" she says.

"Don't know yet, depends on what I find."

"A man with no plan." She raises one eyebrow, he smiles.

"I have a set of possibilities," he says. "It all depends if she wants to come quietly or not. That's why you're here." Catherine smiles inside at the recognition of her expertise and she hopes she is hiding the discomfort she feels about an operation against one of their own.

"Meet me at Berlin Airport tomorrow at nine," he says.

She raises her glass and he mirrors her action, then they chink glasses and drink to their new partnership.

*

Stuart lies in bed and watches the sky through a gap in the top of the blind. Geraldine moves her arm up across his chest; she feels warm against his skin. A midnight bell rings in his distance. She asks him what he is thinking, speaking as quietly as any sound he has ever heard. He doesn't know what he's thinking, it's all new to him. She sits up and focuses on his face to ask if he regrets being here with her. He assures her he's not. She lays back down and they talk about themselves in the intimate way

229

that only lovers know. Secrets shared on a midnight pillow, not utterable in the daytime or with anyone else other than someone so close that the two of you breathe in unison.

They laugh at past stupidities and the times in their lives when they had felt humbled or just been plain wrong. You only share your weaknesses with people when you're sure that they can be trusted, she says. He agrees after thinking about that for the first time in his life. He hasn't spent his years on the planet trusting people, although he might have done if opportunities had come his way.

He asks about her life. She recalls the whole narrative, like it has been taught to her. Branded into her memory after tearful nights initially regretting some of the things she had done, then realising that the things that don't work out are just as much a part of you as the things that do. They compare the greatest moments in their lives and greatest disappointments, or the ones she feels comfortable telling him. Some things are best left as forgotten memories she thinks more than once as they talk. He has few regrets and she finds herself regarding that with jealousy; he has had little pain, but little adventure. She has been married before and only after a while does she want to talk about it. He listens carefully and has more questions in his head than he wants to say. Stuart becomes fascinated by the short time between him thinking some words and then hearing his own voice saying them out loud. She wants to know why he hasn't had many girlfriends; they frightened him when he was young. Women are another country he says and she likes the phrase, but he doesn't tell her it's borrowed from a book he read.

She wants to know what he wants to do with his life. He has never thought about it and she is shocked that that is the case. We all have to do the most we can, be the best we can, she says. Is he passionate about something? She wants to know what makes his soul sing, what makes his heart beat faster, what makes him get up in the morning. He wants to say that she does that to him now, but he isn't ready to be that open just yet. He has never been ambitious, his parents didn't talk to him about dreams, just about exams. Geraldine says that she was lucky; even though her parents were middle-ranking civil servants they aspired to more; but once they had a mortgage and a child they felt trapped inside, not able to realise their potential, so they encouraged her to do that. Is she living out their dreams then? She hopes not, they gave her the drive to think for herself despite the normality of their suburban lives. You have to dream, you have to make those dreams come true, she is on a soapbox in the bed now, she is rolling out her life plan and no one will stop her.

They pause. Her rhetoric ends and it leaves them with thoughts turning on in their minds like the momentum of a vast machine after the power has been cut. They make love a second time in the early hours, an owl hoots to no one, a natural warning left over from living in the wild, now useless in the city. After that they sleep, their hands touching as the waves of tiredness lap across their bodies. She wakes first, somewhere between four and five in the morning, and makes tea and toast then brings it back to bed. They chatter like children allowed to stay up late for the first time.

They doze until dawn, until the sun breaks the grey cloud base over Berlin, but they don't get up, they listen to the passers-by, extracts of lives captured in the broken conversations shared along the gangway outside of the bedroom window. Then they try to guess what the next part of the conversations would have been after they go out of earshot. They have to stop as they can't speak for laughing.

He looks at her while she talks; he is falling in love, he thinks to himself.

*

CHAPTER TWENTY-ONE

The black Mercedes Benz S600 glides along the motorway through the Bryansk region of Russia which sits stoically alongside the Ukrainian border. Sebastian Ulrich opens his eyes after sleeping most of the way through the night on the six-hour journey from Moscow. He looks out of the window at the endless grey of the Russian countryside in the raw dawning of the day. Occasional scattered farms and villages polka-dot the barren landscape as the road cuts hard through the desolation. Before the highway was built, this whole region would have been an unforgiving place to journey through. Many travellers would have succumbed to the biting coldness that strikes out across the land for more months of the year than anyone cares to admit. The people here are hardy, brought up to survive rather than thrive, but they have a solid dependability that comes from a life of isolation, where most people you meet are hurrying through to somewhere else. Even though Ulrich grew up in Russia, this territory doesn't bring him any joy, he has no regrets about swapping the biting winds of his homeland for the summer breeze of the Cote d'Azur.

They approach a road junction that joins their road to the main drag from Oryol and Tula in the east to Kiev in an almost dead straight line westwards. The three-way road layout creates a triangle of land in the centre which houses a café and petrol station. The driver pulls the car off the road and onto the tarmac that surrounds the buildings. Parked up on the perimeter of the car park are two 44-tonne lorries painted in a dirty grey with blue lettering spelling out a fictional haulage company. The driver pulls up next to the wagons and Ulrich steps out. There is a drizzle in the air and he pulls his unbuttoned coat further around him. The front vehicle's cab door opens, a large man climbs down from the driving seat and makes his way over where Ulrich stands across the tarmac. He has a slight limp and rubs his hands together as he walks. When he arrives in front of Sebastian he reaches out a greasy hand and they shake. The second cab door opens and another man gets out, this time tall and thin but no less worn by a life of thundering along the roads of Europe.

The three man huddle together as the rain whips up in the wind and barrels across the adjacent fields, then hits the side of each truck with a whining drone. After they talk for five minutes, Ulrich turns and waves his arm in the direction of another 44-tonner parked up in one of the car park spaces fifty yards away. This new lorry starts its engine and drives toward the other vehicles then turns and backs in to the first two. The drivers break the seals on their juggernauts as four men emerge from the third vehicle. They swing open the back doors and the new driver inches the lorries closer until there is two feet between the back ends. The men drop a metal sheet across to form a bridge and begin to drag and push crates from the third lorry into the first two. Forty minutes later, in which time Ulrich retreats to the warmth of his Mercedes, the transfer is complete. Sebastian clambers out and inspects the work while the men stand in a semi-circle around him waiting for his imperial approval. He turns and gives the thumbs up. One man produces a bottle of vodka and they all swig from it. Ulrich tells the men they need to drive non-stop so will need two drivers in each vehicle. After some haggling amongst the gang, the men regroup themselves, then walk back to the vehicles and all climb on board. Ulrich waits in the rain while the engines roar into life and black clouds of exhaust belch off across the surrounding terrain. The third lorry heads back into the Russian heartland, and the other two growl back onto the road and turn left for the Ukrainian border with their mis-labelled agricultural machinery.

*

The Berlin Brandenburg Airport oozes efficiency from every pore. The buildings shine with newness and people mill about, antlike within the interior. Riverside and Catherine pass through customs and buy breakfast airside in one of the restaurants that overlooks the flat geometry of the runways and departure gates. She has known their destination to be Nice Cote D'Azur since Riverside handed her the tickets as they checked in thirty minutes ago. After they have talked and eaten, Catherine says she wants to look at the shops and leaves him watching the departure boards. She makes a call to a logistics company and confirms that she now has more information on the parcel they are holding for her and could they send it to an address she gives them in Nice on a 24 hour delivery. After that she buys perfume, for a reason she can't work out apart from that it is a learnt behaviour when in airports.

She doesn't feel she knows enough about her new partner on this operation yet, and when she returns to him she knows she needs to prise out more information about him that she couldn't get from her early morning search on Oberon.

"What happened with your girlfriend?" she says as she sits down opposite him.

"It ended, I told you."

"Why did you guys split?"

"Why do you want to know?" he says almost automatically, the way he has been trained.

"I want to know more about you, Rob. Now we're partners."

"Nothing much to tell, she met some guy."

"You knew him?" she says. His head turns rapidly towards her and she knows from that sign that she hit a bull's eye. She waits, watching his hands play out the truth behind the fabrication he is weaving. Riverside nods after a second as though he can't think of words to explain but still feels the need to respond to her.

"You trusted her before that, though?" she says, still watching his face.

"What about you? You got a boyfriend?"

"Why do you want to know?" She echoes his earlier response intentionally. There is a second when he thinks she is serious, then they both laugh.

"I know, spies ask too many questions," he says.

"I do have a boyfriend, but not for much longer."

"Bored of him?"

"Like you, I count loyalty as an attractive trait in partners."

"He slept around?"

She is momentarily shocked, she hasn't thought Rich might have slept with other people apart from the one she knows about. Now the idea has crossed her mind, she knows that it won't go away anytime soon.

"Do you think I'm loyal?" she says.

"No idea. Funny question."

The flight is called; they gather their things and start the long walk to the gate. Her mind flicks to the job in hand. She wants to plan but he is not giving anything away. Maybe he really doesn't know, she thinks, or maybe he knows exactly what he's going to do and what plan he has for her. What Catherine still doesn't know is why he feels he needs backup. It's not unheard of for field ops to call in C9 but this op is different, bringing in an off-grid agent who could be reluctant sounds like a policing job and C9 is a branch that provides brute force, a direct solution delivered to address a direct threat. C9 is not about cosy chats with agents. She needs more information from him urgently or this operation will fail badly.

*

Gabrielle sits in a café on the Rue Grimaldi, one of the streets that makes up Nice's boutique-ridden seafront district known as Le Carre D'Or. The air is light and still around the chic storefronts and customers walk in the roadways to see and be seen. She takes a sip of her Americano and holds her pen a few millimetres above the pad in front of her while she reads her jottings. She had forgotten how relaxing it is to write on real paper and it reminds her of her childhood. The page in front of her has a mass of scrawled words about Marjorie Allardice and what she had meant by, 'Ask in Berlin,' as a clue to where Gabby might find out more on the mole.

She opens a port to Oberon and looks through the list of people in the British Embassy in Berlin. On the clean side there are just names of administrators and clerks, on the dirty side there is the standard array of people with diplomatic sounding titles. She copies all the names and drops them into the Oberon search box, then adds a date range for documents or changes to data around Mac's death. The results gradually click out on the screen in front of her as the system churns through the data and discovers matches. The Belgian GISS operation comes up as a search result and she clicks through to the report. Some of it is beyond her security access level, but the parts that she can see give her more context on why they were there in the first place. The GISS had been called in by Marcus Murphy to provide security for

Klingerfeld, Mac's target. There was little background on why Murphy had done that and why the kill order had not been cancelled. It is perfectly possible to send a simple message with the correct authorisation at the last minute and stop it all, and that would have prevented his death. She reads on through the report, working backwards by date. The moment she reads one particular entry, she can feel her pulse increase. Murphy received a terminate order at 08:35hrs on the day of Mac's death. Mac would have been in the air at that time, plenty of time for cancelling. But Murphy didn't cancel, he called in an ops team from Brussels to attend the location. Murphy, as the senior officer in the Berlin area would have received the message first, but Gabby should have been notified too. All of the day she had spent with Mac had therefore been after the point where London and Murphy knew that the kill order should have been cancelled. Mac received no terminate instruction and no one had told Gabrielle that the need to brief Mac had evaporated. This points to Murphy as part of some sort of operation that was kept secret. Gabby scans the file for who in London had authorised the stop order but the data is blanked out as beyond her clearance level.

She decides to make two phone calls; the first is to Jonas Geelan in Brussels. Gabby walks to a phone box across the street from the café and shuts the hinged door on the outside world. She dials a secure line and types in the access code, then she is through to Brussels on the MI6 private network.

"Geelan," he says as he answers the call. "It's Gabrielle Lane."

"I can't help you anymore," he says immediately.

"Just a quick chat, Jonas. No funny business this time, just tell me something about GISS ops."

He is silent which she takes as agreement to proceed.

"A GISS ops unit was called in by MI6 Berlin on the morning that one of our snipers died. How unusual is that?"

"It's rare."

"Why would anyone do that? There are MI6 teams in Germany who could do the same thing," she says.

"Various reasons," says the Belgian. "No available resources your end for instance, or someone wanted to hide the operation from London."

"Why would it be hidden?" she asks. "The ops detail and the referral to Brussels would all be on the record in the British and the Belgian computer systems, wouldn't they?"

"Not if the call-in was made without authorisation. Only formally authorised requests for assistance are allowed on our system, but if it is an informal request or lacks an authorisation code then you can't create the record here."

"I get it," she says. "I've got some research going on this end, and that's very useful."

"On another topic," he says. "Have you destroyed that record you showed me?"

"Your London person?"

"Yup," he says.

"It was a lucky guess."

"What?"

"I had no information on you, Jonas."

"You showed me the records."

"Typed up that morning," she says. "Interesting that you do have a source in London though."

She hangs up before he can swear at her and calls Hans, this time on her MI6 mobile. They switch to encrypt as he steps outside onto the pavement in front of the Mett Bar to take the call, then makes his way across the road to the bank of the river as they chat. She explains what Jonas related to her and what she found on Oberon, then asks him if he can find more at the Embassy in Berlin; and in particular any unusual activity by Murphy. Hans says he knows Mel very well, who is Murphy's PA, and there may be an opportunity to find something from her that is not on Oberon.

"I need it in 24 hours, Hans."

"I know," he says. "I'm on it."

*

The Petrus Restaurant in Kinnerton Street sits five minutes away from Belgrave Square in London's Mayfair. Sir Bernard sits at a table for four, re-laid for two, and finishes a discussion with his old friend Jeffrey Langley about the likely decisions coming down the tracks from Ministers that will impact the Secret Intelligence Service. Langley is more upbeat that Sir Bernard and has been reassuring during their lunch about the period of time between now and the next election. Langley has to go to a meeting at No.10 and they call for their bill.

Ela has not been to a Michelin starred restaurant before and when Sir Bernard told her to meet him there at 2:30pm she was excited to see inside, although disappointed that she wouldn't be eating. She climbs the steps at Knightsbridge tube station and walks through the streets of London. She arrives too early and waits on the seats by the door as she can see Sir Bernard and his lunch companion are still talking. The other man is given his coat and he shoots Ela a sidelong glance as he passes her, on his way out to a waiting taxi. Ela takes his departure as her cue to join Sir Bernard and walks over to the table.

"Ms. Peretz," he says as he sees her approach. "Do sit. Coffee?"

She accepts.

"I wanted to see you face to face, Sir Bernard," she begins. "I have found something from the trawl of security service databases that you asked me to carry out." She pauses.

"Go on."

"I've found a reference to Petrov."

"Good. Where?"

"Here," she says placing two sheets of A4 paper in front of him. He pulls out a pair of reading glasses from the top pocket of his jacket and arranges them on his slightly bulbous nose. She flicks her eyes between the papers and his face as he reads, letting him take in the information. He reads, then stops, thinking before he utters a word.

"A Russian agent," he says quietly.

"In London," she adds.

He leans back against the purple seating and looks across the tables in the room, now emptying as lunchtime fades into afternoon.

"Who else has seen this?"

"Only you. I thought..., given the information..." She can't think how to complete the sentences.

"So, we have this list of the operations that link to the Petrov source from the European security services," he says thinking out loud. "I need all of these operations pulled out of the system and all of the people involved interviewed."

"That is dozens of people, sir."

"It is, Ms. Peretz. But it has to be done if we're going to find our leak."

*

CHAPTER TWENTY-TWO

Linny stands in the kitchen, cutting vegetables and thinking about her husband. Stephen has seemed unhappy in the last few weeks and it is starting to concern her. He has changed the things he does as a routine, and while she is not particularly driven by the importance of those daily cyclical actions for her own life, she knows that Stephen is.

She hears him coming down the stairs and step into the kitchen.

"I was thinking," he says. "Would you ever want to move abroad?"

The already present expectation of change in him that is orbiting in her mind lays the ground for her muted reaction to the question. She looks at him quizzically. "We've talked about this many times, darling. Would you, then?"

"Maybe."

She frowns and tips her head on one side to get a better view of his eyes to assess his emotion. "Where? I thought you loved it here."

"I do," he says. "But maybe a change of scenery would do us good. You know, I want to retire one day. We've got enough cash to go and explore the world a bit."

"Travel, sure. I don't want to live abroad though, and I don't want to stop my QC work, I haven't got a licence for any other jurisdiction."

He is quiet. She holds out her arm to him but he doesn't respond, and she steps around in front of him and holds both of his hands.

"What is it, Stephen?" Her grey eyes explore his face for some clue of what has prompted a sudden change in his views after all this time. She can see he wants to talk, she knows how people are in court when they are bursting to relate inner thoughts that have clattered around inside their brain without an escape route.

"It's..."

She stands with the person in front of her that she has spent more hours with on this planet than any other. Time hasn't really changed his face, she thinks, a bit more baggy but still the face she fell in love with. His spirit though is a different matter. "Anything I can do?" she says.

His eyes, that have been avoiding her gaze, finally look up to meet hers.

"I'm tired, Linny. Tired of it all." She squeezes his hands and her mouth forms the slightest of smiles.

"Do you want to leave your job?"

"I don't enjoy it like I used to."

"Then get out," she says. "My work pays enough to keep all of our bills paid. Do something different, or nothing. Do what makes you happy."

"Easier said than done, darling."

"You've been through all sorts of challenges and you are always an optimist. Why is it different now?" she says.

"I don't know," he begins. "The same things come around again, year after year. Another new criminal gang or another new threat to our peace. We track them, we infiltrate them and we kill them. The remnants of the movement disperse into different cities, gather more recruits, convince others about the righteousness of their cause and gradually form into some sort of organisation. Then we find out and it all goes in a big circle."

She leans into him and he brings his arms up around her. They stand together feeling the warmth of each other's body.

"I want to help," she says.

"I'm not sure you can."

"Try me. I love you," she says, she raises her head and looks at his face. "I won't judge you, I won't push you into something you don't want, I'll support whatever decision you make if it makes you happier."

"I am so lucky to have met you." His voice softens with the words as he remembers how he would have ended it all years ago if it wasn't for this woman.

"Let's sit down, it's in the oven now for half an hour," she says and they walk through to the sitting room and sit on the sofa that is positioned to give a view of the garden. The residue of the summer blooms sit across the shrubbery and roll on the September breeze as it pours down from the top of Highgate and down the valley towards the Thames.

They talk about irrelevancies as it feels more comfortable at first but both of them want to return to the more important conversation that they have started, and now stands in the house, like a third person in their kingdom of two.

"So, what else would you like to do with your life?" she says eventually getting them off vapid topics.

"Consultancy maybe."

"Consulting about what?"

"Security."

"That's a huge field," she says. "Personal security, governmental security, what?"

"Other country's security."

"What do you mean? Surely you can't advise other countries after being part of the SIS?"

"I don't know."

"I've never seen you so vague, Stephen." He closes his eyes and rest his head on the back of the sofa.

"Tell me about your case," he says

"I'm still being blocked by the Cabinet Office to be honest."

"What did they say?"

"Nothing, that's the point," she says with finality. "I could tell the chap was just playing with me. He was probably sent in to meet me and give the impression of action."

"Depends what you want from your witness," he says, turning and giving her a wry smile.

"To tell the truth, that's all."

"You never did tell me any details."

"Operations in Slovenia, 'contracted private supplemental security resources'," she says, quoting the legal documentation.

"Mercenaries?" he says bluntly.

"How much are they used?" she says.

"More than I'd like," says Stephen.

"We just need this source in MI6 to talk to us," she begins. "That source gave information to my client and can validate the evidence.

"Do you have a name?" asks Stephen.

"Petrov," she says. His body convulses instantaneously, his hand goes to his throat. He leans forward and his stomach wretches but no vomit comes. He is choking and coughing. She leans over him. "My darling!"

*

Gabrielle gets into the bath in her room and inspects the bruising to her fingers and stomach sustained during the battle to get out of the casino in Monte Carlo. Two cuts are irritating her, one on her left hand and another further up just beneath her elbow.

She rests her head on the end of the tub and closes her eyes, thinking through everything that has happened in the days since she went off grid. She is almost there as far as the mole is concerned. Most of the data that helps to prove the identity was uploaded by Hans, and she has one more piece of the jigsaw to find and send to Sir Bernard which she is hoping Hans will also be able to help her with.

She thinks about Murphy. Her relationship with him has always been strained. When he arrived as Head of Berlin Station in 6, he met everyone in German field operations. There is a tension between the individual country Heads of Station and all field agents, as not all security service operations are controlled locally. Gabby has most of her work allocated to her by London Centre, an arrangement that has always particularly irked Murphy. London is the control point where operations are pan-country, whereas Murphy calls the shots if an op is entirely within the Bundesrepublik Deutschland. Murphy is also responsible for day to day liaison with the FIS, Germany's MI6.

They met up in a dingy café in south Berlin on a wet Tuesday afternoon. He was wearing a grey mackintosh and had a black fedora pulled down over his small head to protect him from the rain. Her first thought as she saw him was that he imaged himself as a character from a Le Carre novel and was not to be taken seriously in real life. Some people join 6 because of the romance of spying but soon learn the reality of killing is more bloody and hell than the fiction portrays. Gabby was in full time deep cover at the time and couldn't tell Murphy any details of what she was doing. Her continual referral to London made the man gradually more and more frustrated and they parted on bad terms, Murphy pulling up his collar like Philip Marlow as he ventured back out into the drizzle.

If Murphy is the mole then it will be a surprise to her, but there is no explanation for him not cancelling Mac's kill order.

Her phone thrums out a vibration where it rests on the towel next to her; she opens her eyes and rolls to the side to read the message. It is encrypted and she pushes in the code then scans what it says. Riverside is inviting her to meet him tomorrow at the Observatory in Nice to talk. She knows the place; its isolation makes her feel uneasy but this may be a way to help her identify the mole if he has more information. The first set of data he gave her checked out, so at least he is trustworthy.

*

CHAPTER TWENTY-THREE

The sun scrapes out from the horizon and carves a low, intense light east of the E87 Highway that runs from Marinka in Bulgaria, down through the wooded flatlands of Burgas Province and crosses the border into Turkey high up on the barren mountains at Malko Tarnovo.

The two lorries and four drivers are waived through after dropping cash into the hands of the border guards. They navigate the occasionally narrow and stony lengths of road in the hills then drops down into the valleys of the Turkish plains and make good headway as the light builds for the day. They have planned to stop for twenty minutes in the village of Kirklareli as they have only eaten in their cabs in the twenty-four hours since Ulrich saw them off on their journey from Russia.

The tattered juggernauts pull off the highway onto a side road that leads to the village. The hiss of the brakes cracks through the silent street as they draw to a halt outside a shop with a large Pepsi billboard dwarfing its frontage. The men climb out, go into the café and sit at the only table in the place. They order sukuk and sit facing each other, all different heights and builds, but their clothes consistently the colour of the dusty road.

The oldest man, the large driver of the first wagon, says he hears something and stops their conversation mid-sentence. He stands and walks outside to the road, then squints into the distance but there is no one to be seen in either direction. As the other three men join him and start to tell him that it is nothing and that he is paranoid, a lorry growls around the final bend on the highway before the village. It accelerates down the hill then brakes and follows the route they took fifteen minutes ago. It approaches them along the side road, the lead driver gets more agitated and walks towards his cab; this time his fellow travellers follow suit. The new lorry is all black, from the tar coloured underbelly to its night-dark canopy and the inky windows that reveal nothing of the inside. The intruder slows then stops fifty yards away from the café but there is no movement, no one gets out, no lights come on, no sound radiates from the truck. The leading driver tells the other three men to get the guns from their cabs. They are surrounded by houses that sit either side of the highway, silent and still along the dead-straight road. The leading driver takes his handgun and slowly, step by step, walks from the safety of his own vehicle into the no man's land between him and the newcomer. His colleagues are silent, they watch each other, cycling their view between each man then back to the new truck. Six birds fly without a whisper over the scene in a triangle, heading south; in the distance crickets chatter at the grass-draped roadside. The men wait.

Suddenly the place erupts with the sound of the bolts being hammered back on the doors of the new lorry. From inside, the blows strike metal four times, then a cascade of noise as one back door swings open and a lone gunman with an Uzi, his face hidden with a balaclava, stands watching the men. For five seconds he stands stock still and a slight breeze drifts up from the south behind him and moves the open door by his side. Then the other backdoor slowly swings open and three more armed, masked men stand beside him. They burst out and jump down onto the road, then run towards the drivers who instinctively turn back and run behind their rigs. The first burst of automatic fire rips across the cab window of the leading vehicle, the main driver leans round his lorry and fires rapidly hitting one guy in the shoulder. The attackers fan out the length of the two lorries and skirt around to take up firing positions, all four of the drivers are firing, two are ex-Russian army and are good shots, the other two are useless, and both get hit within ten seconds. The first is sent flailing into the lorry side, his arm a red mass of shredded flesh; the second is hit in the face and falls to the ground, his body quivering as his life slides away into the soil. The two remaining drivers take up positions at the front of their cab, one hits his target and an attacker collapses, they injure a second in the leg, but their luck runs out and the remaining two attackers overwhelm them. The lead driver and his mate both fall onto the front of their vehicle from a sprawl of automatic bullets, their eyes momentarily staying alive after their hearts have stopped beating.

The two surviving attackers stand and celebrate their victory with short yelps and fist-bumps, then tear off their balaclavas to get some cool air on to their sweating skin. The more junior one grins at the bodies in front of him and turns to his companion, and Larry Robinson grins right back.

*

Caroline leaves the house in Highgate earlier than usual and drives to her chambers in Carey Street near to London's Royal Courts of Justice. On the journey, she cannot get the memories of the previous day from her mind. She is glad that she managed to convince her husband to stay at home in bed today as he is obviously going down with something. She makes a note to tell him to visit the doctor when she gets back later.

The building that houses the offices of Milson Laughton Hendry is deserted at this early hour apart from a cleaner rhythmically mopping the black and white tiles of the entrance hallway. The lift is an old-style wire cage that runs up through the centre of a square staircase which spirals round the clanking machine. She pulls back the concertina outer gate on the fourth floor with its accompanying metallic clatter and unlocks the main door to MLH.

She drops her coat and bag in her room and makes a cup of tea in the kitchen area at the back of the ten-foot square room that acts as the chambers' reception area. As she returns to her office, the telephone on her desk rings in a muted warble, she picks up the receiver still holding the steaming mug in her hand.

"Caroline Laughton."

"Clive Tenby from the Cabinet Office, Ms Laughton."

"Mr Tenby. Do you have news for me?"

"Not good, I'm afraid."

She remains silent, knowing what is coming but not wanting to give away her disappointment.

"We have talked to our colleagues in the Secret Intelligence Service and there is no one called Petrov who works there," he says. "Sorry to be the bearer of bad news." He is smooth but she can detect in his voice the fact that he knows that she knows he is lying.

"Can I say?" she begins.

He manages to get in an "Of course" before she completes her sentence, but she ignores it.

"I am minded to request a judicial review on the matter," she says.

It is Tenby's turn to be silent as his brain works through the consequences of what she has said. Also, the silence tells her that Tenby had not prepared for every eventuality of the phone call; he must have assumed, she thinks, that she would just accept his stonewalling.

"I'm not sure that would be a good course," he says eventually.

"Thank you for your opinion, Mr Tenby, but that's not directly relevant in this case." She rolls on, "The decision for judicial review is by way of an application by the claimant or their representative to a judge."

"I'm aware of the process, Ms Laughton."

"Do you wish to reconsider your response to my initial enquiry?" she says.

"Under the Intelligence Services Act 1994...," Tenby begins.

"I'm aware of the legislation, Mr Tenby. There's nothing in that Act that states the SIS can retain information that pertains to a criminal case."

"It is not common practice to go into details of..."

She interrupts him again. "Mr Tenby. I'm not sure you hold the authority needed to make the sort of decisions you're implying to me. Shall we leave it at that? I will talk to my client and follow his direction on an application for judicial review whether it's common practice or not."

More silence at the other end of the line tells Linny she has won this little battle, but she is unsure if it has helped the war.

"Have a lovely day, Mr Tenby." She rings off and redials to talk to her client David McAllister.

*

The Ursprung Cafe sits on the lower levels of the vast cathedral-like Dussmann das KulturKaufhaus book shop on Friedrichstrasse, ten minutes from the bluff yellow brutalism of the British Embassy in Berlin. Vegetation climbs up the walls between steel girders and vibrant lighting picks out the architectural features of the space. Hans descends the escalator to the café floor and sees Mel already sat at one of the tables, her loose dark hair just touching the shoulders of her gabardine jacket. She makes a small wave when she sees him and stands to hug. They order coffees and cake and she explains she can afford a bit of time as Marcus is on a trip to London for a couple of days.

They talk about their work and how it is so good to be able to chat to someone who knows the business, so they don't have to keep tracking whether the facts in any of their stories nudge up against the limitations of the Official Secrets Act. Mel likes him, he can tell from her behaviour. She touches the back of his hand more than once as she talks but he doesn't do the same to her. They are both single, Mel had a long-term boyfriend in her last posting in Paris, but it hadn't worked out. He was married, she says to Hans and watches his face for any judgement, but none comes. Mel already knows that Hans's girlfriend died five years ago in a car accident when he had been driving. She is one of the few people who knows about that. He told her during a cosy late-night drink a year ago when the Christmas office party had gone on to a downstairs bar somewhere near the Brandenburg Gate.

"You should get a girlfriend," she says, smiling at him.

"I dunno."

"You need looking after." Another hand touch.

"If I decide to do that, you'll be the first to know," he says. They acknowledge the flirtiness of the comment.

"Looking forward to it."

"I wanted to ask you...," he begins. For a second, she thinks he is going to ask her out. "How's work?" She rolls her lips inwards together to manage the emotional bounce and sips her coffee.

"Mmm, ok," she says.

"You like Murphy?"

"Bit of a twat." Hans laughs, trying to recover the intimacy of the last minute.

"Will you come to dinner with me," he says suddenly.

She widens her eyes. "Lovely."

"Next week?"

"Sure."

"Why is he a twat anyway?" Hans says just on the limit of too quickly.

"He's secretive," she says. "For no reason, out of the blue. I know all the details of the operations, I see it all, even half of his eyes-only stuff, then suddenly he just clams up."

"Weird. What sort of things?"

"No pattern really."

"When was the last time?"

"That Stranraer op. He went all secret squirrel on me."

"Yeah that was a tragedy," says Hans. "My mate is Brussels told me that they had a team on site that day, he didn't know why."

"Mad, I saw the call-in chitty," she says referring to the R2 Form to requisition foreign resources into MI6 live operations.

"You put it on an R2?"

"Yup. Why?"

"My mate said it was informal," says Hans, keeping his tone and eyes soft so as not to stop her talking.

"I logged the R2 myself," she says. "Why the interest?"

He shakes his head. "He just said it seemed odd, happened with no warning. They normally get at least 24 hours' notice on R2s.

"Marcus behaved weirdly all that day, and for a couple of days afterwards too," she says. "He had two Crows sessions and he was very jumpy before them, but he wouldn't tell me anything." Her disappointment at not being Murphy's confidant is palpable.

"What do you think happened?" says Hans.

"He did something, I think," says Mel, squinting slightly as she scours her mind for the memories.

"Did something untoward?"

She stops and pulls back her lips and drops her eyebrows so that she looks grumpy. She looks up at Hans. "He can't have done, can he?" she whispers.

*

Stephen wakes at 10am. He didn't sleep until four but then fell into a hard unconsciousness and he now feels as though his body has been in one position for the whole night. He showers and has a cooked breakfast, during which time he realises that he hasn't had a day off work for at least six years, apart from the organised holidays abroad that they take. Linny sorts out the details of those vacations, he just turns up.

He decides to walk on the Heath as he is feeling better following the shock of the previous evening. After the panic at the sound of that word on her lips, he had become more rational in the sleepless hours lying next to her before he dozed off. He put a plan together during the night which is simply to deny it all if anything ever comes out.

He turns right out of their front door and down the road than leads directly to the grassland, then he heads for the Parliament Hill viewing point. He and Linny have stood on this spot many times over the years and it never ceases to be breath-taking. He falls into the routine of training his eyes on the farthest horizon he can see and instinctively looks for differences across the city. Like a grandparent noticing that you've grown because they only see you occasionally, he notices the new skyscrapers that have appeared in the City of London and tries to guess which street the cranes are on.

He turns away from the view and walks northwards, then descends into the valley that runs across the park and skirts round towards Hampstead before doubling back to take a wide arc up and over the top half of the Heath. As he starts to make his way home, he drops on to the path that leads down the eastern side of the parkland.

He rounds the final corner before the gate that leads to his road. He can see something lying prone across the track. He walks nearer, step by step, and it seems to be a big dog. The animal must have had some sort of accident. It is not moving and Stephen quickens his pace in case he can save the dog, he doesn't like to see a pet suffering so he may have turned up just in time. He reaches the creature and stops, but as he does so, he can see that it isn't a dog, it's a man, lying face down. Laughton bends down to the bundle of clothes and feels for a neck pulse but finds none, then pulls the man's jacket and rolls him over.

His heart pounds out a rhythm in his throat. Staring back at Stephen is the bloodied and nearly unrecognisable face of Ivan.

*

CHAPTER TWENTY-FOUR

The hotel that Riverside booked for himself and Catherine is a small guesthouse in the hills above the town. Away from the hustle of the glittering lights, the countryside around Nice quickly reverts to greater normality compared to the implausible glamour of the Cote D'Azur's tanned men and micro-thin women.

At breakfast, they talk about the details of the plan for the capture operation they will deliver today. Even sitting down, her height puts her eyelevel slightly above his. Riverside insists that Catherine needs to leave her mobile phone in the hotel, and places a burner phone on the table between them for her use during the op. She knows that removing known mobile devices from an op zone is common practice to avoid any GPS hacking of agent positions by the enemy. What this tells Kate very clearly is that Riverside is definitely not expecting Blackhawk to come quietly or the precaution wouldn't be necessary. Riverside explains that he will meet Blackhawk on his own, and that Catherine will be up in the hills behind them as a security precaution. She will not engage unless he gives her a specific order to do so.

Catherine is still uneasy about the operation, and Riverside repeatedly avoids answering her questions asking for more details about what Blackhawk has done. It is clear in her mind that he is expecting her to just do as she is told, whereas her military training tells her that C9 is most effective when they are given some lateral decision-making powers once you get into a live operation. While technically he is her senior on this mission, they are as near equivalent in rank as is possible. C9 ranks are distinct from the main MI6 officer ranks and that gives them a degree of autonomy which is critical as they hold the power to stop an enemy soldier in their tracks. Intelligence Officers, like Riverside have broader and less specialised training to cope with a broad range of situations, but if you want a death machine, C9 are honed to be the best there is.

The two of them finish their meal and Riverside starts to make moves to go, but Kate cannot start the mission without further details.

"Rob," she says, putting her hand on his arm to stop him leaving. "You need to confirm something to me before we do this." He sits back down.

"OK."

"What is the range of our authorised outcomes here?" She searches his face for his honesty. He looks uncomfortable then takes a large sigh.

"We have authority to shoot to kill," he says coldly.

"Shoot to kill?!" she starts to say at normal sound level, then drops her voice as she remembers the breakfast lounge has an echo that can carry around the room. "That's madness. Who is this woman?"

"She could be dangerous."

"We're all dangerous, Rob. But why is she a danger to *us*? Aren't we all on the same side?"

"Look, I wasn't going to tell you." Catherine's eyes widen and she urges him to go on with a head movement. "London suspects she is working for a foreign agency."

"Why weren't you going to tell me?"

"Not necessary."

"Bollocks it isn't. I'm not some mercenary who you can order about, Rob, for God's sake. C9 is a deadly capability that is deployed in a theatre to enact certain objectives. Going into an op without proper briefing is not how it is done." She stops and glares at him. "And don't give me that 'just following orders' bullshit."

Riverside gets out his phone, selects a screen and places it on the table in front of Catherine. "There, authorisation," he says. She can see an encrypted text from Laughton with the shoot to kill authority.

"Alright," she says. "But I reserve the right to use that authority at my discretion. If I consider it appropriate to only injure then I will do that. This is a member of our own security service, I'm not going to kill unless we are in danger." He nods his agreement.

They sit in silence for a minute and she drinks her coffee. "I'll see you in an hour out the front," he says, and walks out of the breakfast room.

The receptionist calls to Kate as she passes the desk and tells her that a parcel has arrived for her. She waits by the desk as the woman goes behind the scenes and fetches the package. Back in her room, Kate opens the box, inside is an L115A3 long range sniper rifle which she disassembles, checks and reassembles before loading it back into the box ready for the journey. She switches on the burner phone and leaves her own mobile by the bedside to charge.

She packs up her things and sorts her camouflage clothing. As she opens the door to leave, her phone hums on the bedside table as it receives a text and she walks over to it. The message is from Bradley Stewart in the Zurich Consulate and reads, 'Hey Kate, found your DNA sample identity, it's Blackhawk in field ops. Not sure if that helps. Bx.'

She stands looking at the words, not quite believing what she sees.

Riverside and Catherine drive out from the hotel at 10:30am for the half hour journey. He drops her by the Observatory building as it is sited above the location where he plans to talk to Blackhawk. She walks into the trees that create a canopy to hide her from sight and makes her way half way down the slope between the top of the high ground and the low, grey buildings of the Centre International de l'Observatoire which lay on the lower road.

*

Gabrielle parks the Z4 on a side road at the base of the hill that provides the Observatory with the height it needs to supress light from the town at night and give a clear view of the planets and stars. She is in black leggings and top, her Smith & Wesson strapped to her back and a pair of MI6 high powered binoculars around her neck. She dives off into the undergrowth and takes a curving track through the trees. From her scouting reconnaissance yesterday, she knows there is a single winding road that twists up the side of the hill, and various buildings and houses scattered across the upland area around the Observatory. Riverside gave her a grid reference for the meeting which is in front of the administrative buildings that nestle among the trees on the east side of the rising ground.

Gabby runs through the forest, continually watching all directions and slowly makes her way uphill. She reaches the building that houses the telescope itself and scouts around it, but there is no one around. She stops and takes in the view of Nice and the curve of the coastline as it rolls on to the airport in the distance. She runs to the east side of the hill and steps more carefully as she gets nearer to the rendezvous point. She is on the verge of dropping down to the roadway when a single reflection catches her eye. She collapses on to her haunches and scans the area where she saw the flash with her binoculars. At first she sees nothing except undergrowth, the trees and shrubbery on the forest floor melding together into a mass of greenery. Then she sees it, a tiny movement that is out of context. She steps to one side to change her perspective and more in revealed. A woman is lying on the ground wearing camouflage clothing, wisps of blonde hair protrude from a green beanie; and in her hands the standard long-range sniper rifle of the British security services. Gabrielle watches for five minutes and confirms that the woman is bedded in, and fixes her position on the map on her phone.

Dropping down the slope, Gabrielle walks to the edge of the treeline and can see the meeting point ahead on the corner of the road. A long, low building sits at an angle to the road; in front of the entrance, a small car park with no vehicles in it. She can see Riverside standing to one side, looking over the fence at the trees that stretch below and eastwards, outlining scattered tributaries that here feed north into the River Paillon before it turns south and swirls in to the Mediterranean half way along the Plage du Centenaire in the centre of the town.

From Gabby's view, the sniper gives perfect cover for Riverside, assuming they are in this together. Part of her is disappointed as she felt he was an ally, but the view she now has tells her that he is not going to help her get more information on the mole. She can't break cover in this position, so runs across the roadway then down into the lower trees, round behind Riverside and the grey buildings, then up behind his position. There is a second building to his right with a covered entrance that blocks the sniper's view. Gabby jumps the fence and stands in the entranceway.

"Riverside," she calls across the thirty feet between them. He turns.

"Blackhawk, thank you for coming."

"You wanted to talk." They both remain in their positions.

"I was wondering if you had found I gave you to be useful."

"Yes, thank you."

"I have some more I'd like to share with you." He holds up a hard drive.

"What's on it?" Her voice carries on a midday breeze that blows up from the valley and rustles the trees that surround them.

"I'd like you show you, I've got a laptop here, we can go through it."

"Bring it over," she calls. He hesitates, then take a step towards her.

"My computer's in the car as I'm charging it because the battery's shot; but here, come and have a look." He walks back to his vehicle and pulls open one of the rear doors, then puts an arm into the car and produces a laptop from inside. An umbilical lead connects the machine to a socket somewhere in the car. He opens the laptop, places it on the roof of his rental and starts to click on the touchpad.

Gabby is unsure of her best next move. Patently Riverside now needs to be treated as an enemy combatant by her. She doesn't know if he is the mole, or briefed by the mole to capture her, or is part of Ulrich's distributed gang of well-connected people; but she does know that she needs to stop him doing whatever he plans to do.

The day is warm, and the sun beats down on the thirty feet of dirt surface that runs from Gabby's protected location to Riverside's car. She assesses the risk, knowing the sniper is in the woods above their heads. On balance, she calculates, they will want to talk first, so she puts one foot out onto the ground in front of her, revealing her position. No shot comes, and she walks quickly to Riverside, making sure to stand so that he blocks the sniper's shot. He clicks through screens with a narrative of showing her the definitive evidence.

"And here is the proof," he says as he clicks on a final page. The page is blank.

"What's this?" she starts to say, as the muzzle of his handgun raises to her body. They remain stock still, a butterfly skims the car roof and circles their heads, then flies off from where it came.

"Hands where I can see them, Blackhawk." He reaches around her shoulder, removes the Smith & Wesson from her back, and places it on the car roof. Keeping his gun trained on her, he pulls out a zip-tie from his pocket and ratchets it around one of her wrists. He repeats it with a second tie, then pulls out a third tie and starts to lock all of the ties together.

In less than one second, Gabby brings one foot up and round to the back of his knee, it collapses his leg and he falls against the car door. She uses the advantage of surprise to pull his body round and down on to the ground. He pushes up on one leg and lunges for her, grabbing her ankle and bringing her crashes to the floor. Her head hits the dirt with a dull thud and blood immediately surfaces along one eyebrow. She spins and kicks out, hitting him in the face, then she sits up and takes a swing with her fist, landing a punch on his jaw. Riverside's head crashes back on to the ground, giving her time to stand, but he regains his balance more quickly than she imagined, and he gets up and runs at her. Their arms lock, he is stronger than her in the upper body but she is more agile, she punches him in the kidney, and again, until the pain shows on his face. She thrusts in to him with her body weight on a final assault, he falls back and cracks his head on the side of his own car. He pushes him into the open door and rams the door onto his body bringing a cracking sound from his thigh. She re-opens the door, aware that she is angry now, and punches him again. He falls unconscious, half in and half out of the back door.

It is then that the first sniper shot rings out on the hillside. It brings up a shaft of dust on the ground inches from Gabby's right foot. She grabs her handgun and runs for cover, knowing that the sniper will have a bolt-action reload time of between two and three seconds if the woman is a professional. Gabby makes it into the trees at the base of the slope before any more shots are unleashed. Snipers are hampered in warfare if they try and change their position, their strength is in being highly accurate over long shot distances, but they are hopeless on the move. Gabrielle adopts the stealth walking technique taught to her by the Special Boat Service on a weekend training exercise of short bursts of movement, followed by stopping and re-assessing your target. She moves swiftly up through the hill, edging closer to the sniper's position until she gets a clear view of the location where the sniper was bedded in. The bracken is squashed flat but there is no gunwoman to be seen. Gabby crouches low, scanning the undergrowth, the sniper and her rifle cannot be far away. She listens, upper branches sway in the light breeze otherwise the place is deathly quiet, the external sounds dampened by the greenery.

She hears a single twig break fifty yards ahead of her, and runs at pace along a path towards the sound. The sniper breaks cover from her hiding place, turns with her rifle and fires a round towards Gabby then runs off up the path. The bullet skims passed her ear so close that she can feel the air pressure dip then rise as the metal flies by. Gabby has three seconds before the woman is re-armed, she raises her handgun and takes a single shot, but misses, she kneels and steadies her hand, takes a leg shot and the woman falls to the ground. Gabrielle runs to the sniper, picks up the rifle and throws it into the bushes.

"Who are you?" Gabby shouts at the woman, holding her gun to her neck.

"Coniston," says Catherine. "C9 Branch."

"You could have fucking killed me!" says Gabby.

"We were told to bring you in."

"You and Riverside?" Catherine nods. "What the hell for?"

"They think you're the mole."

Gabby laughs and removes the gun from Catherine's neck, then sits down onto the ground, leaning against a tree. Kate sits up and inspects her leg wound.

"You'll live. I shot to skim the flesh."

"Why do they think you're the mole?" says Catherine.

"It's a well-tried internal propaganda technique for double agents," says Gabby. "If you think you're going to be discovered, you send out messages all over the organisation accusing other innocent people of being the leak, then there are so many false flags that the real flag is lost in a sea of counter-accusations. It's clever. Simple and very effective, it plays on human paranoia."

"This bloody stings," says Catherine, pulling at her leggings around the cochineal stain.

"Sorry about that," says Gabby with smile. "Come on, let me help you. My car is down the hill, I'll take you my hotel."

"What about Rob?" says Catherine.

"Who?"

"Riverside."

"Oh, that's his name, you guys know each other then?"

"Not really."

Gabrielle helps Catherine stand, and they slowly make their way down to the Z4. Gabby drives round to where she left Riverside, but he is gone. They turn back and head for Nice.

*

CHAPTER TWENTY-FIVE

The light of the September sun is still strong at 5pm. Sir Bernard sits on one of his sofas in his office, reading the daily reports from the European MI6 field stations. A quiet knock on the door is followed by Lawrence, bustling in with two brown folders.

"Barnet and Red Shark Reports, sir," he says across the office. Sir Bernard grunts acknowledgment which could be construed as rude, but the two of them know each other's foibles, and the noise is exactly what Lawrence had expected. The assistant continues to tidy the desk in silence, butlerlike in his lack of presence. Sir Bernard doesn't notice the man leave but five minutes later he does notice another knock on the door and Lawrence's reappearance. "Sir Stephen, sir."

"Thank you, Lawrence."

Laughton, who was immediately the other side of the mahogany, walks in and crosses the red carpet over to his superior. His normally cheerful eyes have a dullness, the skin on his cheeks dropping down hard to his jawline, his shoulders too are less upright than they have been.

"Have a seat, Stephen. I wanted to talk to you."

Laughton sits on the sofa opposite, Sir Bernard is reading the papers in front of him as he speaks.

"What is the latest on our Hillbank op?"

Laughton takes a second to form the words he needs, long enough for Sir Bernard to look up and make an unspoken enquiry of the other man's face.

"You alright, Stephen?"

"Yes, sir, thank you."

"You're looking peaky."

"Did you hear about the body I found?"

"Didn't. Tell me," says Sir Bernard employing collapsed sentences, the tell-tale signs of his superiority in this situation.

"I was unwell this morning and was at home."

"What was the matter with you?"

Laughton's years of fabricating information to cover his traitorous activities allow him to invent on the spot, with ease. "Dizziness, headache and very tired. Maybe something I ate." Sir Bernard is silent, but watching like a hawk. "I went for a walk at lunchtime on the Heath and found a dead man."

"Do we know him?" says Sir Bernard.

"No."

"Where was this?"

"On the Heath, as I said."

"Near your home?"

"Yes, not far."

"And you don't him?"

"Never seen him," says Laughton, feeling as though he is in the headmaster's study at school.

"Seen the police?"

"Yes, of course I called them immediately. Gave them a statement, but all I did was discover him, I didn't see anyone else near."

Sir Bernard watches a man he knows keeping something unsaid, but does not mention it. Then, after a few seconds, returns to the original subject. "Hillbank?" he asks.

"The contact is today."

"We'll have documents?"

"Not today, tomorrow I think," mumbles Laughton.

"We need to make sure that op is a success, Stephen. There's a great deal riding on it."

"I'm across it, sir."

After a few more minutes of uncomfortable grilling, Laughton drags his tired body up from the seat and retreats to the relative safety of the corridor outside. He walks back to his own office, biting the side of a fingernail on his right hand, his brain won't jump off the merry-go-round of worry which is spinning faster and faster inside his head. He rubs his temples trying to relieve some of the dull ache that has sat there for the last twenty-four hours. In his distraction, he turns the handle of Martine's office and walks in, closes the door and collapse back on it with his eyes closed.

"Sir Stephen!" She stands and rushes to his side. Laughton, surprised that she is there as he thought it was his own office he was going into, pulls back from her with a look of shock and anger. Martine lets out a tiny inhaling noise as she watches his recoil.

"Sorry, Martine."

"You should have stayed at home, you're not well." He closes his eyes again and smiles to anyone who is watching. "Come and sit down." She guides him to the chairs used for waiting guests that are lined up on one wall of her office. They sit down together and, after a second of indecision, she lays her warm hands on his, which are clasped together and white around the knuckles.

"Go home." The words glide out smoothly. He takes a deep breath.

"I'm not sure I can do this anymore," he says so quietly that she leans in to hear the enunciation.

"You're not well," she repeats.

"I've been stupid." Her face frowns, trying to work out his meaning. "I probably knew it couldn't go on for ever."

"Do you want to retire?" she says. "Is that it?"

"I want to end it." Which she takes to be an agreement to what she said.

"I'll call a cab," she says getting up and walking around to other side of her desk.

"Don't think badly of me, Martine, no matter what you hear." She doesn't hear him as she is talking to the man on reception about a taxi.

"What did you say?"

"I didn't think they'd kill him," says Laughton, now lost in his depression.

"Who?" she says and returns to her comforting position by his side. She dips her head to see his downturned face more clearly, her blonde bob drops across her shoulder; but Laughton doesn't answer. Martine helps him stand five minutes later when the call comes from downstairs to say a car is waiting. She leads him to the lifts, stands beside him on the descent, and watches like a mother as the tail lights of the taxi turn out in to the traffic on the Albert Embankment.

*

Stuart rubs his hands in front of the electric fire in the sitting room of the flat. The side windows that look out over the concrete buildings are misted over, proving outside is colder than inside. Geraldine walks through from the kitchen and hands him a glass of wine. Hers is red and his is white. He smiles at her and she replies in kind, her body leans into his and his arm unconsciously curves around her waist, she moves her head to his shoulder and they both stare in silence at the heating bars in front of them.

Their doorbell is a loud shark bite of sound that snaps through the air and crashes their intimacy. They pull away from the embrace and look at each other's eyes. She turns and walks to the door. As it opens, the wind tickles a dream catcher in the hallway which stopped making any sound some time ago due to its age. Standing on the doorstep is a young, blond man, no more than twenty years old. His features are sharp and striking so that you would remember him from a passing glance on a busy train. His hair is short, his eyes a cold penetrating grey; his palette would cause you to turn up the colour on your TV if you saw him on it for fear of poor adjustment.

"I'm looking for Palmer," he says in German.

"I'm Palmer," says Stuart in English from the shadows behind Geraldine. "Come in, Alexander."

They walk in single file to the lounge. "Wine?" says Geraldine. The boy shakes his head.

"I wanted to see you first," says Alexander in accented English, he waits to choose his words. "I wanted to be sure about the deal."

"You'll get any charges dropped," says Geraldine. "As long as you co-operate."

"The information is my co-operating," says the German.

"Yes, but afterwards too, once the gang has been arrested," she says. Stuart is constantly surprised by her bravado these days.

"What information do you have?" asks Stuart.

"Names," says Alexander.

"Gang members?"

He nods. "And further up the tree, details of how they operate."

"That's good," says Geraldine, smiling at him. "When can you get it to us?"

"I can bring it, this time tomorrow," says the boy.

"Why are you doing this?" says Stuart. Geraldine gives him a stark look.

"They killed my brother."

"Who?"

"The gang."

"How do you know?"

"I just know. Shot in his own bed with his girlfriend there."

"Did she see it?" asks Geraldine.

"I don't know, I haven't spoken to her since."

"What was her name?" asks Geraldine.

"Why?" says the boy.

"Just interested."

"Charlotte."

"And she witnessed the killing?"

"I think so." The flow of the discussion dies away as Alexander's nerves climb like larks at dawn, black against a rising sun.

"No matter," she says quietly.

"I need to go," he says. They see him out and he disappears into the dying daylight.

*

Catherine sleeps on the covers of Gabby's bed in the hotel for four hours with her leg on cushions after they return to the Palais de la Méditerranée. By the time she wakes, it is the early evening and she readily accepts Gabby's suggestion to go and eat in the restaurant downstairs. She showers and borrows a dress from the spy which fits but is shorter on her taller frame. They take a table in the sun, they are both wearing black but their hair colour is in contrast to the other. Catherine is restless, Gabby notices, and puts it down to the injury she sustained at the Observatory. They order Prosecco and tiny points of light dance in the glasses and reflect up into their faces.

"You like your job?" says Catherine.

"Sure. Used to it now."

"You didn't like it a first?"

"Just experience I guess. I think I'm better at it now than straight out of training. What about your job?"

"I like the isolation of C9."

"Not a party person?" says Gabby.

"I just like doing my own thing, you know."

"It must be difficult to keep friendships going for you," says Gabby. "C9 gets allocated all over the place doesn't it?"

"I'm based in Zurich, usually the jobs are there. This one's left field."

"Did Rob ask for you then?" Catherine nods. "You two together?"

"No. I've got a boyfriend."

"Zurich's nice."

"He's not in Zurich; London," says Catherine. Her fingers drop to her skirt and she feels the outline of the knife strapped to her thigh.

"How much do you guys get moved around?" says Gabrielle.

"Every couple of years," says Catherine. "They like to change the allocated region."

"Wish they would move me, I've been in Berlin too long."

"Ever get back to London?" says Kate.

"Not often enough."

"You do get back there sometimes though?"

"About three or four times a year."

"Been recently?"

Gabby stops for a moment. "Mmm, yup. Couple of weeks ago."

"Do anything nice?" says Catherine.

"It was just after all this mole shit started. I went off grid and just looked up a few friends." The waitress arrives with their starters and pours them more Prosecco.

"Must be good to catch up like that." Gabby narrows her eyes but says nothing. They eat for a minute without conversation.

"Got a bloke?" says Catherine.

"Nope."

"A few fuck buddies?"

"What?" Gabby stops her fork half way between plate and mouth.

"You know, no strings, bit of a laugh" Catherine's voice gains an edge of anger, slight but identifiable.

Gabby takes a deep breath. "Not really," she mutters.

"You're pretty though," continues Catherine. "Men must be falling over themselves."

"What are you getting at?"

"You know Richard Langley?"

Gabby frowns. "Sure, how do you..."

"He's my boyfriend, Gabrielle."

"Shit."

She is used to situations changing quickly as part of her everyday job, but even Gabby is taken aback by the speed that

Catherine manages to remove the blade from the strapping on her thigh and slit a fine cut in Gabby's skin just above her left knee. Gabrielle pushes the whole table, complete with food, glasses, cutlery and candle across the gap between them and into Catherine's chest. The sniper is caught off-guard and starts to fall back on her chair, and shoves a leg out to the approaching ground to stop her drop. Gabby is on her feet now and lunges for the knife, Catherine pulls it away above their heads. The two couples at the adjacent tables all get up at the same time and move away from the fighting women. The blade comes down in a swerving arc, pivoting around Catherine's shoulder, but it misses the mark and hits Gabby's arm side on. Gabrielle grabs for it and gets a firm grip on the handle; Gabby is the stronger of the two and the knife crashes out of their grasp and clatters away on the floor tiles. Gabrielle twists Catherine's arm round and the women lose balance. They both crash to the floor, Gabby on top straddling her opponent.

"Stop," says Gabby with wide open eyes, dipping her head close to Catherine's and holding both of her hands to the floor. "This is stupid." Catherine strains under the hold for a second, then realises the imbalance between their fighting ability is too great and relaxes. Gabby looks up and three waiters and the maître d'hôtel are standing around them not knowing what do to.

"It's fine," Gabby says to them all. "My sister just got a little upset." She gets up off Catherine and helps her up, then they go out of the restaurant with a promise to pay for any damage and retreat to an outside bar area. Catherine is moody but not violent and walks up and down for five minutes before sitting down opposite Gabrielle.

"Look, I'm sorry. Rich didn't say he had a girlfriend," says Gabby.

Catherine's eyes are half full of anger and half full of regret. She grunts assent to the words from the other woman, they order drinks and then sit in silence for ten minutes. Gabrielle watches the white yachts glide across the silver and gold water of the Cote D'Azur, gashes of light splaying out across the shimmering seascape. She thinks about the one night with Rich and how it hadn't meant anything, it was just sex, as Catherine had said. Gabby wondered if that is the only kind of relationship that works for someone doing her job. She's not envious of spies who are happily married, and mostly she never thinks about relationships; too many ties, too many consequences. But even one night with a man has caused her consequences, and it's not a part of her life that she ever seems to get better at handling.

Catherine clears her throat and Gabby turns. "Let's forget it," says Kate. "He wasn't worth it."

*

The red, yellow and green lanterns in the bar sway in a gentle breeze that comes off the sea. Larry is wearing a blue jacket and jeans, brown loafers with no socks, and his Rolex. He is on his third beer, which is quicker than he would normally have downed alcohol, but he can feel a slight knot in his stomach. His large hands hold the glass captive and his forefinger taps out a Morse message which unbeknownst to him is spelling SOS. He can feel his heart beating a little too quickly underneath the linen on his chest, even its usual cocaine enhanced rhythm is higher tonight. He knows why, exactly why, he is feeling hyper. The text from Sasha had been short and to the point. "Meet me tonight in San Andreas on the waterfront. I want to get to know you better. Don't tell Seb." His heart had started its incessant drumming from that point. He was driven to Varna in Bulgaria after the hi-jack and caught a flight back to Nice, with a three-hour layover in Vienna, during which time the message from Sasha had pinged into his mobile.

He knows when Sasha enters the bar without seeing the moment directly himself as she brings a ripple of energy that sweeps through the patrons. Her large eyes and long dark hair grab their attention and wrestle it to the ground, leaving all comers in her wake. She is wearing a short, green dress, Chanel Butterfly sunglasses and white designer trainers. The teenage boy inside Larry, despite all the women he has been with, cannot quite believe she is walking towards him.

Sasha sinks gazelle-like into the deeply padded seat next to him and shares a sweet, almost innocent smile.

"Drink?" he says.

"I'll order," she purrs from behind her sunglasses, and raises a long, slim arm. The waiter is beside them almost instantly. "Black Russian, please."

"Sir?" The waiter turns, with his eyes only, to Larry.

"Me too, same," he says, and the waiter returns to the bar.

"Lovely to see you, Larry."

"And you, Sash. How are you?"

"Good, you know. Got these Jimmy Choo's today." She elongates one of her legs and pulls up her short skirt to show even more thigh. "You like 'em?"

"Yup." No other words are in his head at that second.

"What have you been up to, then?" she says, moving her bottom towards him on the seat.

"Oh, you know, business."

"Tell me, it's exciting."

"Got some molly coming in tomorrow by road, I was sorting that out today. You want some when it arrives? On the house?"

She nods enthusiastically. "Do I have to do anything to get it?" She takes off her sunglasses and the glitter on her eyelids catches the lights. Her wide mouth soothes into a broad smile, showing her perfect teeth.

"Well, I don't know," he says. "I'm sure we can think of something." They laugh. The waiter brings their drinks and they flirt all the way down from first sip to last drop.

Larry can feel his need for cocaine, and tells her to order more drinks while he goes to the bathroom. When he returns, new drinks are already there on the table, and Sasha is looking at her phone, but puts it away as he approaches.

"Cheers!" she says. They raise their glasses and both drink, she puts her hand on his leg and he can't help laughing.

"What about Ulrich?" he says, the words getting slightly stuck in his throat.

"He's not here, darling," she says, and moves her hand up to his face, smoothing the skin on his cheek.

"Why the sudden change of heart?" he says, coughing.

"I like a bit of variety. I always thought you looked interesting." He feels hot and pulls at his shirt collar. "I thought one day, I'd like to get to know you, before it's too late."

"Aren't I the lucky boy?" He coughs twice, his chest pulls across between his lungs as though he is being hugged by a bear. His hand rises to his mouth that is coughing now every few seconds.

"Larry?"

Robinson tries to stand but his legs have no power; he falls to the side, half on the chair and half on the ground.

"Help him!" she calls out to anyone. His breath is rasping, each intake requires all his strength. He pulls at the table; a man who says he's a doctor comes over and tries to help him. The man says he needs to get Larry to a hospital urgently. Larry grips the man's arm, tries to speak; his body arches up, his face stops mid-breath and he collapses onto the floor. The doctor pounds his chest, attempting to restart his heart for five minutes. Then he stops.

"I'm sorry," he says to Sasha and she cries. An ambulance crew arrives, then a police car. Sasha is comforted, sobbing the entire way through the ordeal. The police let her go for the night as she is so upset and she calls on her mobile for a car. Ten minutes later, a black Mercedes pulls up outside the bar and she gets in.

"Well done," says Ulrich from the darkness beside her. "Very convincing."

*

CHAPTER TWENTY-SIX

It is 11am when Gabby wakes. After their fight, she and Catherine had downed Margarita's into the early hours and pulled apart their love lives to their mutually increasing amusement. She raises her head and can see one of Catherine's long legs protruding from under a duvet on the sofa, her blonde hair a messy cloud drifting across the arm of the furniture. Gabrielle checks her phone and Hans has left a message saying he has learnt some new information from Mel and they should chat. She walks out on to the balcony and puts the phone to her ear. Hans is excited and wants to tell her what he has found. She listens and can feel her pulse rise as he goes through the GISS information. Hans has screen grabs of the comms between Murphy and Brussels, and the string of real time tracer comms that the GISS sent as they were live in the building next to Mac on that day. She tells him to upload it all to Oberon and package it into the eyes-only missive that he created to Sir Bernard.

She steps back into the room and opens her laptop, then logs into Oberon and messages Sir Bernard with the decrypt key for all of the information bundle that Hans has sent. There is two hours left on the time lock, after which Sir Bernard will have the information he needs to identify the mole.

Gabby showers and by the time she is dressed Catherine is awake.

"I need your help," says Gabrielle.

"Cool."

"There's a man who is trying to kill me."

"Great start to a story," says Catherine raising her eyebrows.

"It was a mystery to me at first, but I have now found out that I killed one of his gang members in Berlin."

"And he wants revenge?"

"Yes, but also, I stole his jet-ski and hit him with a bottle of champagne."

"Is this your way of getting a man's attention?"

"I'm serious." Catherine stops her playfulness.

"I want to meet him and put a stop to it, and I need you to cover me, like you did for Riverside."

"Where would you meet?"

I'm going to suggest we meet at the marina here in Nice."

"Not many rooftops for me," says Catherine. "Isn't there a road between the moorings and any tall buildings?"

"Can you do ground cover rather than rooftop?"

"Sure, handgun not rifle. We've got to be so careful though, there are people all over that area."

"I know. I'm hoping no shots will be fired. I just want to talk and clear the air."

"Why would he do that?"

"I don't know, I'm hoping I'm small fry and he'll drop it."

"But you can't be that certain, or you wouldn't want me there too?"

"He's dangerous. He may also be crazy and not respond to logic," says Gabby getting more piqued, "But I have to do something. I'm not going to be looking over my shoulder for ever."

"Fine. When are you thinking?"

"Today," says Gabrielle. "Now."

*

To maintain an air of normality, Laughton goes into the office at Vauxhall Cross. Martine is very concerned about him and tells him three times that he is better off in bed and resting. By lunchtime, he needs some air, and, taking the sandwiches that Martine insisted on buying for him, he walks for half an hour across Vauxhall Bridge, passed the Tate and on through the stuccoed houses of Westminster. The sky is five colours of blue, from a deep cobalt in the west, through sapphire, indigo and aquamarine to a rich navy that stretches over the bustling traffic and the busy people for as far as the eye can see. He walks, unaware of much of the activity around him, his finger nails newly raw, his eyes wet and red from too many sleepless nights. He hadn't expected Moscow to act so quickly and although both he and his Russian friend had known that their lives were at risk each time they had met over the last week, there was a part of his imagination that showed Laughton crossing the bridge from Vladivostok to the islands beyond, standing on the beach at Bukhta Chernysheva with Ivan as they talk of old times, and watching the sun go down over the Sea of Japan.

He walks without purpose, stepping like an automaton with the switch stuck on forward. A woman with a pushchair nearly crashes into him, and says something he doesn't hear, but it pulls Laughton out of his dreamscape. He looks up and he is nearing Buckingham Palace. He crosses the road and walks along in front of the high fencing that allows a view of the forecourt of the building. He stops and watches the guards, standing stock still, never questioning their duty day in, day out. His own loyalty is more complex, he loves the United Kingdom and all it stands for, but also mother Russia. Is he fooling himself that he loves the UK? How can he justify the years of being a quisling, the blood on his hands of his fellow countrymen and women who he had sent to their deaths? He may as well have killed them himself; he is a murderer and he can feel the weight of their eyes upon him. The first tear seeps out on its own, isolated, foreign, uncalled for; but then he weeps, for the first time in years. He cries for the deaths, for the lies and for himself. A little girl is watching him with concern sketched out across her small face. He sees her and turns away, unable to face the innocence of her presence.

Laughton walks to a bench at the edge of the gardens that surround the roads around the palace and sits down. He doesn't notice someone behind him.

"It's not over, Petrov." Laughton starts to turn his head but the stranger snaps. "Look forwards!"

"I can't go on."

"You have no choice," says the voice.

"Why did you kill him?"

"Ivan chose his own path."

"He had given you many years of service, for God's sake!"

"This is a job for life, as you know. Your new controller will be in touch."

"I can't..." whispers Laughton, but no more words come across his shoulder. He turns to look and the bench behind him is empty.

*

Stuart cooks fish pie for lunch using a recipe that he remembers from his childhood. He has always avoided memories from his childhood, not that there aren't any good ones, but he has never had any moments in his life that needed to use the memories, until now. Geraldine has given him much more than love, she has given him a reason to live. Only now can he see that his life up to this point was futile, only days of nothing going nowhere. Now he is the kind of man who needs to recall old recipes to cook, a man who needs to drag up funny stories from his youth or moments when he realised something about himself to throw into conversations with a woman who is interested in him. Now he needs to have opinions that they will discuss and compare, building their understanding of each other and themselves. He has slight regret that is has taken him until now to find someone like this. If he had met Geraldine in his twenties he could have started his new life then.

She walks into the kitchen and hugs him from behind and he puts his hand over her arms on his waist. They stand, moving together but in silence. The buzzer goes off on the oven and he serves the food. They sit at the dining table that has now been moved down into the lounge as it's cozier. They moved the chairs and sofa around last night and made better use of the space as Geraldine had called it.

"After we leave here," Stuart begins. "I was wondering if you would like to move in together?"

She smiles at him. "Aren't you the bold one?"

"You know, it's only an idea." He takes a bite of food.

"It's a lovely idea," she says, moving her little finger out to touch his. "Where would you want to live?"

"My flat is too small."

"Mine too. What about Charlottenburg? That's lovely."

"I don't know it."

"Quite trendy." She smiles as he raises his eyebrows.

"Is it noisy?"

"You're not an old fuddy-duddy, you're the same age as me!"

"I just like peace and quiet."

"We'll find somewhere."

A ring on their doorbell vibrates from down the hall.

"Alexander," he says to which she nods in silence. Neither of them gets up, expecting the other to go, then both get up at the same time and laugh.

"You go," she says.

Alexander is more nervous today than the previous evening, he arrives carrying a sports holdall. He refuses any drink again and sits at the dining table without them offering, so they sit too.

"Did you manage to get the information?" says Geraldine.

Alexander opens his bag and pulls out a pile of A4 documents, each sheet unattached to the other, so creating a messy raft of pages, most folded or damaged at the edges. He puts them down on the table between the three of them. Stuart and Geraldine look through the papers, picking off small bundles and flicking through them. Murphy told them what to look out for in the paperwork; certain names and certain places that MI6 already knew about had to be in there for the haul to be valuable.

"Who's this?" says Geraldine, holding up an image of a man and a woman cuddling in a booth at a nightclub.

Alexander is quiet for a second before answering. "That's Franz, my brother."

"And the girl?"

"Charlotte, his girlfriend." Geraldine looks again at the photo.

"Are these addresses all of the gang members?" asks Stuart.

"All the ones I could get."

Stuart and Geraldine continue to inspect as Alexander watches them, nervously wiping his hand through his hair and shifting in his seat.

"Can we talk?" says Stuart to Geraldine, and they go out to the kitchen.

"Is this enough?" he whispers.

"I think so."

"What did Murphy say he wanted? Gang members' details, locations?"

"Yup."

"We've got most of them." She nods. "Shall we tell him OK?"

"Yes, you tell him. I need to loo," she says.

Stuart walks back into the lounge and sits opposite Alexander. "That's fine," he says.

"And you will keep your side of the deal?" says the boy.

"Of course."

"What happens now?"

"We'll take this back to our people and they'll put a plan together. We'll arrange with you to meet in a day or two and make you disappear."

The boy smiles and nods.

Geraldine walks back in to the room, raises a Grach MP-433 handgun and fires two shots at close range, one into the head of each man. Alexander falls forwards and Stuart falls backwards, hitting his head on the floor and crumpling into a pile.

She runs to the front door and opens it. Ned is standing there with a large bag on his shoulder.

"I heard," says Ned. They go together to the lounge, Ned unzips the holdall and lays out two body bags. Geraldine goes through the flat smashing plates and throwing ornaments onto the hard floor.

"Help me," says Ned. They lift each of the two bodies over the bags and zip them up. "I'll bring the van up." He goes back out and returns a minute later with a rolled-up carpet, he unravels it and rolls Stuart up in the rug. The two of them carry the carpet and Stuart outside, cover him with sheets inside the back of the van, then return for Alexander and repeat the process. Geraldine takes a knife from Ned's bag and, holding her arm over the table, pushes the blade into the skin on her forearm. Her blood drips out next to the pool of Alexander's that is already staining the papers he left there. She wraps a bandage around her arm, collects the papers together, has a final check around the flat then runs out and pulls the door shut.

Outside, Ned is waiting in the van, nervously tapping his fingers on the wheel. She jumps into the passenger seat and they drive away.

*

CHAPTER TWENTY-SEVEN

Seven white super yachts move gently on the tide, straining on their mooring ropes in the Port of Nice. It is mid-afternoon and the crowds of people who flocked along Quai Cassini on their way from lunch are starting to thin out. A few tourists admire the boats and take their pictures in front of the giant craft.

Gabrielle sits in white jeans, white shirt and trainers at a small round metal table outside one of the cafés that sit next to the marina. A half-finished latte in front of her provides the reason for her to sit there without being bothered by the waiting staff. The day is warm. She can feel heat on the outside of her body and a sense of trepidation inside it. Her training for field operations gives her the mental and physical abilities to be calmer than a civilian, but this particular meeting has become personal for reasons she can't quite fathom. It was personal before the fight on the MV Quarrel, but at last now she can clear the air.

Two black Porsche Cayenne's appear on the Boulevard Carnot at the far eastern end of the port and crawl around the road that circles the water. They stop, the back door of the first vehicle opens and Sebastian Ulrich steps out, the blackened car windows reveal nothing of who else might be inside. He walks on his own across the tarmac and approaches Gabby. Catherine, three tables away in the café, nurses a holdall at her feet.

"Charlotte," is all he says as he sits. She remains silent. A waiter approaches but Ulrich waves him away.

Gabby licks her lips. "I want to clear the air, Sebastian." Her voice is clear and calm, not nervous, not pleading.

"You owe me a jet-ski."

"There's something you don't know." Her words slide out towards him.

"Oh yeah?"

"You have a contract out on a British woman."

"I do," he says still not connecting, a frown appears between his eyes. "She has proved slippery."

"Why do you want her dead?"

He pauses before answering, still unsure of his ground. He seems to be weighing up why this crazy woman who fought with him on his boat would know about the contract. He relinquishes. "She killed a friend of mine."

"Franz Keneely?"

He says nothing but his eyes narrow, his brain trying to compute how two distinct parts of his life seem to be connected.

"You knew him?" he says, starting to play chess in his mind.

"I killed him."

"Then came looking for me?" He is still nowhere near working it all out.

"You sent your gorillas after me, I had to do something." He wipes his open hand across his face.

"What do you want?" he says calmly with the faintest whisper of threat mixed in.

"Like I said, clear the air. Call a truce."

"Why would I agree to that?"

"I can destroy you," she says. Ulrich laughs and Kate turns her head at the very edge of Gabby's peripheral vision.

"You're way out of your league," he sneers, showing an insecurity about his status.

"Lost any drugs recently?"

"What?" he says.

"One of your imports went up in flames, I hear."

He smiles. "That was you?"

"I can destroy you," she repeats.

The words between them pause. They sit, not always looking at each other, weighing up what they need to do. Seagulls bounce and glide on the warm air above the calm water of the marina, each gull alone and yet mutually dependent, if only for a fleeting moment.

"I can keep doing that until you remove my contract," she says. "That's the deal."

He says nothing. A bead of sweat sits on his hairline, he moves his fingers as though warming up for the piano in a display of what he thinks shows his control.

"Let me think," he says after a minute. As he stands and turns back to the two Porsches, a silence seems to envelope the whole area, no sound emanates from the yachts or the cars in the vicinity. Ulrich takes four steps, then, as Gabby and Catherine had predicated when they had been planning an hour before, he swings round, his Grach Yarygin handgun drawn. His first shot is wildly wide, Gabrielle dives under the table and de-holsters her Smith & Wesson; Catherine already has her Beretta in her hand. Simultaneously with the first shot being fired, all four doors of the Porsches open and seven men dressed head to toe in black emerge at speed. Ulrich's second shot is closer and hits the table above her head. Catherine fires one round, a warning shot only. The bullet hits the ground three niches from his left foot, he turns and only then realises Gabby is not operating solo. He runs towards the group of seven who are spreading out across the width of the road. Catherine lets off two more rounds and takes down two of the men, they fall injured but not killed, the way she prefers to operate. The five standing gunmen respond to the two hits and scale back their ground as Ulrich reaches the relative safety of the group.

Catherine waves two fingers in the direction of the sea as a move out signal, and she and Gabby run alternately, each covering the other, constantly under fire, until they reach the Place Guynemer that occupies the corner of land at the edge of the marina and stretching westwards along the coast. Ulrich's men follow on foot, unsuccessfully trying to hit the women. Catherine hits a third man in the leg and he falls to the ground. Ulrich regroups his troops and with much arm waving he pulls together a battle plan. They split into two groups and attack the flanks of Gabby and Catherine, who take cover behind each side of a low building on the quay.

"You take that group, Kate," yells Gabby. Catherine signals acceptance of the order. One shot from Ulrich's men skims off the wall and Gabby is showered with concrete chips in her face, the speed of the impact slits her skin in three places and blood comes to the surface on to her eyebrow and forehead. She wipes it away and returns to the attack. Kate's superior weapons training continues to pay off and she hits a fourth man leaving just two groups of two, but the remaining four are narrowing the gap between Gabby and Kate, and making headway towards the building that provides their cover. Gabrielle signals again to Kate and the women run further along the coastline and onto the roadway that stretches from the marina to the beaches. They sprint to a set of motorbike parking bays set on one side of the road, then pick the locks of two BMW R1250 bikes that have been left there. They drop the clutches and ride off towards the old town leaving Ulrich and his henchmen in the distance. As Ulrich reaches the bike racks, two tourists arrive on Ducati Scramblers, the gang attack them and take their machines.

Ulrich and one gunman mount up and chase after Gabby and Kate.

The four motorcycles cascade through the traffic on the Quai des États-Unis, weaving each side of vehicles, and swerving to avoid errant members of the public who are trying to cross the road between the cars. Even though the Ducatis are less powerful than and BMWs, Ulrich and his sideman are slowly making ground. The machines fly out of the heavy traffic and onto the Promenade des Anglais, the main drag through Nice and alongside the beaches that are full of bathers and sun worshippers. On the open road, Ulrich pushes his bike to the limit and, when the gap is fifteen yards, draws his weapon and fires at Gabby. Meanwhile Ulrich's man is nearing Kate and follows his master's lead by letting off a round which hits her fuel tank. Ulrich fires again and hits Gabby's wing mirror. Kate's tank starts to spill out the noxious odour of petrol but she pushes the machine further.

They hit a patch of heavier traffic and return to their swerving approach to get through the density of vehicles. Gabby and Kate draw up level with each other and Kate signals to turn off. They drive up onto the pavement and down onto the grey pebbles of the beach. It gives them thirty seconds of breathing space before the chasers catch up.

"My tank's hit," shouts Catherine. "I'm losing power." Gabby signals to stop.

"Time to face the music," says Gabrielle and they both put their machines on the stand and duck down behind them. Ulrich and his +1 appear at the top of the beach. They stop when they see the women waiting.

"Where are we?" says Catherine, inspecting her handgun and reloading.

"Almost at the airport."

"What are they waiting for?"

"Wondering where our weak spot is, I imagine," says Gabby.

"You're bleeding," says Kate.

"Ricochet."

Ulrich and his man restart their bikes and slowly drift down onto the pebbles, then stop again twenty yards away.

"Let's talk," calls Ulrich.

"OK," Gabby shouts back.

He makes a big play of putting his handgun down on the stones.

"Cover me," says Gabby and she gets up from behind the bikes.

The two leaders walk out towards each other and stop when they are ten feet apart, each facing the other.

"Your friend is a good shot," says Ulrich.

"MI6 trains us well."

"You're MI6?"

"Did you think we were just some random women out to ruin your life?"

"I get it now." He smiles. Gabby can sense his henchman in the background with weapon drawn.

"We know all about you, Sebastian."

"What do you want?" he says again.

"I told you the deal. We know all your operations, we know your contacts; we are ready to move on your whole organisation."

"OK, I'll cancel the contract on you." He holds out his hand. She waits, then offers her hand too. As soon as her fingers near his, he grabs her wrist, pulls her towards him and tries a hold on her, but Gabby twists out of it. He draws his arm back and lands a punch on her cheek, she is momentarily stopped, she wavers, then her blood rises and her focus comes back. She turns and throws a kick to his kidneys, then another on the other foot. Ulrich's henchman starts to fire and walk forwards, Catherine returns fire, resting on the BMW but a bullet hits her shoulder. She continues to fire at both Ulrich and the other man. Ulrich runs back from Gabby to his bike, restarts it and rides away, leaving his man to finish the job. Catherine can see the blood through her jacket, she takes aim with a last surge of bravado; in her sight, the muzzle wavers as the pain makes its presence felt. She unleashes a shot, it hits the man squarely in the chest and he keels over. Gabby runs to the remaining Ducati, opens the throttle and gives chase to Ulrich.

She pushes the machine as fast as it will go. Ulrich is thirty yards ahead but Gabby is closing the gap. The yawning space of the sea stretches to their left; on the horizon the Nice Cote D'Azur airport looms as they speed their way through the September afternoon. Ulrich looks back repeatedly, and minute by minute, mile by mile, Gabby is gaining on him. They swerve down to a route near the water's edge, churning up spray from the shallows as their machines hurtle through the water. Gabby takes the opportunity of a smooth stretch to take out her handgun and fire off some rounds, to Ulrich's obvious surprise. She doesn't land any and he accelerates the bike to escape the onslaught.

Gabby suspects that Ulrich doesn't realise that the beach ends at the airport. As the grey buildings that provide storage and services for airlines grow steadily nearer, Gabrielle thinks through the choices that Ulrich has. In end he takes the obvious one and storms off the pebbles and onto the access road system around the airport. She follows suit and is glad to be on solid tarmac as she can control the bike more effectively. She scouted the area two days ago and knows that all the roads are dead ends and terminate with fencing around the airport. Ulrich takes one turn and, frustrated by no through route, swerves away wildly and along the fencing. The machines roar at frightening speed along the wire wall; Ulrich searching for freedom, Gabby waiting for closure. The fence turns an abrupt left and Ulrich skids round. A grass bank sits between road and fence, built up to provide a measure of protection if any accidents happen on the carriageway. Ulrich's mind races and he is pushed into his only option. He throws the throttle wide, leans back, runs up the grass bank and launches his machine at the fence, it rises with its momentum, up off the earth; the tyres nearly hit the fence but clear the top with half an inch to spare. Gabby sees his jump, stops her machine, assesses her own ability to jump the bike, then rebalances, opens the throttle and heads for the fencing. Like Ulrich she leans back as the wheels go skyward; with the same power and a lighter frame, she sails over the barrier. Her impact on the other side is less skilful and her bike jumps over taking her with it and she tumbles painfully across the concrete on the other side of the fence and hits her knee.

Ulrich fell too but is already back on his motorbike. Gabby hauls up her machine; the pain from her leg throbs and the lower half of one leg of her trousers is red with blood. But she has to go on, she screams out loud as she pulls together all her remaining reserve to get back on the bike. She is damaged now, she knows it. Her psychological motivation is undimmed and will now have to override the physical pain. She speeds out from behind the service buildings and looks for Ulrich; he is fifty yards away, she gives chase. Ulrich decides to take a route across the airport and breaks out in the direction of the taxiways. He drops his speed to navigate his way with caution and Gabby makes up some ground. She is near enough for a shot with her Smith & Wesson and pulls out her weapon and release one round, it hits him on the arm but he doesn't lose focus, she takes another shot, this time at the bike, but misses. Ulrich's attention is drawn towards her and in that instance he realises too late that he has stopped on the landing strip. An aircraft coming in doesn't see him there. Gabby watches as the undercarriage catches his head and his frail body is thrown up into the air, then down with a sickening bloody bounce onto the runway.

*

CHAPTER TWENTY-EIGHT

Stephen Laughton stands looking out of the window at the Thames. From his office in the MI6 Building at Vauxhall Cross he can see the grey water, tidal from the sea until Teddington as it flows up and down in a regular cycle each day. He has never thought before about how he echoes its natural rhythm, he's never thought before about how he has followed a cyclical ritual of repetition just like the water every day of his life for longer than he cares to remember.

A knock on the door echoes around the room.

"Come in, Martine," he calls and hears the door open behind him but doesn't turn as Martine will do her work quietly without disturbing him. Laughton continues his rapt attention on the river.

"Stephen." The voice beside him is not Martine, Laughton turns his head.

"Sir Bernard. I thought..."

"We need to talk."

"Of course, sir." Laughton turns away from the glass, the other man is shorter than him but it doesn't feel like it.

"Shall we sit?" says Sir Bernard. They move to the sofas and take places on opposite sides of the low table that separates the seating.

"Some evidence has come to light," begins Sir Bernard. "Evidence about a mole in 6." Laughton can feel his body relax as this means he is out of scope of any investigation, otherwise he wouldn't be being briefed on it.

"You remember the meeting a couple of weeks ago when Blackhawk went off grid after the location of a kill was leaked and one of our C9's was killed in action?" continues Sir Bernard.

"Of course."

"Do you remember that we sent Riverside to bring her in?"

"Yes, naturally."

"Do you remember that he met her in Switzerland and they were attacked and the location of that meeting must have been leaked as very few people knew about it?"

Laughton stops responding to each question as Sir Bernard seems to building a narrative.

"Do you remember that we put untrained embassy staff into a live operation after Blackhawk disappeared, so we could continue her work of turning a member of the criminal gang operating in Berlin? Well those embassy staff are dead now, murdered. The information on that operation was leaked as well. We responded of course and the Crows have been interviewing people searching for this Petrov character."

The more senior man stops and let's time drift on inside the room, like the water outside.

"It turns out that Blackhawk has spent two weeks gathering evidence about these leaks."

"Excellent," says Laughton.

"She's a good agent. She has sent me a file of evidence, and Ms. Peretz has filled in the details from her interviews."

Sir Bernard stops again and turns his head to the light coming through the window. He adjusts his spectacles on the end of his nose, then turns back to Laughton.

"We know you are the mole, Stephen. We know you are Petrov."

"That's ridiculous! Blackhawk is trying to frame me, obviously. She has never been dependable, and this just shows she has a streak of revenge about her, I never did trust her."

The other man watches the bluster. "Stephen!" says Sir Bernard sharply, then more quietly. "You're embarrassing yourself."

"But..."

Sir Bernard raises his palm to silence Laughton. "You have two options as far as I can see," he says. "Remain in post and we feed Moscow false information from you to them. Or you spend the rest of your life in prison somewhere and likely meet a Russian assassin one day when you least expect it."

Laughton has thought about this moment repeatedly over the years of being a traitor. What would he say when the evidence is too compelling? What would he say when the final dead end is reached? The Moscow advice is to deny everything, every time, and never admit to even the slightest misdemeanour.

"Does Linny know?" says Sir Bernard.

Laughton's mind is in pain, he wants his thoughts to be clear but they won't sort themselves out. Images of Linny and Ivan and the agents he has sent to their deaths swirl inside him. His mouth opens to speak but words are not there, his fingers can feel the outline of the tablet in his pocket. He searches for anything that will make it all stop.

"I assume she doesn't know," says the more senior man.

Laughton, finally, acknowledges what he has spent twenty years lying about, and the sounds croak out from his gullet, "She doesn't know." His eyes are fixed on the floor, he can't look at Sir Bernard. He feels a wave of relief and a wave of sadness and his eyes water but he stops himself from crying.

Sir Bernard sits patiently. He has known Laughton for five years and has not suspected anything like this. The acting has been extraordinary and he has seen many moles before, but never at this level, never with over twenty years' service.

"Was it from the beginning, Stephen? At Oxford?"

Laughton clears his throat. "Yes."

"Was the man you found dead on the Heath your Russian controller?"

"Yes."

"Are you prepared to feed Moscow false information from now on, and stay in post?"

"Yes," he says with no hesitation.

"You'll have to de-briefed by the Crows over the next few weeks of course. We'll need every detail, every leak, every meeting."

"I understand." He finally raises his head to the other man.

"I assume you are carrying the standard issue Russian arsenic tablet? If you would be so kind..." He holds out his palm and Stephen pulls out the capsule and hands it over.

"Is Martine part of it?" says Sir Bernard.

"No, not at all."

"She'll need to be changed nevertheless. I'm going to bring Murphy in from Berlin on this for now. He will make all decisions pertaining to the official role but you will still have the job as far as the outside world, and Moscow, are concerned."

Sir Bernard stands. For a second, the two men look at each other, both with no discernible emotion on their faces, then the more senior man turns away and walks out of the door.

*

The traffic on Highgate West Hill is heavier than usual as it winds its way up from the Swains Lane shops and restaurants, passed Karl Marx's grave in Highgate Cemetery, and curves round to the village's South Grove at the summit. Laughton sits in the back of the cab and watches the lights of the cars coming down the hill; his heart still beating fast as it has done in the two hours since Sir Bernard confronted him.

The taxi drops him off on the corner of the road and he walks to his front door. A slight rain is in the air, carried on a breeze that blows across from the Heath. He turns the key in the lock and goes in.

"In here, darling!" Linny calls from the lounge.

He walks through the house to her. "I have had a very odd day," she says. "You know that case of the mercenaries? My client was being charged with handling secret information? I had a call just as I was leaving tonight. It was the chap from the Cabinet Office, said he had spoken to the Attorney General and the case against my client has been dropped! Just like that!"

"You must have scared them," he says quietly.

"You think?" He nods and she notices his sadness. "How are you? You look tired, my darling." She holds out her hand to him and he sits next to her on the sofa. "How was *your* day?"

They talk for half an hour then Stephen makes them dinner while Linny has a bath. They eat in the dining room and set places at the far end so they can see the remains of the day slide away into dusk. Linny clears the plates and Stephen decides to take his bag into the study from where he left it by the front door. On the door mat, a small square piece of paper sits dead centre. He didn't see it when he arrived home, and stoops to pick it up. He unfolds it and inside the message reads, 'Outside at 9pm.' He checks his watch; it is 8:50pm. He puts his bag in the study, then says to Linny he is going to get some air. She is listening to the radio and waves a silent hand to acknowledge message received.

He turns the handle and steps out in to the night. It is colder now than it was when he arrived home, and he buttons up his coat, the one that Linny bought him for Christmas.

Laughton walks into the road as there is no traffic. He stands, waiting for something, but he isn't sure what. The street lights stand guard, marking out the route down the hill in one direction and on to the Heath in the other. There are few sounds; only a distant drone of traffic creating a permanent London background noise that no one notices after a few weeks of living there.

"Petrov." The word comes at him like an arrow. He turns and a figure is standing in half shadow only ten feet away.

"Who are you?"

"Your new controller. I wanted to introduce myself."

"I can't see your face," he says.

"All in good time."

"What do you want?"

"To hear from you that you will continue in your service to the motherland."

"I will."

"So your thoughts of stopping? You have changed your mind?

"Yes. Ivan was the one who encouraged me to think like that," he says towards the shadow.

"We suspected as much."

"It will continue, just like before," he says.

"They will be glad to hear it. I'll be in touch. You can go now." Stephen obediently walks back to his house, turns the key and shuts the door firmly behind him.

The headlights of a vehicle that has been waiting in the dark suddenly illuminate the roadway. It moves and pulls up alongside the other figure who is walking away from the meeting. She opens the door and, for a split second, Marjorie's face is lit up by the street lights before she disappears from view into the car.

*

EPILOGUE

The shower is warm on her back. Gabrielle stays under the water longer than normal, letting the memories of the last days and weeks run through her mind.

She was angry when she heard that Murphy had put untrained people into the field to try and complete Project Hillbank. The deaths of two embassy staff is unforgiveable. They would have stood no chance when the professional killer had struck in the safe house. The loss of Alexander too is a tragedy, particularly given his age. Already, intelligence has started to come into MI6 about how Sebastian Ulrich's empire is being carved up by the criminal fraternity. There have already been deaths as a consequence but Dima Lebedev is the one who seems to be gaining the most from Ulrich's demise.

She wraps herself in her dressing gown and takes her coffee to the balcony to let the day seep into her consciousness. Berlin is mulling over whether to be warm or cold. Flecks of white mottle the navy-blue sky, and the sun basks weak and low over the broad cityscape.

The conversation with Sir Bernard Macintosh two days after he received the mole information was one of those unique opportunities to discuss matters openly that only come about rarely in the SIS. She had sat on a secure video link on the dirty side of the Berlin Embassy, just her and Sir Bernard. They went through all of the data and information that she had sent via Hans. He wanted to know all the details, every nuanced fact, every second of the operational tracking data that she had unearthed. The intel revealed the mole, but she was surprised herself when Laughton's name had emerged from what she discovered. The Berlin link is still unclear to her though, and Sir Bernard implied that there was data that the Crows had found that gives a bigger picture, and he didn't share that with her.

Riverside sent her a message the next day too, almost but not quite apologising. It was of no consequence, they are both soldiers doing a job, and sometimes the job needs objective action no matter what you feel personally.

Hans invites her to lunch and she drives across town to the Mett Bar. There are only two customers in the place as she arrives. She and Hans talk about Nice, and the mole, and their lives and dreams. He looks younger, she thinks, and he mentions three times how he needs to get back into real field operations.

"Murphy's going to London, did you hear?" he says.

"Promotion?"

"Unclear," says Hans. "But he seemed pleased, so I guess so."

"Did you know those two who were killed in the safe house?" she says.

"Nope."

"Why would Murphy put them on it?"

"Crazy," says Hans.

"And he got promoted for that!"

"I know!"

"And Murphy made that weird decision to call in GISS when Mac was killed," she says. "What was that about?"

"You miss him?" says Hans.

"Yeah," she says looking down. "He was a good friend, we'd known each other since the beginning. He was the one who encouraged me to think that there is a life beyond MI6. A way to stop, you know? That idea, that there can be an escape hatch, has kept me going for years."

"Don't you like the job?" says Hans.

"I love the job," she says. "That's not it. It's the idea that you can press the button someday. Living like this is as tough as it gets; lying, fighting and killing, pretending to be someone else, having no outside life to speak of, telling your friends and parents that you're an anonymous clerk somewhere in the British civil service. But it's what I live for, every day. It's what I am."

Hans watches her come down from her emotional rise.

One of the men in the café approaches them. "I'll get your bill, mate," says Hans and goes to the till.

"I couldn't help over-hearing what you said," says the man.

"Oh, I was just ranting about my job, sorry if I disturbed you."

"I agree with what you said, you must always have a way to get out. It's essential, or what's the point of..."

She stops and turns her head to the man. "Mac?" she says.

"Hello, Gabby."

THE END

BLACKHAWK WILL RETURN IN
THE KILL ORDER

Printed in Great Britain
by Amazon

58958863R00196